REAP3R

BOOK DESIGN BY Kevin Barrett Kane

People seeking the meaning of life get it backward.
You don't ask life for an answer.
Life asks you.

PROLOGUE

THE TARGET ENDED THE CALL, slipped the phone into her pocket, and looked out over the shimmering infinity pool. Walter Klein followed her gaze through the binoculars, but beyond the cliff's edge, there was nothing but the Pacific Ocean stretching away into blue-gray haze.

What would a person like Dr. Alice Tufekci be thinking about as she stared into the distance? What memories haunted her? What anxieties plagued her? The CZ 75 dug into his ribs. Walter shimmied up a few inches so the gnarled trunk of the Torrey Pine didn't rub against his shoulder holster. It was always tempting to imagine that targets were thinking profound thoughts, that they had some intuitive premonition of what was coming and used what little time they had left to consider the path their lives had taken, the moral quandaries they'd navigated, the fears they'd fled from or overcome. But Walter knew he was projecting. Alice was probably just mentally reviewing the latest experimental results or wondering whether she had time to take a shit before heading to the lab. Movies used music to build tension before major twists, but real life didn't have a soundtrack to clue you in to the fact that everything was about to change. Everything was just normal until it wasn't. Sometimes Walter wanted to scream at them: *Can't you feel the crosshairs on the back of your neck? Stop being an idiot and appreciate the gift of existence before I snuff it out. The end is nigh, asshole.* But of course he never did, because he was a professional, and professionals shut up and did the work. Nobody wanted a dentist who decided to improvise in the middle of a root canal. So whether or not ignorance was in fact bliss, targets went to their graves without ever knowing the jig was up.

Alice spun and walked through the French doors into the house. Walter checked the time. If she stuck to the routine—and she *always* stuck to the routine—she'd be flying out to the lab in five minutes.

It was strange how well he got to know targets. Alice loved the *perrones* at Tacos El Yaqui in Rosarito, an hour's drive down the coast from San Diego. When she was working on a particularly tough technical problem, she listened to the Taylor Swift song *marjorie* on infinite repeat. Habitually celibate, every once in a while Alice would pick up a Marine in an Oceanside dive bar, hustle him off to a boutique hotel in Rancho Santa Fe, and fuck his brains out for a weekend before returning to her default life as if nothing had happened. Last night, Walter had woken up with an erection from a dream that conjured one of these irregular bacchanals in graphic detail. He sighed. There was a peculiar kind of ache accompanying this one-way intimacy. He knew so much about her, and she knew nothing about him. But he was here to fulfill a contract, not the possibility of human connection.

The target came out of the front door at the five-minute mark—probably not enough time for a shit—and boarded the chopper. Through the binoculars, Walter could see her checking diagnostics. The rotor began to spin, kicking up dust in the native-plant garden that surrounded the helipad.

Walter admired Alice. She'd been on the legendary team that headed straight for the epicenter of the original Bakunawa outbreak. It was during her time in the Philippines when, as the pandemic raged across the globe, she'd been helivaced out of a quarantine site under attack from a local militia. After Geoff Rossi, Alice, and their colleagues had managed to defeat the virus, she'd used some of her share of the proceeds from the vaccine to buy a helicopter and learn to pilot it. Now, she flew back and forth from the lab every day. Walter could appreciate what it might mean to feel like you always had a means of escape, and how such feelings could ultimately betray you.

Individual blades faded into collective blur.

Walter unlocked his tablet and ran the script.

The chopper rose smoothly off the ground and hovered in place for a long moment.

His mouth was dry and he was sweating under his denim jacket. Not even people who had saved the world were safe from people like him. There were sheep, and there were wolves, and neither lived forever. You could survive a lot of things, but you couldn't survive life.

And then Alice dipped the nose of the chopper and swung it out to sea and the drones Walter had kept carefully hidden beneath the cliff's edge swarmed up around it and dive-bombed into her rotor mast and air intakes. The helicopter listed to one side as the target desperately tried to regain control—the slate of Alice's mind wiped clean by existential dread—and then flames shot out the back of the engine and the tail swung around fast, carving a chunk of sandstone out of the cliff before the failing machine plunged out of view. The ground under Walter shook when it hit the beach, and then again when it exploded.

Time to move.

He pushed himself to his feet, stowed the tablet in the backpack stuffed with ephemera carefully curated to simulate a generic grad student, wiped his hands on his jeans, double checked that his jacket was covering the CZ 75 in its holster, ran a hand through his ginger hair, and slipped away from the grove of wind-sculpted trees.

Despite his racing heart, Walter forced himself to stroll past the opulent La Jolla Farms estates. Incoming sirens wailed as he crossed the main road onto UC San Diego's campus. He allowed himself one glance over his shoulder as he followed a pedestrian path past the undergraduate dorms. Oily black smoke billowed up over the bluff, darkening the baby blue sky.

Down the rabbit hole, Alice.

Walter's phone buzzed.

Reap3r notification: Payment received.

Walter wondered what Alice had done to earn the enmity of whoever had posted the gig, but clients were anonymized behind layer upon layer of encryption, the transaction facilitated by smart contract instead of fixer. Was there a spurned lover? A conspiracy-addled anti-vaxxer terrorist cell? A secret beyond the scope of the dossier he'd collated? Walter would never know and frankly, it was easier that way.

A target was a target.

A job was a job.

Anyone who claimed life was priceless wasn't paying attention.

Three years later…

1

SANSOME HAVERFORD FORCED HIMSELF to let out a long-held breath, set his shoulders, and strode onto the stage.

Lights blazed. Applause swelled.

TED.

He had worked so hard to get here. He wished he were anywhere but here.

Sansome smiled with his eyes just like Esteban had coached him. He didn't need to look at the slides or the prompter. He didn't need to look at the clock. He needed to look out at the audience—meet all those other eyes behind the glare.

Some people loved being the center of attention. There was a hunger in them that could only be sated by sating the hunger of an audience. Sansome was not such a person. The hunger of an audience made him feel like a meal. Far better to be a center of influence, to direct events from the sidelines, to move the world with the gentlest of touches.

Speak.

Speak.

Speak.

Self-flagellation roused Esteban's training and Sansome spoke. Stories took shape and interlocked, loaded with carefully calibrated logos and pathos, each successive piece revealing the puzzle's overall design to be stranger, grander, more counterintuitive.

Sansome resented his fear of public speaking in no small part because it was so cliché. The butterflies. The burgeoning nausea. The dreams shot through with anxiety. To feel crippled by such a common phobia was humiliating, and knowing such a sentiment was unworthy made it that much worse. He fought back the rising tide of stage fright by focusing on the rhythm of the words.

Remember why you're here.

He'd give anything to be holed up in his study with a biography of Florence Nightingale or Genghis Khan right now, and whatever narcissism smoldered in Sansome's heart wasn't stoked by adulation. No. He was here to be of service, not to the beau monde gazing up at him with bated breath, not to the faceless millions streaming this talk online, but to his portfolio, his people, his family.

Nobody liked raising capital, least of all those whose profession was to manage it. But by corralling money from pension funds, sovereign wealth funds, endowments, and billionaires, Sansome could guarantee that a lack of cash would never stand between those under his wing and the futures they sought to realize. And the staid shepherds of the wealth Sansome wanted to deploy liked to think of themselves not as fungible cogs in a machine to turn money into more money, but as strategists of insight and initiative who chose to put their weight behind the kinds of people with ideas worth sharing, the kind of people who earned standing ovations at places like TED. So Sansome would do this little dance for them, to spare his own investees the trouble. And who knew? The next Florence, or the next Genghis, might watch this talk and see in Sansome a potential ally.

So he told them about Human Capital's humans. Geoff, who had saved billions of lives with his vaccine. Safaa, who was the highest grossing professional athlete of her generation. Farzona, whose databank had rewired the information architecture of the entire internet. Lauren, who had singlehandedly revitalized *Star Wars* for Disney. Samuel, who had built a new nation from the remains of what had once been Venezuela. Molly, whose pioneering work in genetic engineering was poised to revolutionize biotech. On and on and on. For every example he mentioned, Sansome glossed over many more whose positions or projects were sensitive. And of course, he couldn't mention Luki's top secret advances in quantum computing, much less Reap3r.

Sansome walked back and forth across the stage, hoping movement would quiet his nerves. He explained that in ancient Rome wealthy patrons had financially supported writers and artists, providing them with room, board, gifts, stipends, and social access. In return, these artists served as *anteambulos*, literally clearing a path for their patrons as they walked the bustling streets, and metaphorically clearing a path for their patrons by ferrying messages, offering favors, and generally nudging life in the right direction.

And here was the lovely reversal Esteban had suggested: the audience expected the anecdote to resolve with Sansome as patron—investing as he did in artists, scientists, inventors, and entrepreneurs. But Human Capital's *real* work was that of anteambulo: clearing a path for their portfolio to make the greatest impact they possibly could. It was the kind of narrative sleight of hand that might show up in podcasts like *Akimbo* or *Rabbit Hole*.

Sansome stopped, faced the audience, and sank into the moment, reaching for the kind of inspired spontaneity only achieved via relentless practice. "At Human Capital, we don't bet on technology. We don't even bet on companies. We bet on people."

Repressing the pain it caused him not to fill it, he let silence expand into the room for a long beat—that was the bit Esteban had drilled him on hardest: holding space for silence.

"It's tempting to look at the world and see governments and businesses and schools and hospitals and institutions, but that's all a convenient fiction. The truth is that organizations are just a bunch of people trying to move in the same direction, and technology is just the way that people do things. Special relativity didn't change the world. Einstein did. So we dispense with the theses that guide so many investors, and think of ourselves as a special breed of *New Yorker* profile writer who just happens to invest in the subject of the story. We find the best people in the world, figure out what makes them tick, write them checks, and give them free rein to do what only they can do."

He opened his palms as if revealing a present. "That's it," he said. "That's the Human Capital formula. Only people can change the world."

Silence.

Blind panic: Had he misread the room? Had he fumbled this crucial opportunity to reach the right people with the right message? Had he failed himself and those who depended on him?

The crowd rose to their feet.

Sansome might not relish public attention, but there was no denying that the roar was electrifying. The wave crested and broke. He feigned embarrassment, letting it wash over him. Against all odds and in violation of weeks' worth of stress fantasies, he hadn't fucked it up.

He bowed. Waved. Bowed again.

And then he was backstage and out of the hot glare of the lights and checking his phone and—yes—Esteban. This time, Sansome's smile didn't require media training.

"I fucking *killed* it, thanks to you," said Sansome. "LPs will slit each other's throats for a seat on the bus."

"It's Geoff," said Esteban, his urgent tone wiping the shit-eating grin off Sansome's face. He didn't want to deal with this right now. He wanted to sit back with a well-deserved whiskey and reread Devon's grant application. "I'm forwarding you the feed."

"Nightmare?" asked Sansome.

"Harrowing," confirmed Esteban.

That was the problem with investing in people.

Numbers were clean.

People were messy.

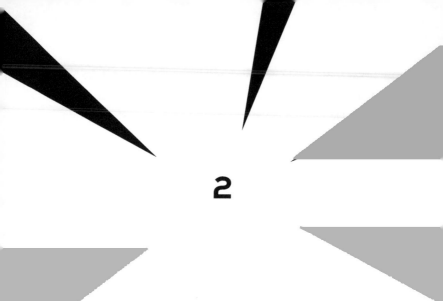

2

THE PHONE CALL ruined an otherwise perfect lunch at Saul's.

Geoff Rossi wasn't on planet Earth. At least, not quite. While he was technically sitting in a booth at the best deli to have ever graced his palate, he was also—thanks to Terry Pratchett's indefatigable imagination—sneaking through the fetid alleys of Discworld's infamous, conspiracy-ridden, fantastical city of Ankh-Morpork. After another bout of night terrors, Geoff had needed an escape.

He reluctantly lay the novel down on top of the stack of dissertations he was supposed to be reviewing. He remembered how full of vim and vigor he'd been in graduate school, how eager to advance the cause of science, to unlock the secrets of life. Now when he wasn't busy steadfastly refusing the never-ending flood of offers to commercialize his patents—this being the best lever Geoff had to head off the existential dangers his discoveries heralded—he struggled to summon the energy to coach the brilliant students so eager to work in his lab at UC Berkeley. He knew what the tools they developed might be used for. Japan had outlawed guns for three centuries. Italy had outlawed silk spinning for two centuries. France had outlawed printing for two decades. Technological prohibitions could work, if only for a little while. Geoff's only hope was to buy some time for people to think through the implications of his invention before remaking the world with it. While he took every opportunity his celebrity afforded him to champion the *Protocol for Ethics in Synthetic Biology*, he shuddered at the fact that he'd been the one to write it. What would people do if they found out the truth? Nothing made Geoff's skin crawl like admiration, which was why their complete indifference to his Reputation was the greatest gift Saul's staff could offer him.

Their second greatest gift was the Pastrami Ruskie—from which he took an enormous bite while pretending to ignore the phone buzzing in his pocket. Fatty and mouthwatering, the owners sourced the grass-fed beef from Bill Niman's ranch in Marin County, brined it for days, rubbed it with spices, long-smoked it, steamed it and served it on warm, handmade, fermented rye. Then there was the Swiss cheese, Russian dressing, coleslaw, and pickled vegetables. In other words, perfection. Geoff would award the sandwich one of his godforsaken Nobels if he could.

But the food wasn't the best thing about Saul's. The best thing about Saul's was that it wasn't trying to be a New York Jewish Deli. The only thing Saul's was trying to be was itself—a luxury unimaginable to Geoff. He sometimes resented having outlived Alice and Frank, his closest collaborators on the Bakunawa vaccine.

Wishing he could shut the damn thing up through pure force of will, he snatched the vibrating phone from his pocket.

His jaw froze mid-chew as he stared down at the screen.

This was the one number Geoff never, ever wanted to hear from.

He had almost managed to convince himself that the caller didn't really exist, was just yet another hungry ghost in the faceless 220-million-strong pantheon that haunted his dreams.

Geoff forced down the masticated lump of sandwich.

He'd known this was coming.

It came every year, without fail.

Island hopping through the Aegean.

Shooting the Northwest Passage.

Rounding Cape Horn.

The lap of waves against hull.

Unfamiliar pelagic birds circling overhead.

Air thick with ocean-tang.

And people. People Geoff didn't care to know. People he couldn't avoid thanks to a promise he'd lived to regret.

He wanted to decline the call. He wanted to drop the phone on the floor, crush it under the heel of his Birkenstock, and get a fresh number from a new carrier. He wanted to escape back into Discworld.

Geoff accepted the call, if not the fate he knew he more than deserved.

"Sansome?" the tremor in his voice calcified Geoff's self-hatred.

"Geoff, my man. I come bearing the invitation of a lifetime."

3

LUKI ZUBIRI WALKED the path that ran along the edge of the bluff.

To his right, the full moon dipped toward the Pacific, out of which rolled waves the size of houses—monsters born of some howling Aleutian maelstrom shooting the gap between the Channel Islands to reach all the way to this protected stretch of coast. The waves stacked one behind the other all the way to the horizon, jacking up as they swung around the rocky point before dashing themselves against California like so many other builders and dreamers and fortune-seekers had before them, destiny glinting in their mad eyes.

To his left, the sun rose winter-pale over snow-dusted mountains. Luki wondered how many millennia of uplift and erosion it had taken for these humpbacked ridges to form their peaks and valleys, to draw their stark line across the dawn.

Inhale: the air was crisp and clean with a touch of brine.

Exhale: a ghostly puff of breath briefly rendered visible by morning chill.

Today was the day.

Ten years of work. Ten years of secrets. It could take an eternity to live a decade and barely a moment to reflect on it—the mechanical regularity of clocks belied the changeability of time, something that human intuition understood and yet rebelled against. But there was something in that subtle dichotomy, in the expansion of reality to encompass many and contradictory possibilities, that was fundamental to the quantum computer that was buried under Q's unobtrusive Santa Barbara headquarters, supercooled to just above absolute zero by a cryostat, built by the best minds and protected by the best spooks of a generation.

No.

It might *feel* like a miracle—especially to Luki who saw in Q a realized dream—but it was in fact the opposite: the scientific achievement of the century—an accomplishment to rival electricity, antibiotics, and the steam engine.

And yet the researchers he'd recruited from Caltech, MIT, Berkeley, and UCSB, who painstakingly furled and unfurled reality in the layer cake of subbasement labs, had won no Nobel prizes. They could not publish. To even whisper of their work was a death sentence. They could be launching a technological revolution, but instead they toiled in obscurity to further the even-more-obscure political ends of whatever scheming Intelligence Community powerbrokers were footing the obscene bill. And for what?

So spies could chase their own tails? So Paul could maneuver to gain fleeting advantage in the Great Game? So the dream of empire might survive another day?

Luki unfolded the piece of paper that had been burning a

hole in his pocket and stared at the chicken-scratch. Notes from reviewing logs he wasn't supposed to have access to, logs that revealed what Paul was using Q to do. There was the predictable stuff: stealing foreign military plans and weapon designs, setting myriad traps, and all manner of SIGINT espionage. But Paul was also scraping the accounts of senators, agency staff, and federal judges who might threaten his budget or undermine the program. And harassing his ex-wife by sabotaging every device she touched. Q had invented a wonder of the modern world, and Paul had perverted it before anyone else even knew it existed.

But the scariest part was what Paul was building toward, what Q's contract extension would enable. He didn't just want to be able to break into any computer system. He wanted to create a rolling permanent record of everything on every computer system on the planet—a private mirror of the entire history of the entire internet and every device that had ever connected to it so that he could reach back through time to dredge up whatever secrets the past might offer to tighten his grip on the future. Catching lightning in a bottle meant he could smite people with it at will.

A shiver ran down Luki's spine. Using unprecedented means to such disturbing ends was simultaneously awe-inspiring and profoundly petty. He tore up the notes and let them scatter in the wind like so many dandelion seeds. Paul had reduced Q to a Machiavellian plaything when it should be powering an upgrade to civilization itself.

The problem was that building the quantum computer hadn't been cheap. Sansome had written the check to get Q up and running and then introduced Luki to Paul, who had become their first and only customer, providing the clandestine government contract that had paid for them to go from prototype to the real thing. Silence had been Paul's price: the unholy quiet he needed to use Luki's invention to pry open the internet and play voyeur.

Luki knew he had made a deal with the devil, but the devil was apparently the only one willing to pay the price of progress, and anyway, it was only a temporary measure. Luki had obtained the resources he needed to build Q. Paul had bought five years use of a digital master key. Today the contract would officially cross the finish line, and Luki would officially decline the impending extension. As a result, Q would finally be free to share their long-held secret with an unsuspecting world, kickstarting the quantum computing revolution that Luki did not want to admit he wanted so badly for fear that admission might somehow jinx it.

Sansome wouldn't approve of Q jettisoning their only customer on the brink of a lucrative tender, but Luki would make him see how much more valuable it would be to democratize access to the technology so that new industries could be built on top of it.

"Oy, mister, you wanna miss your flight or what?" Dexa called from the little beach-access parking area. She was leaning against her yellow Jeep holding two insulated mugs of homebrewed coffee. An experimental physicist with a meticulously organized mind, Dexa had quickly become Q's chief operating officer, freeing Luki to invent the software necessary to harness the qubits their breakthrough had unleashed. She was the rare kind of person who could dissect human systems as surely as mathematical ones. She was also, inevitably, his ride to the airport. "You all set? Cuz I can tell you the troops can't *wait* for the next act."

Luki hefted his backpack, hoping he hadn't forgotten

anything important, knowing he probably had. It was an odd trip to pack for. First stop was D.C., to close out the contract with Paul. Second stop was *The Liminal*, for Sansome's mandatory annual soiree. Third stop was back here where Luki belonged, to raise the curtain for that next act—whatever it might prove to be.

"I'll be right there," he said, taking a fortifying breath.

Down on the beach, snowy plovers darted across quicksilver crescents of wet sand. Gulls wheeled overhead. Out to sea, a black speck bobbed over the first wave of a set: a lone surfer. The second wave lined up and the figure pivoted in the water, paddling across the rising face at an angle and then down the sloping back to get into position for the oncoming third wave, which rose huge and shuddering and scary like the sudden shadow thrown by the beam of a flashlight.

Offshore wind blew feathers of spray from the cresting peak of the blue-gray giant and the surfer—pitifully small against the rising mass of water—paddled with single-minded ferocity, popping up onto her board, dropping in vertiginously, and arcing into a smooth bottom-turn just as the lip hurled itself out and forward, crashing into churning froth.

When he was a boy, Luki had visited an uncle in Durango, Biscay for the local feast day. The entire town had gathered around the naked oak trunk erected in the middle of the square—stripped of limbs and bark and topped with flowers. The swords of the Dantzari Dantza dancers had flashed as they stepped and wheeled through their ancient, mesmerizing choreography. The memory still burned bright in Luki's mind, even though the rest of that year was shrouded in the haze of pre-adolescence. Now, watching the surfer carve fluent, loose lines across the mirror-smooth face, feeling that he was somehow not just observing her but moving *with* her—tasting the salt on her tongue, leaning back to let her fingers drag along the heaving wall of water, ducking under the diamond curtain into the roaring singularity of the barrel—he experienced the same strange jealousy he'd once known gazing at the dancers: wanting desperately, impossibly, to *be* them, to embody grace as they did.

"Ready to break a man's heart?" asked Dexa.

"Ready as I'll ever be," said Luki.

Right when the wave was about to close out, the surfer swooped up to the last open stretch of lip and let her momentum carry her up into the air where she disappeared into a blast of spray that the rising sun infused with crosshatched rainbows.

As he turned toward Dexa and the coffee and the Jeep and the flight and Paul and Sansome and Q and the future, a pregnant melancholy overcame Luki at the implausible yet unequivocal knowledge that he was living a moment that would burn bright in his memory for years to come, as the dancers had.

4

THE ONLY THING Devon Chaiket could hear was her own voice.

That was the whole point of lining every square inch of the closet with soundproofing insulation and acoustic foam. The only problem was that they made the already small closet that much smaller, so that with her stool and laptop and recording equipment, Devon could barely fit inside these narrow walls covered in little black pyramids that swallowed sound like a black hole did light.

She turned off her mic, and then the light.

Silence.

Darkness.

Rabbit Hole: an oubliette of her own design.

Shit. With the guilty certainty of the frequently tardy, Devon realized she was running late for her meeting with Kai. She checked the time, glowing numbers confirming her intuition.

As soon as she opened the closet door, sounds flooded in from the restaurant below: clattering pans, muffled voices, the jingle of the bell attached to the front door.

Devon emerged into the bedroom that had been hers since childhood. Thirty years old and still living with her parents. She couldn't pretend that this was where she imagined she'd be by now. There was the Lynn Chevalier quote taped above her unmade bed: *We all know that stories spread, sometimes apotheosizing into memes. But much more interesting than straight sharing and reproduction is when stories inspire the telling of other stories in a cultural daisy-chain.* There was the crack running up through the plaster that for some strange reason she'd always imagined to be an extension of the San Andreas Fault. There was the battered dresser that was doing double duty because her closet was taken. There were the boxes of faded manga. There was the teetering stack of research notes. Beloved and pathetic. All of it. Desperately, predictably, comfortably pathetic. Her room was a shrine to the fruitless striving of the starving artist she had promised herself never to become.

Devon shrugged on her lucky jacket on her way out and, through force of habit, skipped the squeaky step on the way downstairs before entering the familiar chaos of the kitchen. Soup bubbled. Noodles fried. Her mom was chopping basil, the herb's fresh scent merging into the ambient smellscape of lemongrass, curry, and makrut lime. Her dad banged through the swinging half-doors calling out an order. Beyond him, the King beamed down on the restaurant's guests from the sepia photograph that enjoyed pride of place above the potted palms.

"Devon!" her dad was endearingly incapable of speaking her name without an exclamation point.

"Can you pick up shrimp?" asked her mom, green-stained

steel blade poised, as Devon unhooked her bike from the rack by the back door.

"Yes, *Mae*," Devon called back over her shoulder. "I'll stop by Tokyo Fish Market on the way home." She would pay for the shrimp herself, a rare opportunity to contribute to the family finances in some small way.

"Charge it to the restaurant account," said her dad in a tone that preempted objection.

Berkeley rushed past.

Devon loved this town, loved exploring the hills above it. There was a path that hugged the scientific research facilities of the United States' first national lab, dipped into the dappled shade of gnarled oak groves, and offered spectacular views of San Francisco's skyscrapers rising silver-blue across the ruffled bay. From up there you could see Adeline, the street down which Devon was racing, slash diagonal across Berkeley toward Oakland.

Pump. Pump.

Brake for a stop sign.

Pump. Pump. Pump.

The problem with having no money was that you couldn't think of anything else. You couldn't plan. You couldn't work toward something better. You could still dream, but they were nightmares born of anxiety. There was only the next bill, the next credit card payment. Your time horizon shrunk with your checking account. But Devon's future wasn't the only thing poverty devoured. Her parents were unfailingly supportive. They wouldn't let her pay for rent or even groceries. And yet Devon could feel their generosity curdling into resentment within her, throwing her self-doubt into stark relief. By accepting their support, wasn't Devon effectively stealing from the restaurant's slim margins to fund her podcast? It was one thing when your failures undermined your work and quite another when they began to sabotage your relationship with your family.

Red light.

If something didn't change soon, Devon would have to do the unthinkable: abandon *Rabbit Hole*. When you pour your whole self into something, you don't expect to have it shatter and spill you out across the floor. Actually, that's exactly what you expect, but you lie to yourself because otherwise you'd never be able to make the thing in the first place. Now that she could no longer deny how fast she was running out of time and money, Devon was left trying to convince herself that her heart wouldn't break when her project did.

Pump. Pump.

Forward. Always, forward. Wind in her face. Sweat on her back. A good ride got your blood moving. She needed to clear her head. Plus, she wasn't wasting her dwindling cash on Lyft.

Overpass.

Pump. Pump.

Turn. Zig-zag.

Pump. Pump.

Hop up onto the curb. Swing off as the bike's momentum carried it the last few feet. Lock it to the rack.

Here.

"'They were so desperate to document their lives that they forgot to live them.' -*Going Viral: A History of the Social Media Age*" was stenciled across the cement block wall in foot-high yellow letters surrounded by a cloud of meticulously illustrated internet iconography: the Facebook thumbs-up, the Twitter verified account checkmark, the Reddit upvote, the Mozaik mosaic, the Instagram heart, the YouTube comment speech bubble, and a dozen others that Devon didn't recognize but might have been real or invented.

Every time she visited Palimpsest, Kai's infamous café-bar, the graffiti covering the outside wall changed, fresh paint layered on fresh paint, the result of a never-ending series of commissions. It was the street art equivalent of a mandala—Tibetan monks laboring for months to create intricate patterns of colored sand, only to wipe them away upon completion and begin anew.

Taking one last look around at the bleak industrial wasteland that she knew Kai believed was the only appropriate context for Palimpsest, Devon stuffed her hands into the pockets of her lucky jacket and stepped across the threshold and into the bar.

The space was a single enormous open-air patio. Picnic tables were scattered everywhere, shade structures soaring above them in intersecting geometric shapes like the vast sails of a surrealist galleon plying urban seas. In the middle of it all was a square bar with dimensions that were a precise scaled-down version of the outer wall. A square within a square. But the wall was the star of the show. The interior was just as lushly decorated as the exterior: death's heads, tags, declarations of love, psychedelic fantasias, and philosophical aphorisms all bled into each other. Countless cans of spray paint were scattered at the base of the wall so that any patron could pick one up and participate in the creative melee.

Devon spotted Kai, who waved her over to a picnic table.

As Devon's boots crunched across the gravel, she rehearsed her pitch. With nearly a hundred thousand downloads per episode, it drove her crazy how close *Rabbit Hole* skated to insolvency, how dependent she was on soliciting major donors. But this story needed a real production and travel budget, and Human Capital was one of far too few actually writing checks for this kind of thing. Devon tried not to imagine what she'd be able to achieve if she was awarded the grant. Instead of jinxing herself, she needed to focus on getting ready for the all-important interview.

And who better to help her prep than a rare artist whose income matched the diversity and quality of their output?

5

THE CORK SHOT OFF into the unseasonably warm night with a jaunty *pop* and champagne spilled onto the napkin Paul had carefully folded around the neck of the sweating bottle. They stood on the back porch of his appropriately nondescript house on an appropriately nondescript suburban cul-de-sac in Northern Virginia. Dogwoods stretched skeletal branches in dark profile against faint stars straining to shine through the dull city glow of Washington D.C. across the Potomac.

Leaning against the doorframe, Luki watched the golden liquid arc into the waiting flutes and felt a burgeoning nostalgia for the straightforwardness that had characterized Q to date, a simplicity conferred by the clandestine program of which it was but a part. Thanks to Paul's bottomless black budget, they had been able to ignore everything but their work.

For all Luki's resentment of the use to which Paul put their invention, he couldn't deny the value of the gift the old spook had given them. Q wouldn't be what it was without Paul. Without Paul's contract, Q would have been just another startup crushed beneath the weight of its ambition, just another write-off in Human Capital's ledger. So as eager as Luki was to embark on the next stage of Q's journey, it was good that he was here taking a moment to commemorate the end of an era with the man who'd made that era possible.

Paul offered Luki a flute and then raised his own, saying, "To Q."

"I'll drink to that," said Luki with a grin.

Clink.

They drank, savoring the sharp effervescence.

"Remember the night Sansome introduced us?" asked Luki.

Paul chuckled. "I thought you were so full of shit."

"The feeling was mutual," said Luki.

"A g-man and a mad scientist walk into a bar…"

"Good thing Sansome was there to play ambassador."

Paul nodded. "I know it sounds silly, but part of my initial skepticism stemmed from the fact that Santa Barbara seemed too unlikely a birthplace for quantum computing. Beaches. Wine country. Tourists and celebrity weekenders up from LA."

"And I thought the promises you made were just braggy hand-waving," said Luki. "Sansome had to sidebar with me after you left to convince me it was real."

"Hey," said Paul, catching Luki's eye. "We made it real."

"I guess we did, after all," said Luki with a small smile.

They gazed out at the night in contemplative silence.

Luki thought about how solving mysteries inevitably seemed to reveal deeper mysteries, how so much of science was built on the careful monotony of precise experimentation, and so much could change when a burst of new theory cast old results in a new light. He thought about how often he emerged from the depths of the lab and stepped outside expecting it to be midnight and discovering it was in fact noon, or the other way around. He thought about apples hanging like glossy planets in his parents' orchard. He thought about how the next leg of his journey would take him back aboard *The Liminal* to see Sansome and his stable of chosen ones. He thought about anything and everything that might distract him from the fact that—as dangerously and inevitably as that surfer's wave—this conversation was building toward the moment when he would have to decline the contract extension Paul had been so long orchestrating, an extension that would fill Q's coffers but tighten its gag.

"Now," said Paul, meeting Luki's eye with sudden intensity, "I have great news."

Luki held the other man's gaze with far more assurance than he felt.

"Ten years. Ninety billion dollars," said Paul.

Luki opened his mouth and found he had nothing to say.

Paul grinned hugely. "The Select Committee on Intelligence handed down final budget approval last week. Locked and loaded, baby." He raised his flute. "To new beginnings."

Incompatible futures fanned out before Luki like a hand of cards. Seal the deal with a *clink*, secure unimaginable resources to further their secret toil, return to Dexa and the team with his tail between his legs. Would they stay to continue their work if it remained at the mercy of Paul's dark purposes? Or he could inform Paul that what for him had been prologue had been epilogue for Luki: Q was declining the extension. They had already been quietly laying the groundwork to publish their discoveries and reinvent themselves and their business—stabbing their benefactor in the back. That image prompted Luki to remind himself that despite this man's carefully cultivated innocuousness, he was the spymaster who oversaw an unprecedented digital surveillance program that Luki was loath to admit Q had enabled.

As the possibility space of those divergent futures collapsed into the finite present, Luki looked down at his flute. Champagne might just as easily christen a ship before a voyage as celebrate a long-awaited arrival on a foreign shore.

"Paul," he said, trying and failing to wish away the crack in his voice as sought-for conviction arrived, not with the unfiltered glare of certainty, but faint as starlight through city glow. "I'm sorry. Really, I am."

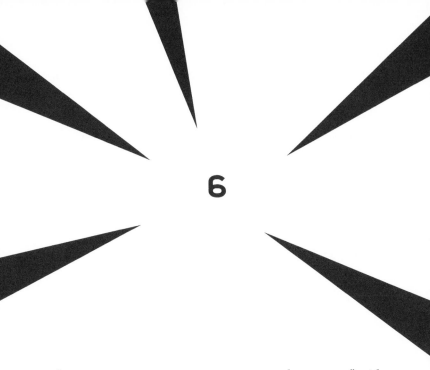

6

"I VISITED THE HAGIA SOFIA over the summer," said Kai as they walked a circuit around Palimpsest to inspect the latest artistic contributions. "Tourists everywhere and hot and sweaty as Chewbacca's butt crack, but it was worth it—all domes and arches and cultural collage." Kai illustrated the scope of the grandeur with expansive gestures. "They built it in 537 and since then it's been a cathedral, a mosque, a museum, and a mosque all over again. Empires, fortunes, and governments rose and fell around it. Holy Roman Emperors were crowned there, sultans prayed there, and now it's the backdrop for billions of selfies. Which of those do you think is the most important?"

"I have… no idea," said Devon, taken aback.

"Exactly," said Kai with a wicked grin. "Not knowing is what keeps it interesting."

Devon snorted and glanced sidelong at her friend. When they'd first met, Devon had been immediately fascinated by the extravagant breadth and depth of Kai's thinking. Only afterward, when she was making notes on some of the rabbit holes into which they'd burrowed over the course of that initial four-and-a-half-hour conversation, did Devon realize that she had no idea what Kai's last name or gender was. Another realization followed hot on the heels of the first: that the reason she hadn't noticed any ambiguity was that neither cultural category could hope to contain someone like Kai. The only appropriate pronoun was plural.

"What are you drinking?" asked Kai.

Devon shrugged. "I'll just take a water, thanks."

"Pregnant?" asked Kai.

"No!" said Devon. "It's only, I'm…"

Kai raised an eyebrow. "It's on the house, okay?"

"No, no," said Devon, blushing. "Seriously."

But Kai signaled one of the bartenders.

"I…"—*say thank you*, Devon told herself—"thank you."

"Come on now, don't be silly," said Kai with *tsk*.

"Your level of comfort with the unknown never ceases to amaze me," said Devon, trying to steer the conversation back on track. "I feel like I'm always wishing the world was more tractable, that life made more sense."

From a certain point of view, that feeling was the driving force behind Devon's vocation. But reality was too complex and changeable for even the most diligent research to prove more than a temporary salve.

Kai's golden eyes widened. "But I'm *never* comfortable," they said. "I actively seek out *discomfort*. It's only when we're out of our depth that we can find out what we're truly capable of, right?"

"You're living my best life, Kai," said Devon, shaking her head in admiration. If there was any truth in the truism that you gravitated to the mean of the people you surrounded yourself with, then Devon was glad to count Kai a friend.

"You're living *my* best life, dude! I would never have been inspired to open this place if I hadn't listened to that episode you did on the neuroscience of creativity. I'd been dreaming about doing something like Palimpsest forever but your story was the kick in the pants I needed to actually buckle up and do it. Hey"—Kai grabbed Devon's lapels and shook her gently—"stop selling yourself short."

"Selling myself is the reason I'm here, actually," said Devon. She had labored over the application for weeks, vacillating between manic excitement over the prospect of being selected and deep-seated frustration at having to do so much work in order to do so much work—not wanting to fully admit either sentiment even to herself. Some people lived lightly: navigating triumphs and defeats with easygoing composure, facing whatever life threw at them with a twinkle in their eye. Devon was not such a person. It wasn't that she didn't have a sense of humor. She just approached things with earnest intent. The weight she attributed to them was a sign of respect, an aspect of her unrelenting curiosity.

"Well, there you go," said Kai. "Hot tip number one: Sell yourself *long*, baby."

Devon laughed, despite her ambient anxiety. "Okay," she said. "Seriously, though, I need your help." Kai was one of the few artists Devon knew who managed to make a living making art. "Everything hinges on this grant interview. If I don't get it... I honestly don't know what I'll do. I've burned through my savings. Sponsorships aren't filling the gap." She was racking up overdraft fees. And she'd already let her health insurance lapse and lied to her parents about it. "I'll have to scrap the story and..."

Months of research, piles of annotated books and scientific articles, Devon had poured everything she had into this one. Scrapping it was inconceivable. This was the problem with making a podcast with only one or two monster episodes a year.

Go against the grain, she'd thought. *Instead of obeying the demands of the market, make something weird and wonderful that you want to exist in the world.* She should have added a peppy, *And have fun going broke along the way! Mad props for becoming a cliché!* Devon disgusted herself by swiping away an unwelcome tear. For fuck's sake.

Kai knelt and scooped up a can of spray paint. They gave it a good shake, cocked their head to the side, and attacked the wall with neon green calligraphy: "The struggle is real. The struggle is the work. The struggle is everything."

Then they turned to Devon and shrugged in a way that was somehow both tender and knowing.

Devon pressed her lips together and managed a small smile.

The bartender arrived with the drinks.

"Okay," said Kai. "Tell me about the goats."

7

LUKI'S FINGERNAILS DUG into his palms as Paul sped along dark roads, cone after cone of streetlight flickering by, tires squealing as they took corners too fast, engine whining as they accelerated out of them.

When Luki had informed Paul that Q was declining the extension in order to take their quantum computer public, Paul's gaze had turned inward. He carefully set down his champagne on the railing, gripped Luki's upper arm, marched him to Paul's appropriately nondescript sedan, backed out of the driveway, violently spun the car around in the cul-de-sac—no doubt raising questions in the minds of his neighbors as they were drifting off to sleep or settling into a Netflix binge—and roared off into the night.

Paul's face had turned to stone as surely as if he had glimpsed Medusa, but instead of petrifying him into a statue, it had spurred him to action. Now Luki was trying and failing to divine anything from the dashboard-illuminated frozen expression of the driver beside him.

Terror was not a feeling Paul had ever inspired in Luki before. The man might work for a three-letter agency, but he was a bureaucrat, not a secret agent. Luki couldn't help but wonder whether Paul's very blandness had been a carefully cultivated front.

Paul's silence was the scariest part. He hadn't said a single word since setting down the flute. The quiet opened like a chasm between them that Luki, even though he knew that running his mouth had never won him anything, was madly, desperately, unceasingly trying to bridge with apologies and explanations.

"Paul, this isn't Bletchley Park. Think of the good we could do."

"Paul, I'm sorry, but we fulfilled all the terms of the initial contract, and now we're ready to go in a different direction."

"Paul, we both know this isn't remotely Constitutional. How long are you planning to keep this up anyway?"

It wasn't that Luki's words landed on deaf ears. Instead, they piled up until they collapsed under their own weight.

Shut up, Luki told himself, *shut up, shut up, shut up.*

Logic would not stem the flood.

Logic fell apart when you were at the mercy of the director of an intelligence program so secret that you didn't even know what agency it was a part of or whose oversight, if any, it might be subject to. Even if he could sneak his phone out of his pocket, what could Luki do, call the cops? Paul would text their boss's boss's boss's boss's boss and Luki would be back to square one, or worse.

Not even the cold, hard realization of the staggering depths of his own naïveté could snatch the words from Luki's lips. Instead, what finally did was the seatbelt cutting into his chest as Paul screeched to a halt in the middle of an empty parking lot.

Luki hyperventilated in the passenger's seat as Paul rooted around in the trunk. What was he looking for? A nine-millimeter? A improvised garrote? An oiled leather case of neatly arranged scalpels and bone-saws? Realizing this was his chance, Luki pulled out his phone. It slipped out of his shaking hands, and he snatched it up from the floor. He might not be able to call anyone, but at least he could find out where they were. But when he finally managed to unlock the phone, there was no service.

Fuck.

This wasn't how Luki's life was supposed to have turned out. He still remembered the musty smell of the library tucked into the rugged hills of Basque country. Sick of the endless chores at his parents' cidery, he'd made a habit of sneaking off to scramble up peaks and explore misty oak groves. But one day when he was eleven or twelve, Luki had peered out of the undergrowth to see that the side door of the tiny village library had been left ajar. On a whim he still couldn't quite fathom, he'd slipped inside.

The book he'd pulled off the overstuffed shelf at random was a translation of Richard P. Feynman's memoir *Surely You're Joking, Mr. Feynman!* Luki had sat cross-legged on the floor and started flipping through it. He had been so absorbed that he hadn't noticed the librarian standing over him and was doubly shocked when instead of kicking him out with a beating, she offered him a slice of homemade cheesecake and helped him sign up for a library card so he could borrow any book he liked.

Luki's parents hadn't understood their son's newfound fascination with the legendary physicist, but the story of a loner defying the odds to construct theories that changed the world lit Luki's mind on fire. Feynman led Luki to Knuth and Turing and von Neumann and Lovelace. He became obsessed with Silicon

Valley, a fantastical kingdom of ideas and inventions and fame and fortune that existed in a different dimension than the mud and sheep and gossip of Basque country, which now seemed impossibly parochial. He studied math, then physics, earned a doctorate in quantum computing from Stanford, and was in the middle of a UCSB postdoc when Sansome had come knocking on his door.

Everything had been so much simpler in academia. Sure, you were always desperate for funding and the departmental politics were as vicious as they were inconsequential, but at least your mandate was clear: Publish. Then publish more. And then publish even more after that. It had felt like a burden at the time. And yet now Luki was willing to sacrifice everything to gain the freedom to share his work. What was the point of advancing the vanguard of science, if not to share the fruits of discovery?

The trunk slammed shut.

Luki hastily stuffed the useless phone back into his pocket and smelled the sour tang of his own cold sweat.

Sacrificing everything was all well and good in theory. In practice, it was another matter altogether.

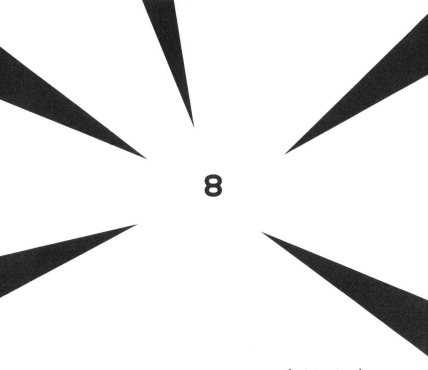

8

DEVON WORE HER LUCKY JACKET to the interview, but she had definitely not put the glasses in its pocket. They certainly weren't hers. She didn't even wear glasses.

Thanking the driver, she got out of the Lyft, glanced around at the converted waterfront former military buildings of Fort Mason, and pulled out the mysterious specs.

She had never seen anything quite like them before. Thick, round, tortoiseshell-patterned acetate frames, subtly shadow-boxed. Mirrored turquoise lenses. Turned tubular temples extending through the front with a sleek hinge maintaining a continuous line. They were unnaturally heavy and looked expensive. Devon turned them over in her hands. No branding. In fact, no numbers or marks of any kind. *Very* expensive, then.

How had they found their way into her pocket?

She should be rehearsing her pitch. She should be hustling across the parking lot to The Interval to make sure she was a few minutes early to meet Veronica, the Human Capital associate who would decide her fate. Instead, Devon donned the glasses experimentally.

They fit surprisingly well. The lenses were polarized but not corrective, shading everything in a delicate blue-green hue. Devon leaned over and peered at her reflection in the cracked window of a dilapidated Rivian.

The glasses were almost painfully cool. Seriously though, whose were they? She did a double take on her reflection. Something was moving on the wall of the building behind her. The mullioned windows were—impossibly—expanding across the cream stucco of the surrounding wall.

Devon spun around, but it hadn't been a trick of the light. New panes were popping into existence one after the other, the red metal frames extending like telescopic batons up and down, left and right, until the entire facade of the long, low building became a giant grid of glass. Was she having a stroke? Had someone laced her breakfast parfait with LSD?

Devon snatched the glasses off her face and, to her immense relief, reality reasserted itself. The building was just a building, complete with stucco walls and tiled roof. The laws of physics were no longer in abeyance. She sucked in a deep, briny breath and tried to slow her racing heart. Then she carefully tried on the glasses again.

The wall was an unbroken grid of windows once again, but something was off. Devon stepped forward. Upon closer inspection, each pane was itself made up of a grid of smaller panes, and each smaller pane was made up of yet smaller panes, on and on and on into red-framed infinity.

Dizzy, Devon retreated. She tore her gaze away from the fractal hallucination and looked back toward the city. Behind a line of trees rose the refreshingly normal hills of San Francisco. But even as she watched, the blocky houses and apartment buildings began to replicate and stack themselves like so many pieces of Lego, climbing higher and higher and higher, the towering geometric assemblage curving up and over the dome of baby blue sky—Escher on steroids.

With another tremendous act of will, Devon un-craned her neck. Beyond the marina's forest of masts, the fog rolling in around the towers of the Golden Gate Bridge began to stretch itself out like silly putty, tendrils reaching in all directions and twining around each other like the thousand tentacles of some mythical sea creature. The fluffy mass pulsed from within across every color of the rainbow.

Then the strobing fog-tentacles arranged themselves to scrawl a note across the sky, each word dissolving into the next:

A little present to cheer you up from a project I'm working on. If things get desperate, sell 'em on the interwebz. They're going for serious $$$ right now. Oh, and don't even bother asking for deets. The NDA is tighter than skinny jeans.
XOXO, Kai

Kai.

Devon had last worn her lucky jacket to Palimpsest three days ago. Kai must have slipped her the glasses then. They must be part of some new augmented reality art project. It was hard to fathom the cost of developing whatever custom hardware and software made these seamless, fractal visions possible. Then again, Kai's CV included plenty of wild stunts. Devon would never forget the ethereal sight of a life-size neon green Godzilla stomping through the midnight streets of downtown San

Francisco. The apparition was made up of thousands of drones flying in precise formation—orchestrated by Kai in flagrant violation of gods knew how many laws. Kai had told Devon afterward that a VP at Sony had funded the entire affair on the sly in what turned out to be a misguided guerrilla marketing effort for yet another reboot. Kai's work had gone viral, the movie hadn't.

Speaking of funding, trippy technophile experiments could wait. Devon had a grant to secure.

Veronica.

The interview.

This was her chance. An opportunity to escape the hamster wheel of crushing debt and net-sixty sponsorship contracts and barely being able to pay her freelance audio engineer and living and recording in her parents' house when her friends from college were collecting stock options like poker chips and debating which was the best labradoodle breeder. *This was her chance,* as long as she didn't fuck it up.

Devon removed the glasses, eyed them suspiciously—otherworldly portals that they were—folded them up, and stuffed them back into her jacket pocket. Damn. She would never be able to bring herself to sell such a singular gift, however much enthusiasts might be shelling out for them. Kai was too generous.

Get in the zone, Chaiket. She hurried toward The Interval and tried to remember Kai's equally generous advice. *Sell yourself long, baby.* Yes, that was it. *The struggle is real. The struggle is the work. The struggle is everything.* She could do this. She *would* do this.

Devon squared her shoulders, opened the door, stepped into The Interval, and had to pat her pocket to make sure the glasses were stowed because the space inside looked like it might have been the product of their uncanny transformations.

Directly in front of her was a large model solar system in

which intersecting steel circles held miniature planets in their orbits. Behind the display, a two-story floor-to-ceiling library was stuffed with books, a spiral staircase rising to access the upper shelves. On the far wall, a small frame-mounted robot was writing complex mathematical equations across a massive chalkboard. The shapes and colors on a painting behind the bar morphed so slowly that it took Devon a second to realize they weren't static, and a small group was playing a board game atop what was apparently intended to be a table: an interlocking set of steel gears large and intricate enough to be a physical manifestation of a steampunk horologist's wet dream, covered by long sheet of glass.

"Devon?" asked a woman in a leather apron carrying a tray of lushly garnished cocktails.

Devon nodded.

"Back room." The woman nodded to indicate where Devon should go and then proceeded to serve the board-game players.

Devon walked past the bar, injecting as much purpose into her stride as she could muster while reviewing her mental checklist one last time. It wasn't about her. It was about the story. She just needed to show them why it *needed* to be told.

The door to the back room opened and a tall man wearing a gray Patagonia vest over a pink button-up gave her a wide grin and extended a large hand. His hair and short beard were charcoal peppered with white, his smiling eyes auburn. A hale fifty, give or take.

"You're not Veronica," said Devon, taking his hand and realizing belatedly that she recognized his face from the Human Capital TED talk she'd watched in preparation for this interview.

"She was kind enough to let me take the meeting," he said with an apologetic shrug. "My name is Sansome Haverford. And I'm a *huge* fan of your show."

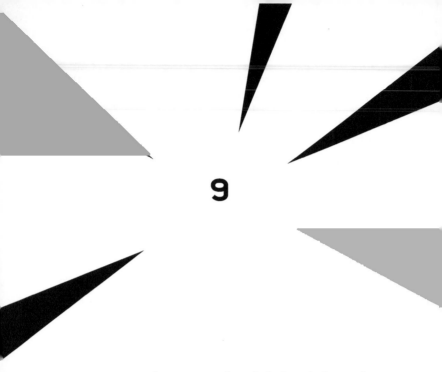

9

PAUL OPENED the passenger door, flicked on the heavy-duty flashlight he'd found in the trunk, and pointed the beam out into the darkness beyond the parking lot. Trying not to piss himself, Luki took the hint, unclipped his seatbelt, and got out of the car. Paul strode off, then looked over his shoulder, and Luki made to follow, trying not to wonder whether he was walking to his own execution.

It was hard to figure out where they were going when Luki could only get a good look at whatever the harsh, juddering beam touched, but it seemed to be some kind of campus or office park. Gravel crunched under his shoes. Lawns encroached on the pedestrian path. A hunched building slipped away into the darkness behind them.

Luki had exhausted his cascading justifications on the ride to… wherever they were. Now it felt like uttering a single word would require Herculean effort. The lump in his throat, the tightness in his chest, the cramp in his stomach, everything conspired to lock him up within himself, the final refuge from whatever horrors awaited him here.

How he wished that the rules governing the quantum realm might seep up to infect the human, that reality might prove malleable enough for him to bend it toward escape.

Without warning, Paul turned off the path and onto the grass and Luki followed, struggling to keep his footing on the uneven ground. Maybe he was asleep on the flight to Reagan National and this was just a dream born of anxiety and discomfort. Maybe this stumble was his mind's way of justifying external turbulence. Oh, the joy he would feel to open bleary eyes and see the back of a tray table.

Luki almost ran into Paul as the older man stopped in front of a tall stone wall that had appeared out of nowhere. He stepped close and shone the flashlight directly at it.

"Marquette, Michigan," said Paul, the first words to come out of his mouth since he'd set down his champagne. He reached out and touched a stone embedded in the wall.

Luki steeled himself for a hidden door to spring open revealing stairs leading into the bowels of a clandestine facility complete with an operations center plastered with screens displaying a cornucopia of intelligence feeds, a maze of tunnels through which those with the right clearance could spirit themselves anywhere in the capital, and the interrogation chamber that would be the last room he would ever see.

"Look at it," said Paul, tapping the stone again.

Luki realized with a start that this imperative was meant for him and not some unseen guard. He peered at the red and gray brick that had been warped by sun, wind, and rain into a miniature topography worthy of Gaudí.

"Sandstone from a quarry in Marquette, Michigan," said Paul. "That's seventy years of erosion." He tapped a different, yellowish brick that resembled the shattered crust of a creme brûlée. "Marble from Coimbra, Portugal." Stepping back, he pointed the beam of the flashlight at various mismatched stones embedded in the checkerboard wall above them. "That black one's basalt from Puebla. There are fossils in that marble from Austria—ancient corpses buried in the Alps. That there's Pompton Pink granite from the fine state of *New Jersey*." He pronounced the name of the state with an obnoxious imitation of the local accent.

Gooseflesh rising on his arms, Luki wondered whether his refusal to accept the deal had come as such a shock to Paul that it had triggered psychosis, though this line of reasoning didn't clarify how such a possibility might impact Luki's odds of survival. What would Dexa do if Luki never returned? Would she and the team question whatever plausible explanation Paul's people would use to justify Luki's disappearance? What would become of Q? What would his parents think when the son who had already ventured so very far from home vanished altogether? He had a sudden, visceral memory of the funky-sweet smell of rotting apples.

"There are more than two thousand samples." Paul ran the flashlight beam around the edges of the wall—meticulously constructed from stones that didn't match, like a toddler had assembled it out of multicolored blocks—which Luki now saw stood alone and incongruous in the middle of the open lawn.

"It's the longest running stone weathering experiment on the planet," Paul continued. "Builders knew they couldn't always trust lab tests. They wanted to see real-world results."

Every stone was indeed unique—an individual patch in a rocky quilt held together by Portland cement mortar. Standing out here by itself, the technicolor wall felt more like a surreal-ist art installation than a National Institute of Standards and Technology experiment.

"I don't understand," said Luki as cracks began to spread through what was left of his sanity and the vice around his chest ratcheted a notch tighter.

"They built this thing to demonstrate that American rock was as good as anyone else's," said Paul. "People used to import stone from China and Europe because they thought our own deposits weren't good enough. Domestic quarry owners wanted to prove them wrong, and Washington was happy to help."

Reeling and disoriented by this impromptu lecture, Luki touched a piece of limestone for support, cream shot through with curved slashes of black—a product of some unimaginable act of geological violence. The rock was cold and coarse against his skin. The sensation yanked him back into the moment.

Paul cocked his head. "I look at this wall and I see a world map," he said. "Each square is a people, a nation. The experiment tests whether and how they weather history, who will stand the test of time."

Paul turned to Luki and his face—rendered angular and ghostlike by reflected light—came suddenly and vividly alive, as if he had swung back into close proximity after arcing through a long orbit.

"My job"—he said in a voice so quiet that Luki strained to hear over the roar of his own blood in his ears—"is to see that *we* do. Your invention is our scrying glass. You do not *lend* such an artifact to an empire. So I will shower you with riches. I will re-write laws on your behalf. I will clear any obstacles that stand in your way. But if you ever so much as *hint* that you are considering snatching back your arrow from this great nation's quiver, by the powers vested in me as one of its defenders, I will damn you to a personal hell developed with the same obsessive rigor as your precious quantum computer. Your fate will make Prometheus weep in sympathy as the eagle rips out his liver. But"—Paul's voice rose to normal volume and found a relaxed, affectionate cadence—"this is all clearly a simple misunderstanding. You must forgive my little excursion. A man is entitled to his eccentricities. Shall we head home and raise a toast to celebrate this new chapter in our historic collaboration? I have another bottle of the '90 Salon stashed away."

Forces gathered in the night around them, darkness pressing in against the flashlight's beam. Destiny was not a muse, but a wrestler that grappled you into submission. You couldn't win. You couldn't even escape. You could only tap out and hope to live another day.

"So, whaddaya say?" asked Paul with such apparent warmth Luki half-imagined that despite the leading edge of the freshly sharpened guillotine brushing the hairs on the back of his neck, this was all, in fact, a simple misunderstanding.

Luki swallowed the lump in his throat and, hating himself even more than he hated Paul, spoke the two words that cut most deeply against the grain of his soul: "Yes, sir."

"That's my boy," said Paul, clapping him on the back. "One day, we'll look back on this and laugh."

In the verdant tangle of Luki's heart, the future withered on its vine.

10

TRYING TO SHAKE OFF the sense of dread that Sansome's call had left in its wake, Geoff lowered himself onto the steps of UC Berkeley's Doe Library. Ionic columns studded the Beaux-Arts facade. The campus architect had designed it to be an exemplar of his vision for an "Athens of the West" in an era when such aspirations seemed within the realm of possibility—before history intervened.

Students tossed a frisbee on the well-groomed lawn in front of the steps. Laughter. Music pulsing from a portable speaker. The orange disc sketched wide arcs from hand to hand and all Geoff could think about was the ten thousand viruses that embarked and disembarked every time it touched a palm, the manifold bacteria that hitched a ride whenever it fell to the grass. Immune cells waging their endless wars of attrition. DNA reproducing and recombining, every random mutation capable of flipping symbiote to contagion.

It was wrong to look at the students and see people. They weren't just people. Each was a civilization, an ecosystem, a universe unto themselves. Trillions of cells dancing to an impossibly complex tune. Humans weren't unitary creatures, but waveforms rolling through the medium of life. A person was an organizing principle.

And what principle organized Geoff's life? To ask such a question was to touch your reflection in a dark pool, only to throw the surface into rippling chaos.

Chaos seemed to be what Geoff was destined to sow.

Bakunawa had torn the world to shreds. In Cebu, the local, provincial, and national government had lied about the outbreak to protect the tourism industry, and then to cover their own asses, even as those tourists dispersed to the far corners of the earth bearing their deadly cargo. Then the hospitals were overrun, and medical staff began to die. Panicked people emptied grocery store shelves, and disrupted supply chains failed to refill them. Rumors snowballed into conspiracy theories compounded by grifters who saw an opportunity to carve out new factions based on blood or ideology. The power went out. Wastewater treatment facilities flooded. That's when people started reaching for their guns—all too plentiful in a country that had grown to rival the United States in firearms per capita.

Geoff and his team worked through it all, sweating in their bunny suits, hoping against hope for a cure, their hastily constructed field laboratory protected by special forces and superstition.

Most people thought of disease as a biological problem. If the right doctors and scientists tried hard enough, they could fix the body like a programmer debugged code. But epidemiologists knew firsthand that social dynamics often trumped microbiological dynamics. A society was only as strong as its systems were resilient.

Sunlight broke through the marine layer to highlight a student in profile as she released the frisbee, arm extended like Pallas Athena.

Geoff's heart skipped a beat.

It was Molly.

A group of chattering undergrads engulfed Geoff, flowing around him like a stream around a boulder. Had she seen him too? Could he make it into the library without her noticing? Was he really so afraid to face a former graduate? The arguments had been bad, but the long slide into silent resentment had been far worse. He'd tried his best to do right by her, to be the mentor she needed, but Molly had wanted to continue the work that he had made it his mission to derail. She hadn't been there in Cebu. She hadn't seen what these tools could do. She knew they needed to be controlled, but she didn't *feel* it. Frustrated, she'd left the lab to start her startup, but even autonomy couldn't help the fact that Geoff controlled the patents for the IP she was so eager to put to use. Her enthusiasm terrified him. As the group around him dispersed, Geoff found himself on his feet, buzzing with anxiety.

But it wasn't Molly after all. Just another young woman throwing herself into the academy's maw, replete with dreams.

Geoff pivoted to face the library.

The Athens of the West.

A place where new ideas glittered like sequins in the fabric of a city-state governed by a nominal democracy, riven by internecine struggle, and manipulated by fickle, impenetrable gods.

Perhaps the architect hadn't been so deluded after all.

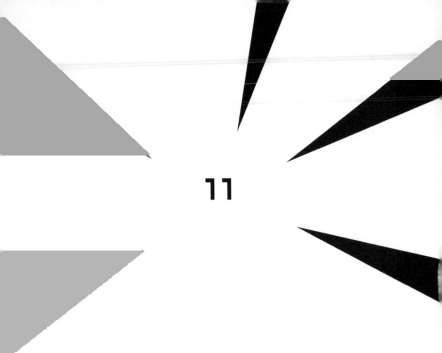

11

"THIS ROOM IS TOO SMALL for an elephant," said Sansome. "So let's address it up front. We've already awarded you the grant. The full amount is being transferred to your account as we speak."

Devon opened her mouth. Closed it again.

Warm afternoon light poured in through the window. The room was a single enclosed booth, a photograph of some kind of spiral fossil mounted on the ceiling. Her hands cupped the flat white on the table in front of her—complete with winking-emoji foam art.

Her mind should be racing. Instead, it refused to start as stubbornly as her mom's 1992 Volvo.

Sansome leaned forward.

"Look," he said. "I subscribe to a lot of podcasts but the only ones I actually *listen* to are *Song Exploder*, *Akimbo*, and *Rabbit Hole*. There's a reason for that. You're doing things differently. Whenever I listen to your show, I realize that everyone else is barely scratching the surface. It's like reading Twitter your entire life and then discovering that there's such a thing as books."

His fingers drummed on the table eagerly. "Like your episode on the Distributed Heist? Stealing $781 million worth of art from private collections in a single operation coordinated remotely by a single guy and executed by dozens of gig economy workers with no knowledge they were even participating in theft. Pumping the proceeds into similarly orchestrated civil rights and resistance efforts in China." Sansome touched his temples. "I mean, harpZkord is a genius. And maybe the most impressive part of the whole thing is that you managed to actually interview him." Devon smiled inwardly at the misgendered pronoun. They had algorithmically camouflaged harp's voice as male neutral for the podcast, and the fact that it confirmed hacker stereotypes strengthened the disguise. "It's as good as getting Banksy or Satoshi."

Devon would never forget working on that story. The taste of fried dumplings would forever be associated with clambering up the dizzyingly steep learning curve of opsec that kept highest-level targets like harp alive and free. There had been so, so many hoops to jump through. It had taken years to earn her trust, and months for Devon to get herself clean enough that harp would risk direct contact.

Okay, those were actual thoughts. However reluctantly, Devon's brain was finally starting to turn over.

"Can we back up a minute?" she asked. "Did you say that you've already awarded me the grant?"

Sansome nodded impatiently and Devon's head spun as she did her best to rein in expectations that were champing at the bit.

"Don't get me wrong," said Devon. "I'm thrilled to accept it, but wasn't this interview supposed to be competitive?"

Despite her valiant efforts at self-control, Devon's brain was already doing logistics—and having finally gotten in gear, it wouldn't stop accelerating. Airfare options. Setting up interviews with sources at the national park, the research centers, the ministry, the various villages, the conservancy, and veterans of the program itself. Reef-safe sunscreen. Confirming with Juan Jose and chartering a boat. Pelican cases for the recording equipment. Shoes that could handle broken lava fields. Her parents would freak. She couldn't wait to tell Kai.

Sansome grinned. "You know why I chose this place?" He tapped the tabletop. "It's not the coffee or the cocktails, though both are excellent. It may be the only bar in San Francisco owned and operated by a nonprofit. That nonprofit is dedicated to fostering long-term thinking—the gear-gasm-table out there is part of a prototype for a clock designed to last ten thousand years. But the coolest project the founder, Stewart Brand, is involved in is using synthetic biology to bring back the woolly mammoth from extinction. And you know why? Because when humans killed off all the mammoths, there weren't any other six-ton beasts stomping around the far north. And no more stomping meant the ground became less compact, which made permafrost melt much faster once global temperatures started rising because of climate change. And when permafrost melts, it releases methane, which is a super potent greenhouse gas—further accelerating climate change."

Devon frowned. "So Brand wants to revive the mammoths so they can stomp around the Arctic, pack the permafrost tighter, and break the positive feedback loop so the planet doesn't broil?"

"Ding, ding, ding!" said Sansome. "Exactly. It's brilliant. But it also points to a much bigger issue. The mammoth project is only possible because all the advances in genetics and computing over the past few decades have given science a new suite of tools to experiment with the building blocks of life. China is pumping ungodly sums into R&D. So are Russia, India, and South Korea. I mean, shit, even *Canada* is getting in on the action. Even though it had a lengthy head start, the U.S. is falling dangerously behind. Plus, we have the highest regulatory hurdles. Basically, the government is saying we won't invest in this *and* we won't let you do anything. So all the best talent is moving elsewhere where they can get paid better to do more interesting work."

"As an investor, that must be frustrating," said Devon. Sansome's cv was a uniquely Bay Area amalgam of venture capital and kiteboarding humblebrags. But he was more than a typical VC. Human Capital didn't just invest in technology startups, it backed pop stars, screenwriters, scientists, and other movers and shakers whose influence scaled according to a power law and whose work might yield OUTSIZED? exponential returns on investment. To some extent, in addition to being a financier, the man across the table from her with his pink shirt and silver tongue was also a kingmaker—or at least that seemed to be what he aspired to be, and the breadth and depth of his portfolio showed that while such things were difficult to gauge, in his case it wasn't wholly bluster. The grant program Devon had applied for was a kind of farm team for up-and-coming talent. If things went well, she'd advance to the big leagues. Locked doors opening. Was this what things going well felt like? Maybe she'd finally be able to afford her own place. Maybe she'd be able to record at an actual studio or build her own in a room larger than a closet. But if she was honest with herself, more than anything she just wanted this digression, and this meeting, to end so that she could start packing.

"Right," said Sansome. "So it's obvious why I care, but I'm convinced that the real problem is *education*. If people understood biology better and could wrap their minds around the promise of all this new technology—and the ethical quandaries it raises of course—there wouldn't be so much knee-jerk regressivism out there. If we fear the unknown, then making these issues *known* would mean we can stop hiding from bogey men and actually have a thoughtful, informed debate about the future. And nobody, I mean *nobody*, can make a complicated issue compelling and comprehensible like you. So when Veronica forwarded me your proposal, I told her right then and there that we were funding it. Your goats might not have CRISPR, but they've got damn near every other ingredient. You tell this story, tell it well, and it'll change how your listeners think about humanity's relationship with biology. And alongside our other content investments, maybe it'll move the needle for enough people to save this country from itself—and others."

Devon's heart fell. The plans she was making in her head melted like ice cream under summer sun. She wanted this so badly. All she had to do was say yes. But she hadn't gotten into this business to become a shill.

"Look," she said. "I appreciate your interest. Really, I do. But this is a complex story, and there are many aspects of it that may shine a light on how more thought and oversight are needed, not less. I never know where a story will lead until I chase it, but this one very well may lead to a conclusion that undermines your goals, or a conclusion irrelevant to your goals, which I won't change the story to suit. So I'm going to have to respectfully decline your generous offer."

He raised a hand. "Hold on," he said, shaking his head. "Sorry for subjecting you to that rant. I must have let my enthusiasm get the better of me. But I'm not asking you to do a puff piece. I'm looking to help spark a conversation that our culture needs to have. I don't want to lean on the scales. I want you to do this story *your* way and reach whatever conclusions you reach. Having read the proposal, I just want to *listen* to the damn episode already. And anyway, the money is already in your account, and I'm not taking it back."

He paused, then cocked his head to the side. "Is it weird that I feel like I know you even though we've never met before just because I'm so used to hearing your voice on the podcast?"

Devon smiled sadly. "Sometimes when I hear my own voice on the podcast, I'm not sure I know myself." She took a sip of her flat white. Where was the line between ethical reporting and self-sabotage? Was her knee-jerk hesitation a manifestation of high moral standards or just another way to hide from the success she didn't believe she deserved? "So. Full funding. Complete creative control. Sounds too good to be true. What's the catch?"

"The catch," said Sansome, "is that you keep the entire budget, but don't book your own travel. Instead, come with us. All expenses paid. Your grant application inspired this year's annual Human Capital excursion."

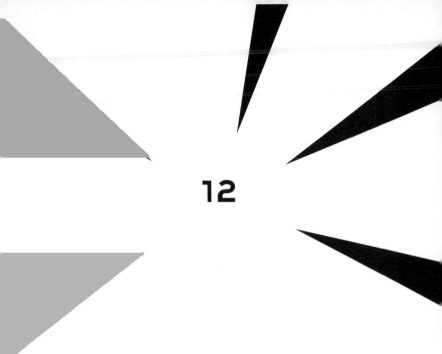

12

WHAT DID YOU BRING to the meeting that might force you to betray everything you stood for? Geoff unzipped his canvas duffel carry-on and stared vacantly into the empty bag. The thick green fabric had faded to olive, and the shoulder strap was fraying at the edges, but it would still serve, even after twenty years of frequent use. This was the bag he'd taken with him to Cebu.

The bunny suits had been shipped separately.

Geoff strode out of the bedroom, opened the liquor cabinet, poured himself three fingers of gin, and tossed it back, wincing at the searing heat in the back of his throat.

He poured another three fingers, ordered Alexa to play Radiohead's *In Rainbows*, and stepped out onto the balcony. Some people hated that album, said it represented a crucial and disappointing break from their previous work. Some people had fallen in love with the band because of it. Geoff suspected that while he appreciated losing himself in its haunting, dreamy soundscape, the divisiveness of the album itself was the real appeal.

That was what art did: divide people. Those who loved it, those who hated it. Those who got the joke, those who didn't. People liked to talk about the connections art forged without acknowledging that any *us* cast a shadow of *them*.

Geoff and Sansome had been an *us*, once.

Geoff and Molly too.

If art divided people, ideals atomized them.

A fog bank had engulfed San Francisco and was creeping across the Bay. He watched as it swallowed Treasure Island and the traffic-choked Bay Bridge. He sipped the gin. It was harsh and grassy. He imagined the warmth in his belly expanding to fill his entire being until he floated away—no longer a person but a person-shaped balloon filled with herbaceous fumes.

The wall of fog devoured downtown Berkeley and the university campus. The top of the Campanile pierced the surface of the white blanket, until even it was enveloped by the encroaching billows. And then the fog was rushing up into the hills toward Geoff's balcony, erasing neighborhood after neighborhood, seeming to accelerate as it approached, until it washed up and over him.

Geoff stared out into damp, gray blankness.

He wasn't sure there was a world out there anymore.

He wasn't sure he wanted there to be.

Shivering, he downed his tumbler and went inside. He poured himself another gin and took down the *tenegre* sword from where it hung above the mantel of the nonfunctional fireplace. The pommel was carved into the head of a Bakunawa— the dragon whose movements defined the geomantic calendar of ancient Filipino shamans. The mythical beast was said to have controlled eclipses, earthquakes, rain, and wind. It had eaten six of the seven moons. Its namesake had eaten 36 million times as many souls.

Geoff grasped the hilt and unsheathed the sword. The blade was curved and beautiful and cruel, expertly crafted.

The eerie music swelled.

Raising the sword, Geoff pricked the fleshy pad of his thumb.

He didn't pop.

Instead, blood welled up.

So. Not a balloon after all.

He sucked his thumb, tasting iron, then dunked it into his gin. It stung—wisps of red seeping out into the clear alcohol, millions of cells dying, the glorious machinery of their genes and enzymes and proteins coming apart, descending into entropy.

He clamped his mouth shut, only then realizing that he'd been speaking—a meandering soliloquy careening into hoarse shouts. Whatever meaning his words might have contained faded like the memory of a passing dream. His throat was raw. His mind blank. Swallowing the blood-pink gin, he spun and flung the sword across the room. He'd thought it might sink into a beam, quivering cinematically, but it just left an ugly notch in the drywall and clattered to the floor.

Returning to the bedroom, Geoff regarded the abandoned canvas bag lying crumpled on the unmade bed. He tossed in his passport and the dogeared Discworld novel and zipped it shut. Then he slung the otherwise-empty duffel over his shoulder and walked downstairs to catch a car to the airport.

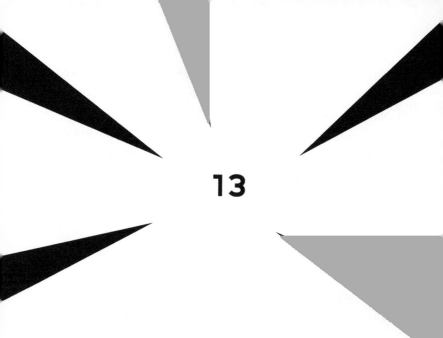

13

"LOOK, I PREFER to burn bushes rather than beat around them," said Molly. "We need those patents."

Sansome looked up from Zoom. Beyond his office window, manicured gardens progressively transitioned into grassy hills and sheltered forest. The further from the house you went, the wilder the ranch became. Tigers stalked dappled oak groves. Gazelles drank from fresh springs fed by the Mount Tamalpais watershed. Komodo dragons, giant otters, chimpanzees, and even a polar bear made their home on this little piece of Northern California that Sansome had carved out for them— the menagerie a living illustration of the ideas that Darwin had first drafted on the very papers lining Sansome's office wall.

It was amazing how far paying attention could take you.

"I didn't know your scientific sensibility had room for religious allusion," said Sansome, recognizing the evasion even as he voiced it. The jet was fueled and ready. Adventure beckoned.

He wanted to enjoy the company of his flock, watch Devon do what she did best, hear the lilting tones of Luki's queer accent. Now was not the time for yet another problem.

"I contain multitudes," said Molly, trademark intensity sharpening her delicate features. "And what these multitudes are shouting in unison is that it's time for you to go biblical on his ass."

"Yes, well..." Sansome faltered under the weight of all the things he couldn't say. He wanted to help, wanted to reach down and sweep the obstacles from her path. "These things take time, but we'll get there."

"Not good enough," said Molly. "My lawyers have dissected this thing every way they can. I hate to admit it, but without those patents, we're shark chum."

Molly was one of those people whose personality was a force of nature. Fate bent to her will. Sansome loved to invest in people like her, though he'd found that fate, however bent, still managed to surprise even the most headstrong. Her team was pioneering a new genetic engineering technique to develop food crops resilient to the accelerating extremities of climate change. Her almonds required thirty percent less irrigation. Her pears could handle both higher temperatures and a wider temperature range. Her wine grapes resisted smoke taint. She was even growing corals that could thrive in an increasingly acidic ocean. But commercializing Molly's advances required licenses to the patents on which her work was built, patents controlled by the one man who would never grant them: Molly's one-time post-doc adviser, who also happened to be the first person Sansome had ever invested in.

There was a quiet knock on Sansome's office door.

Esteban wouldn't be interrupting if it wasn't important, and when Sansome pivoted to meet his cappuccino eyes, the urgency behind them was readily apparent.

Sansome turned back to the video call. "Some battles are won with brute force, others require patience and subtlety," he said to Molly. "Let's continue this conversation aboard ship."

Molly raised her eyebrows. "Shark chum," she repeated before signing off.

Esteban reached Sansome's side in three quick strides. He leaned over the desk and called up the surveillance feed. Geoff stood on his porch, tumbler in hand, staring out into impenetrable fog.

"Speak of the devil," Sansome said under his breath, and felt Esteban shift beside him.

Spectral music Sansome recognized but couldn't place played in the background. Geoff slugged the drink, turned on his heel, and went inside. The feed shifted to a camera with a view of the living room. Sansome had hired a team of former FBI agents to rig Geoff's house three years ago. He hadn't wanted to, and still felt terrible about it. Geoff was a friend, even if he wouldn't admit it. His vaccine had made Human Capital what it was, earning Sansome billions. They'd been through hell together. Spying on him was wrong, but it was necessary. Geoff was unstable, and the stakes were too high.

Geoff refilled his drink and set it on a side table. He looked up at something out of frame, then crossed the room and took whatever it was off the wall, body blocking Sansome's view.

Esteban was saying something.

"Quiet," snapped Sansome.

"Him, not me," said Esteban.

The murmuring was coming from Geoff, interpolating itself into the music. Sansome raised the volume, but still couldn't quite make out the words. Then there was a flash of movement and suddenly Geoff was holding a naked sword. The empty sheath fell from his other hand.

"Shit," said Sansome, the curse catching in his suddenly dry throat. The ranch fell away. The world narrowed to the screen in front of him.

Geoff gazed down at the blade and words tumbled out of him. A chill ran through Sansome. Names of people long dead. Lingo from field hospital procedures. Epidemiological statistics. Lines from the Nobel acceptance speech. All of them tangled into a knot that was only comprehensible to those who knew what to listen for. This was worse than the footage of Geoff's thrashing nightmare Esteban had sent Sansome after his TED talk. Much worse.

Geoff raised the blade and Sansome found himself gripping the sides of the monitor, wanting, impossibly, to thrust himself through it to still Geoff's hand.

But Geoff lowered the point and pricked his thumb. He sucked the wounded finger and then dunked it into the tumbler. All the while, his monologue accelerated like a runaway train. Case rates. Symptoms. Death counts. Headlines. Tenets of the Protocol for Ethics in Synthetic Biology. And more names. Always names. What had started as a whisper was now a hoarse, ragged shout. Geoff's face was livid, his eyes bulging.

And then, abruptly, silence.

Geoff looked surprised, as if overcome by a flash of self-awareness he hadn't bargained for. Then he wound up and flung the sword across the room. Sansome jerked at the sudden violence. The curved blade gouged the wall and clattered to the floor.

Sansome leaned back and covered his face with his hands. The Spanish Flu killed more than three times as many people as World War I, yet the deadliest pandemic in history—until Bakunawa usurped it—was glossed over in history books because humanity facing an invisible virus lacked the drama and political freight of Great Powers lining up against each other. It was hard to relish victory over a mindless thing you couldn't even see with the naked eye. That was why the world could never find out the real story behind Bakunawa: as long as the virus was a product of natural evolution, it remained a bitter tragedy with only fate to blame.

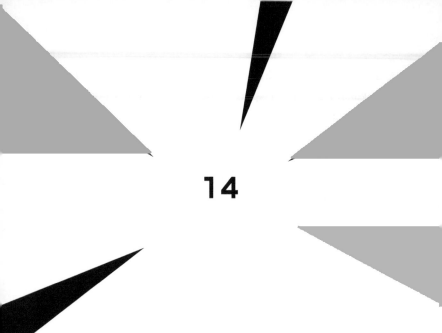

14

THE SOFT SHUSH of wind through candelabra cactus spines.

Devon leaned in close, adjusting the mic. These were the sounds you couldn't anticipate or replicate, the texture of the world she would build in listeners' minds.

For years people had been waiting for virtual reality goggles to make good on the promise of the digital metaverse. But, as with so many paradigm shifts, the VR killer app had slipped in via a side door: audio. AirPods had ushered in a new reality as surely as the iPhone had. The metaverse was the internet whispering in your ear.

Devon pitched her voice low so that her words mingled with the wind instead of running over it, "Humanity has turned wilderness into garden, fearsome beast into zoological curiosity, and famine into plenty. But we have yet to adapt instincts honed by millennia of scarcity for a world of abundance—with all its unintended consequences."

Broken lava fields extended in every direction like the shattered crockery of an angry god—the jagged edges of pitted black rock ready to tear away flesh as easily as a cheese grater. The tropical sun beat down and its heat radiated right back up, with Devon baking in the middle. She might as well be standing on the surface of a distant world. If she told this tale just right, might her listeners glimpse the sublime wonders of their home planet through fresh, alien eyes?

She was here.

Here!

She still couldn't quite believe it.

"Galápagos." The word rolled around in her mouth like a Jolly Rancher. "Galápagos. Galápagos. Galápagos!" The origin of *The Origin of Species*. Supply depot for explorers and conquistadors. Refuge for pirates. Setting for Kurt Vonnegut's madcap apocalyptic novel. Home to a veritable cornucopia of endemic species. Beads strung across the equatorial Pacific by liquid magma welling up through ruptures in Earth's crust. "*Galápagos*."

Devon reached out and touched a cactus spine, instinctively yanking her hand back when it pricked her finger. This wasn't a dream. It was strange and wondrous and very fucking hot.

This *wasn't* a *dream*. Not only was she here, she hadn't even had to draw on the Human Capital grant to do it. She could come back to do even more research. Maybe she could even stretch it to cover whatever story she tackled next. Or maybe she could pay down some of her loans. Maybe she could even afford a desk in a coworking space. Or hire a research assistant. And Sansome had intimated that if the project went well, they were prepared to "invest in her career and expand the scope of their working relationship." Was this how successful people talked? Honestly, how did they not snigger at themselves? Well, if finally making it was actually on the table, she could fake it with the best of them.

The radio on her hip squawked. Static hissed and then a voice crackled through. "We leave in half an hour, people. Back to the boat."

Devon checked her watch. *Shit.* She had lost track of time. She couldn't be late for the big welcome party. She stuffed her mic into her backpack and began to run. Or rather trot, which was about as fast as she could manage on the treacherous terrain. Sweat slicked her skin. The radio bleated. The sun edged closer and closer to the horizon, blinding her with glare.

Devon snatched Kai's glasses from her pocket. There. She could see again.

But after a few steps the world began to bend and fray. Instead of staying where they ought to, the pockmarks on the lava rock swirled, forming almost-but-never-quite legible ruins as if some sorcerer-scribe was writing an epic poem across the papyrus of this otherworldly landscape.

A slab of lava rock crumbled beneath Devon's boot and she stumbled, catching herself on a phallic spire that tore open her left palm. Shit. She looked down at her hand, blood oozing from a network of small cuts that rearranged themselves to mirror the same runic patterns.

Maybe Devon was wrong about audio winning the virtual reality race. Maybe the killer app required distilling an acid trip into a wearable. She took off the glasses, but the sun was even lower, and the glare even more blinding. She put them back on, let their magic reassert itself, and started jogging again.

It took some trial and error, but if she didn't let herself get absorbed in the visual fuckery, she could maneuver just fine. The glasses unraveled the surface of the world and wove it into spectral collage, but they didn't interfere with any edges that were crucial to the Newtonian physics of Devon's awkward scurry.

When the smell of guano became sufficiently nauseating, she knew she was close. There were the blue-footed boobies, their webbed feet flickering through a psychedelic rainbow of colors. There were the marine iguanas napping on the exposed rock, the flames flickering out of their nostrils confirming them as the diminutive dragons they already appeared to be. There was the crystal-clear freshwater pool with the enormous antique engine inexplicably rusting away in the middle, now resurrected to its former glory with every wheel, cog, and piston in furious motion.

And then, abruptly, Devon arrived.

The other guests that had joined for this particular terrestrial excursion were already packed shoulder-to-shoulder in the Zodiac and the annoyed crew member was waving Devon down to join them. Sea lions barked their zombie pinniped barks. And there, across the waves, outlined against the glowing ember of the setting sun that the glasses distended into a fiery halo, sat Sansome's yacht.

The Liminal.

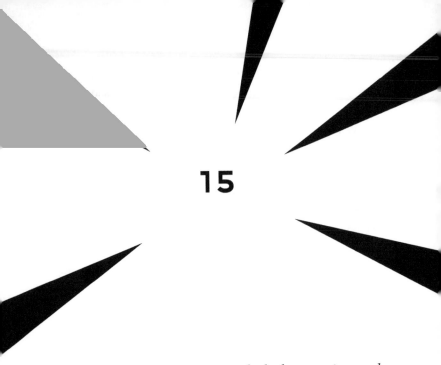

15

SANSOME LEANED TOWARD the bathroom mirror and snipped away a stray nose hair, reminding himself to introduce Devon to Geoff before the scientist got too blasted to offer a quote. The grant had gotten Sansome's foot in *Rabbit Hole*'s door, but to earn Devon's loyalty Sansome would have to prove his usefulness. Access was one of the implicit promises Human Capital made to those it invested in. Everyone was here so that their ideas and endeavors might cross pollinate, and Sansome was the buzzing pollinator, darting from flower to flower.

"Run through it one more time?" Esteban's voice came in from the cabin.

"Will you give it a rest?" Sansome couldn't quite keep the exasperation from his voice. "Whatever happened to enjoying a moment of quiet before the storm?" He imagined the people out there waiting for him to give his big welcome speech, all those bright eyes boring into him.

"You don't *enjoy* the moment of quiet," said Esteban. "You *use* it. That's the difference between amateurs and professionals."

"So you're calling me an amateur?" Sansome stepped back from the mirror, examined the reflection of his naked flesh. His chest hair might be completing the transition to gray, but the body beneath it was still lean.

"If I didn't push you to be better, wouldn't *I* be the amateur?"

It was always like this. A dance in which each of them was always trying to lead, neither content to follow. It held their partnership together and kept them reaching for new heights. But it was also why Sansome had long since installed his dead-man's switch. Unless, when prompted, Esteban input a special password—which Sansome needed to update, come to think of it—the system would automatically publish a cache of evidence implicating Esteban were anything to happen to Sansome. Just in case. He'd be surprised if Esteban didn't have a similar contingency in place—such was the stuff of nightmares. Then again, trust had been built on shakier ground than mutually assured destruction.

There was a sharp knock at the cabin door.

"My dear Ms. Bisset, how lovely to see you," said Esteban, his voice assuming the obliging politeness appropriate to his public station. "But I'm afraid Mr. Haverford has asked not to be disturbed."

"Esteban, my *man*," said Molly. "Don't worry, this'll only take a minute."

"But—"

"It's alright." Sansome stepped out of the bathroom and into the cabin. Molly didn't so much as bat an eye at his near nakedness. "What is it, Molly?"

"You said we'd continue the conversation aboard ship."

"Shark chum, yes, I haven't forgotten." Sansome raised his

eyebrows and gave her a look that said, *you've made your point: you feel this is important enough to break social decorum.*

"Fan-fucking-tastic," said Molly with a wide grin that said, *and you know I'll keep doing it until I get what I want because even if I don't know why, I can almost hear the tinkling infinite loop of hold music.* "Just making sure it says front of mind. Thanks, boss."

Molly winked and was gone.

As soon as the door clicked shut, Esteban's shoulders loosened, and some subtle aspect of his energy shifted to reestablish equal status. Esteban's chameleon nature was a superpower, and his outward-facing role as Sansome's assistant allowed him to observe from the background and avoid scrutiny in handling particularly sensitive tasks, yet Sansome couldn't help but suppress an occasional shudder at the ease with which his longtime partner could slip between worlds. When you changed color so frequently and expertly, might you forget your true colors? Ultimately, were any colors true?

"They circle," said Esteban, a predator acknowledging fellow predators.

"So first it's practice, practice, practice, and now we're going to deconstruct competitive dynamics?" Sansome said, exasperated, as he donned the linen suit Esteban had laid out.

Esteban cocked his head to the side, raptor like, his high-bandwidth gaze encompassing covert hordes of cryptocurrency, informers spilling secrets in anonymous hotel rooms, scandals smoothed over, surgical Reap3r hits—all the facets of Human Capital that didn't make it into the TED talk.

Leverage. The world was built on leverage.

"I can handle them," Sansome said gruffly.

"I know you can," said Esteban, with surprising tenderness. "And I know how unpleasant that can be."

Sansome pressed his lips into a thin line.

Esteban nodded once and turned to go. He paused, hand on the door handle, and said over his shoulder, "By the way, Q won their contract extension."

And then Sansome was alone.

He thought of Luki with his slight build, intense eyes, paradigm-shifting ideas, and now, apparently, virtually unlimited budget. He thought of Geoff with his dedication and his pain. He thought of Devon with her boundless curiosity, her finger on the zeitgeist. He thought of Molly with her vision, determination, and tenacity.

In 1781, Spanish colonial authorities in Peru had ordered the execution of indigenous rebel leader Túpac Amaru II—eponym of Tupac Shakur—by dismemberment: each limb would be tied to one of four wild horses that would proceed to tear him apart. Sansome populated his stable with people who displayed the idiosyncratic wildness and strength that made them contenders to shape world events as Túpac had, but every so often he felt bonds straining at his wrists and ankles.

Sansome snatched the belt from the drawer and snapped it like a whip. Then he sighed and his pride slackened like the strip of oiled leather dangling from his fist as he imagined what lay ahead.

Slipping on the belt, he unfolded his prepared remarks. *Welcome aboard The Liminal. Strange name for a boat, huh? Barely plausible niche ideas. The outskirts and underpasses of a megalopolis. Burgeoning self-awareness. The cultural fringe. Technologies that appear to be nothing more than toys. The fractal outline of a fern frond. Marginal returns. Emotions that are just barely ineffable. Border towns. The moment just before you lean in for a first kiss. Coastal ecosystems. The lucid dreamscape halfway between sleep and wakefulness. The ragged edges of things are always the most interesting part. That's the liminal. And you, ladies, gentlemen, and everyone in between, are its brave explorers.*

Too purple? Too philosophical? Too weird? But eccentricity cast a useful shadow, and the line between making an impression of arrogance or mastery was dangerously thin. More than anything it needed to feel *true*. Not true in the sense of factual, but true in the sense of speaking from the heart.

I know you can. And I know how unpleasant that can be. He glared at the spot where Esteban had been standing. The best partners are those with whom you can and do share hard truths. And one hard truth that Sansome didn't want to admit even to himself was how much Esteban meant to him. No one else would have known that Sansome needed a pep talk, or would have been able to deliver it with the proper level of irony—banter to calm frayed nerves.

The deck was stacked. The cards were dealt. It was time to make his move.

16

LUKI ACCEPTED ANOTHER cocktail he couldn't name from a server whose deference made him uncomfortable. He was playing his favorite party game: how few people could you manage to actually talk to? Mostly it involved loitering between groups and then strategically striding away with apparent purpose just as people were about to invite him to join their conversation.

He sipped his drink and grimaced. He'd hoped the liquor would calm his nerves, but instead it was making him sick with nostalgia. He remembered a sunburnt Canadian pilgrim who had wandered through his parent's village on the Camino de Santiago and, after drinking an impressive quantity of Luki's parents' cider, had asked whether they could ship cases of the stuff to his home in British Columbia. Luki had explained that unlike the posh wineries up in Saint-Émilion, Basque cideries didn't have an overinflated opinion of themselves, and certainly didn't ship internationally. His were a seafaring people, and they had started fermenting cider because fresh water went sour on long voyages, while alcohol stayed potable. So each sailor had his allotment of three gallons of cider per day, and orchards sprang up across the wet, mountainous valleys of Euskadi. That's why French wine would tap out your bank account, while Basque cider was cheaper, and far tastier, than water. Of course, right now there was no price Luki wouldn't have paid to replace his unfathomably expensive cocktail with even the dregs of his parent's barrels.

Tink, tink, tink.

The live band quieted with a flourish, the chatter faded, and Sansome Haverford raised his highball.

"Welcome aboard *The Liminal*," his voice boomed out as Luki carefully avoided his roving gaze. Q wouldn't exist without Sansome, who had first approached Luki after he'd presented a paper at a physics conference, asking probing questions of a different sort than Luki's colleagues. They'd talked for hours after the hotel bar closed. Sansome had started to drop by Luki's lab whenever he was in town on business, always with new questions, always with suggestions that transcended the scope of the experiments Luki was running.

The Santa Anas had been blowing hot and dry out of the east when Luki had finally, in a minor fit of pique, said of one such suggestion *that's a great idea, but I'll never be able to get a grant for it* and Sansome had thrown down the gauntlet: *leave the university, start a company, and I'll supply all the funding you need.* Sansome had made good on his word by investing in Q, and then, once they had a working prototype up and running, introducing Luki to Paul: their first customer who was so determined to be their last.

And now here he was, drinking a fancy cocktail on a boat, as if the accoutrements of success might camouflage the profundity of his failure. He felt awful about ignoring Dexa's increasingly urgent emails and texts asking about how things had gone with Paul. But as long as she didn't know, as long as the team didn't know, they could keep imagining that freedom was within their grasp, that Luki hadn't consigned their shared dream to permanent captivity. Wasn't keeping them in suspense the kind thing to do? Or was it cruel? Was there a difference? Suspense: the closest human analog to quantum indeterminacy, the tension that held Schrödinger's cat in purgatory. Standing there, a powerless instrument of power, Luki experienced a flash of blind fury at the gauche opulence of the yacht—anger feeding on his disgust at how easily he'd allowed himself to become a pawn.

There had been a three-hour layover in Guayaquil on Luki's flight here from D.C. As he sat under merciless fluorescent lights in the cheaply constructed terminal, in a valiant effort to avoid thinking of the immensity of what he'd just agreed to, Luki's mind dredged up memories of the few news headlines from his youth that featured this Ecuadorian port city: *Bakunawa ravages Guayaquil*, *Corpses pile up in the streets as virus surges out of control*, *Hell surfaces in South America*. Luki didn't remember the details, only that the community this airport served had consumed itself as contagion cascaded into a complete institutional breakdown as if the virus had plucked the crucial block in a game of Jenga: electrical blackouts, overwhelmed ICUs, police riots, empty grocery stores, mass looting, flooded wastewater treatment facilities, and on and on. Despite years of hard work and extraordinary luck, Luki's grand vision for Q, just on the cusp of its realization, had collapsed in on itself as surely as Guayaquil had.

"...I first heard the Magma Chamber Orchestra on an

episode of *Song Exploder*, and immediately binged their entire discography." Sansome nodded appreciatively to the band. "Chamber music is often called 'the music of friends' because of its intimacy—it's meant to be played in living rooms, not concert halls—and because for more than a century it wasn't considered a distinct form of performance so much as a way for musicians to enjoy making music for its own sake. It is in that spirit that I invited the band and your-esteemed-selves here tonight…"

Luki glanced around at his fellows. There were the people: the band—a tuxedoed string sextet, staff darting around delivering drinks and offering trays of canapés. And then there were the People: the founders of companies that had disrupted industries ranging from pharmaceuticals to telecom to agriculture, the writer-director whose production company had resurrected the *Star Wars* franchise from reboot hell, a deputy commissioner of the FDA, the most recent MVP of the NBA, a two-time Nobel Laureate, a petite woman in jeans and flannel pointing what looked like a microphone toward Sansome, the creator of an open-source project that had grown into an integral layer of internet infrastructure, the Youtube star whose channel commanded billions of views, et al—Human Capital's dramatis personae.

It was into these People that Sansome poured his millions, and from them that he earned many multiples on that investment. He picked winners, and then leveraged the portfolio to ensure that new members *became* winners—a network effect that the mandatory annual voyage aboard this yacht represented and encouraged. Luki wondered what it felt like to be Sansome, the invisible node of a vast web of influence that spanned technology, art, business, and politics, facilitating others' success in countless forms, noticing holes in the world that people might fill, finding people that pried open new worlds thick with danger and promise, setting them in motion and watching sparks fly as grand aspirations collided.

Your-esteemed-selves. Was Sansome's arrogance sincere and sincerely shared by these glittering celebrants? Was Luki the only one interpreting it insincerely? Or did Luki's bitterness stem not from Sansome or his People at all, but from the long shadow Paul had cast across Q? How many revolutionaries had been seduced into aiding the very cause they had set out to combat, finding cold comfort only in jaded cynicism?

Sansome's gaze swept across the crowd and his voice dropped an octave. "...and remember: the only people who change the world are those who choose to believe they can."

Applause.

Toast.

Music.

And then Sansome was right there beside Luki, leaning close to whisper in his ear, "Hey kid, a little bird told me you closed a mega-deal with the g-man. Rocket fuel, baby. Time to shoot for the moon. Kudos, seriously."

Sansome pulled back and the genuine pride evident in his auburn eyes curdled Luki's bitterness into self-loathing, which he strove to cover with mumbled thanks and a hasty smile. Who was Luki to pass judgement on this man with his yacht and his exotics collection and his grand ambitions? The Pauls of the world armed themselves thanks to the Lukis of the world. Sansome was only playing mentor-matchmaker.

17

DEVON RECOGNIZED the band from NPR's *Tiny Desk Concerts*. They had talked about chamber music as conversation, one instrument introducing a melody and another responding with a similar motif approached from a new angle—all of it a joint experiment in intonation, syncopation, and ego submersion. Looked at sidelong, culture itself was an extended conversation in which many great works of art or scholarship were simply intriguing digressions.

This party certainly felt like a digression. There was so much to do. Making notes. Reviewing transcripts. Editing audio. Planning tomorrow's field expedition. Rescheduling the interview with Jaime from the Galápagos National Park Service. Double checking the *Capra hircus* eradication paper in the *Journal of Wildlife Management*. Choosing pull quotes from Paolo Coelho's popular novelization of Mata Hari's life. Then again, one thing Devon had learned making *Rabbit Hole* was how sometimes the bits that initially felt like digressions ultimately turned out to be crucial to the story.

Time to get to know her fellow voyagers.

Steering clear of Sansome's glad-handing, Devon approached a slight man with sharp features and a shock of thick dark hair. She smiled and extended her hand. "Hi, I'm Devon."

"Luki," he said, then his face froze and his gaze darted down to her mic and back. His palm was cold and clammy. He looked like someone who was far more comfortable in front of a computer than a person.

"It's okay," she said, laughing lightly, trying to put him at ease. "I'm producing a podcast that explores some of the natural history of the islands. This"—she nodded to indicate the yacht and the party—"is just background. Sorta like the establishing shot in a movie or something. That's my story. How'd you land a berth?"

"Pardon the interruption," suddenly Sansome was there, magnanimous and apologetic, squeezing Luki's shoulder and then looking at Devon with those laughing auburn eyes. "But there's someone I want to introduce you to."

The kid—Luki must have been about her age but for some reason Devon still read him as younger than his years—seemed to wilt with relief.

Devon shrugged. "Okay," she said. "Who?"

Sansome led her through the crowd, politely dodging efforts to engage him in conversation. "Geoff Rossi."

"Wait," said Devon. "*The* Geoff Rossi?"

They skirted the bar and there he was, leaning against the railing, sullen and aloof. The man who had defeated the Bakunawa virus, saved millions of lives, and brought a terrified world back from the brink. One of three laureates to ever win two Nobel

Prizes, alongside Marie Curie and Linus Pauling. Author of the *Protocol for Ethics in Synthetic Biology* which underpinned global biotechnology policy and research guidelines. He had written bestselling books that shaped the dreams of a generation, was the subject of a critically acclaimed biographical series on HBO, and ran a lab at UC Berkeley that generated papers with enough citations to justify an independent research university.

And here he was on this boat.

"I thought you might want to ask him a few questions for the podcast," Sansome said softly. Then louder, "Geoff, meet Devon Chaiket. Devon makes the incomparable *Rabbit Hole* podcast and she's here working on a story that's right up your alley. I know you two will hit it off." And then Sansome was gone, fading into the bustle of the soirée as seamlessly as he'd emerged from it.

"So," said Geoff flatly. "You're a podcaster."

"Yes," said Devon, wishing she sounded a little less breathless. "Every episode is a deep-dive into an unlikely but fascinating topic. It's not about breaking news, it's about sparking curiosity."

Even though his expression didn't change, a barrier fell into place behind Geoff's sea-green eyes like a shutter rolling down a storefront. See? This was why Devon didn't interview famous people. They assumed everything was about them because most of the time they were right. Coaxing them out from behind the buttresses of their media training was rarely worth the effort. If she wanted to be a siege engine, Devon would be covering the politics or entertainment beat.

"And what's the topic of the moment?" asked Geoff.

"Goats," said Devon.

Geoff raised an eyebrow. "I'll give you unlikely," he said. "But what makes them fascinating?"

"When Europeans first stumbled on these islands out here in the middle of the equatorial Pacific, they realized they could use them as a supply depot for long voyages," said Devon. "Darwin camped out to study the local fauna, and when Captain FitzRoy picked him up on the *Beagle* for the trip back home to England, they took along endemic giant tortoises to feed the crew. Other captains set livestock loose on the islands, letting them run feral and returning to hunt them whenever they needed to stock up. The goats they dropped off were so successful that they displaced local species, gobbled up every plant they could find, and fundamentally reshaped the local ecosystem. So a while back a coalition of public and nonprofit groups launched an eradication effort to kill off the goats and give native species space to thrive. We're talking everything from packs of hunting dogs to satellite tracking to gunning them down with assault rifles from helicopters. Naturally, there were as many environmental groups opposing the project as supporting it. The whole thing is this super weird case study of humans attempting to engineer nature toward contradictory ends, from Age of Sail pirates up through modern wildlife managers—and the whole fraught experiment is taking place on the islands where we first caught a glimpse of evolution." Devon bit the corner of her lip. "And, clearly, I can't shut up about it."

"No, no," said Geoff. "That's captivating, really. I spend most of my time trying to get people to think deeply about these issues, and stories are vectors for ideas. You can't just explain something directly, it doesn't stick. You have to wrap it in narrative like a capsid around a virus. To be perfectly honest, it drives me crazy. I wish I could just speak directly about the ideas and have done."

That might make for a pull quote, but Devon could tell that

Geoff's mind was elsewhere. He looked beyond her, into the crowd. "And why are you *here* here?" he asked.

Good question, mister. "Human Capital provided a grant to support the show," said Devon, cycling between pride, embarrassment, and feeling like an impostor. "And Sansome invited me to tag along for the Tortoise Center ceremony." Which she'd dutifully record, knowing that she'd probably trash the metaphorical tape even though her benefactor would doubtless love to hear himself make a cameo on the show.

"I see," said Geoff. There was something happening behind his shuttered eyes, something seismic, but Devon was at a loss for how she might tease it out of him. "I need another G&T," he said, rattling the ice in his empty glass. "Good luck with the goats. Let me know if you decide whether exterminating them was genocide or salvation."

"I—" Devon started, but he was gone.

She watched him wind his way to the bar. That had been... odd.

A young woman with delicate features in an understated black dress posted up next to Devon.

"I deeply, truly despise that man from the bottom of my aching heart," said the newcomer with a rueful shake of her head. "I hope he ends up in a bespoke wing of hell with lots of thumb screws and death metal and a pervasive smell of fart." She guffawed. "Please don't quote me on that. But if you do, I'll stand by it. Oh, and if you do, don't you dare make it anonymous. I'm Molly, by the way. And I'm really not as horrible as I sound."

Devon chuckled. "Devon," she said with a nod. "So"—she raised her eyebrows—"what exactly has Geoff done to earn your everlasting hatred?"

Molly tossed her dirty blonde hair with evident irony. "Let

me count the ways," she said. "One: he saved the world, inspired me to go into biotech, and was the best adviser I had in my post doc. Two: his research has opened so many new frontiers in synthetic biology. Three: he refuses to license any of his patents, effectively making those new frontiers off-limits for creating anything of actual value to society." She sighed theatrically. "It's like if Prometheus stole fire from the gods and travelled around using it for parlor tricks, but never taught humans how to make it."

Devon tried to remember the gist of Geoff's manifestos. "I gather that his reluctance stems from concern that his discoveries might be the means to terrible ends," she said. "A la Einstein's Special Theory of Relativity leading to the development of the atom bomb."

"So you're saying Prometheus should keep fire to himself so that humans don't accidentally burn down their houses once in a while, and forgo cooked food, warmth, light, and everything else that fire empowered us to achieve?"

"You know what burns easy?" asked Devon. "Straw men."

Molly was midway through a sip and snorted into her drink. She narrowed her eyes at Devon and raised a finger. "You're good," she said. "I like you."

"Well, I'm pretty sure nobody else at this party has used the word 'fart' yet," said Devon. "Which is a refreshing change of pace, so I guess it's mutual. How'd you end up on this boat?"

"Oh, Sansome's an investor in my startup," said Molly. "He does this every year." She dropped her voice to a baritone and made air quotes. "'Meeting of the minds.' Mostly we just go kiting and get wasted. He said to expect something special this year, but he says that *every* year. And if you ask me, writing a big check to get a tortoise sanctuary named after you might be *cute*, but isn't *special*."

Tink, tink, tink.

"For fuck's sake," said Molly. "*Another* speech?"

The crowd's attention spiraled onto Sansome.

"The captain has informed me that the La Cumbre volcano on Fernandina is erupting," he said, and there was something sharp and eager in his expansive smile. "Naturally, I told him that we need to see it for ourselves."

Beneath their feet, the engine rumbled to life, sending tremors up through the deck. Devon steadied herself on the railing, wondering what exactly she had gotten herself into.

18

THE YACHT SAT at the base of a moonlit tower of steam. The rippling fumes rose up and up and up to feed a cloud of noxious gas fanning out across the stars. Lava bubbled out of fissures, flowing thick down the slopes of the island, igniting scrub in distant, short-lived flashes and painting the underside of the billowing vapor a feverish red. The molten rock spilled over the edge of the squat bluff into the boiling sea in viscous globules that detonated explosive geysers. The reek of sulfur poisoned the air. The ceaseless gurgling roar was unlike anything Geoff had ever heard—as if the planet itself was preparing to hawk a loogie.

Geoff slugged his gin and tonic and imagined the Earth's crust tearing itself apart, magma surging up from the mantle to consume the boat, the island, the whole archipelago.

If only.

An arm fell across his shoulder.

"'Whereas the beautiful is limited, the sublime is limit-less,'"—said Sansome—"'so that the mind in the presence of the sublime, attempting to imagine what it cannot, has pain in the failure but pleasure in contemplating the immensity of the attempt.'"

Geoff tried for another gulp but ice clicked drily against his teeth. The party buzzed on the upper deck. He'd come to down here to be alone. "Kant makes me thirsty," he said.

"Any reading of *The Critique of Pure Reason* unlubricated by alcohol is unlikely to produce much insight," said Sansome. "And no field of human endeavor owes more to liquor than philosophy."

"Is this what you're like when you're drunk?" asked Geoff. Was he strong enough to heave Sansome over the railing into the roiling depths? Was he brave enough to heave himself?

"This is what I'm like when I'm *happy*," said Sansome. "When I'm among *friends*."

"Fuck off," said Geoff. He wanted to be back in his cabin. He wanted to lie on his bunk, pick up his book, and escape into Discworld. Novels were mosaics in which every tessera was a window through which to catch a fleeting glimpse into someone else's life—a glimpse that offered temporary relief from living your own.

A beat.

"What happened to us?" asked Sansome, the palpable melancholy in his tone catching Geoff off guard. Melancholy seemed anathema to the driven, indefatigable man Geoff knew. Geoff's palms began to sweat as he remembered the fateful call he'd made to Sansome all those years ago.

Geoff had been standing outside the field lab, barely notic-ing the mosquitos eating him alive, shock divorcing him from himself so he seemed to be looking over his own shoulder as he spoke the words: *It's ours. No question.* Sansome hadn't argued with the impossible reality. He hadn't bothered with denial. Or even blame. He had taken Geoff at his word—a gift Geoff hadn't realized he so desperately needed at that critical moment—and immediately started executing contingencies.

Sansome had a bias to action so strong that it displaced reflection. He generated his own momentum until everyone got caught up in it, which was why the nuanced minor chords of melancholy sounded so odd coming from him, like hearing a freight train recite poetry.

"You never stop," said Geoff. "You never, ever stop."

"Motion is *life*," said Sansome. "All this"—he indicated the lava, the steam, the moon, the boat—"is what we fall through. We're all falling, all the time. Death might catch our bodies, but our souls just tumble out and keep on falling forever. You can't stop, you can only close your eyes."

"Yeah, well, you move that fast, sometimes you leave people behind," said Geoff.

Sansome sighed and squeezed Geoff's shoulder. "That's what you think of me, huh? That I dumped you by the side of the road." Shadows shifted beneath Sansome's words, shadows Geoff had never noticed before, and didn't want to acknowledge. There were depths to the man that were easy to forget when you were caught up in blaming him.

"I think you had higher priorities," said Geoff, which made him feel uncomfortably like a petulant child jealous that his best friend had found new friends. But this frustration was laced with a countervailing sense of being handled, of not being able to quite keep up with whatever subtle game Sansome was playing. Because there was always a game. Always.

"Yeah? Well, I think you have the *wrong* priorities," said Sansome. "You want to make things right, sure. You think you do that by drowning yourself in that"—he gave Geoff's empty tumbler a pitiable look—"by trying to pretend the world doesn't move on even though you won't?"

"Fuck off," said Geoff again, with more vehemence this time. *You are the* only *person not allowed to judge me*, he wanted to scream. A heart attack took Nassim. A helicopter crash took Alice. The brain cancer finally took Frank. *Besides Paul, we two are the only ones left to share the moral low ground.*

"You're not *behind*," said Sansome. "You're *beneath*. You are the springboard, you sad old man. Molly will build great things on the foundations you've laid. You just have to *let* her."

Molly. Geoff's star student who had refused to be reined in. In her willfulness he had seen an echo of his younger self, and hoped he might teach her how restraint was the better half of brilliance. He'd noticed her in the crowd and done everything he could to evade her—that irrepressible grin another notch on his long list of failures. His pride in her venture was tempered by his terror at the possibility that it might succeed.

"With your patents in hand, she'll be able to eliminate disease, revive bleached corals, and develop crops that thrive even as the climate changes," said Sansome. "She'll unlock the secrets of life itself and build a better world along the way. Imagine an end to cancer, hunger, and privation."

Geoff spat. "Imagine genocidal viruses targeting an ethnic group's DNA. Imagine inequality written into genes. Imagine a world in which life itself is nothing more than intellectual property."

Sansome shook his head. "Gin makes you dour."

"Gin makes me honest," said Geoff. "A condition that I can neither abide nor avoid."

"Then let's be honest with each other, shall we?" said Sansome. "You think refusing to license your patents is helping anything? You know better than anyone how few fucks are given about IP at legit bioweapons labs. It's the national security carte blanche. And it's not just Washington. It's anyone who can field the right equipment and postdocs. So sure, pharma isn't commercializing your shit, and everyone golf claps for your precious Protocol, but all you're really doing is guaranteeing that *only* well-resourced bad guys get to leverage your ideas. Your chastity isn't virtuous, it just reduces the net potential for good sex. Loosen up. Let younger, better people do what you couldn't. At the very least, get out of the fucking way."

Geoff sucked in a sharp breath.

"I'm sorry, but it had to be said," said Sansome. There was genuine pain in his voice, but no regret—a lack that kindled Geoff's envy.

"I know what they're doing with my ideas," Geoff whispered. "I'm just doing what I can."

"I know you know," said Sansome. "Your knowledge makes you complicit. 'Doing what you can' isn't nearly enough. In fact, it's worse than nothing. You're blocking any good that might come of it, giving evil free rein."

"No." Geoff shook his head. So this was the game. "No. No. No. No. No."

"Want a team of your own, it's yours," said Sansome. "Or if you want to provide guidance from a distance, I'm sure Molly would love to have you as an advisor. Who knows? Maybe second time's the charm. With your ideas, skills, and reputation you could spin up your own goddamn Manhattan Project. Or just leave it to the kiddos and enjoy haranguing postgrads between well-pulled cappuccinos. Do it your way, whatever you want your way to be, but do it."

"I won't say it again," said Geoff, suppressing a sick urge to cave-in Sansome's temple with his tumbler. "Fuck. Off."

"I think we both know you'd rather Pandora's box stayed closed," said Sansome.

"You're the one who's opening the damn box," snapped Geoff, staring at the man who had been his partner.

Sansome just shrugged with a tightlipped smile.

Power was the ability to offer false choices.

Purple lightning crackled through the tower of steam.

This was where dedicating your life to science got you. He had become nothing more than a celebrated tool of powerful men. The most heartbreaking part was how banal and short-term their goals were. When confronted with infinite and wondrous reality, they chose to seek quarterly profits, personal fame, or national aggrandizement. The human condition could be so infuriatingly sad sometimes.

The bloated corpses of strange fishes—many of which must be new to science—bobbed to the surface, poisoned and poached by the volcano's submarine exhalations.

"Tomorrow," said Sansome. "The sharks will feast."

19

THE LIMINAL CUT THROUGH rolling groundswell, leaving the drama of the eruption behind. Stars wheeled beyond the ragged edge of overhanging steam and smoke. The band had long since packed up. The guests had returned to their cabins. But Luki sat at the prow, one leg to either side of a railing pole, forehead pressed against the smooth steel so that it bisected his eyes, feet hanging off the edge of the deck.

One cocktail had followed another until the world loosened around him, rocking on a different axis than did the boat. Luki navigated this complex motion with the agility of a rodeo clown until it turned sickening and he sought refuge here at the apex of the V *The Liminal* inscribed across these dark Pacific waters.

Luki faded into the long lineage that lay behind him: fishermen fighting North Atlantic gales, young men setting out to seek their fortunes in the New World, desperate sailors embarking on hopeless campaigns against imperial armadas, all these cider-drunk Basque brothers-across-time peering out over night-shrouded waves trying to catch a glimpse of… what? A clue to what fate held in store? The hint of a path forward? The answer to a question they couldn't articulate? The sea was vast in its promises and its dangers, but most of all in its indifference.

Luki's stomach spasmed and he stuck his head out to vomit over the side. Acid burned the back of his throat. His head swam. The pole was his anchor and he gripped it so hard his arms shook. Nausea swelled again, and he gave in, knowing that fighting it was hopeless. Once, twice more he emptied his stomach into the water below, and with that it was as if a pressure valve had finally been released and he was light-headed and drained but no longer ill.

"I've been there, kid," said a voice. "Hell, I *live* there."

Luki looked up to find Geoff Rossi looking down at him, holding a bottle of gin in one hand and drumming long, elegant fingers on his thigh with the other. Geoff seemed to mutely consider something, then slid down to sit next to Luki, his movements stiff and a little sloppy.

"Rabies is a sneaky motherfucker," said Geoff. "It starts by infecting muscle tissue around the bite, biding its time for a month or two while it hijacks your cells and replicates itself in secret." His cadence was expansive, as if any topic he broached ran the risk of accruing idea after idea until it became an avalanche. "Then it begins to spread, racing up your neural pathways toward your central nervous system, setting off all kinds of red flags along the way. Your immune system kicks into overdrive trying to fight it off, causing splitting headaches and a brutal fever. Once the symptoms emerge, they accelerate. Soon you're confused, agitated, paralyzed, or twitching uncontrollably. You descend into paranoia. You attack anything that comes close.

Hallucinations terrorize you, but nothing scares you more than water. Eventually, the delirium swallows you whole and you go into a coma. You're dead within a week. Nobody who shows symptoms survives."

Geoff paused and Luki wondered whether this strange man was himself a hallucination, along with his soliloquy. They saw each other every year on Sansome's annual cruise but had never traded more than a few words. Luki was shy and introverted. Geoff was notoriously ornery and standoffish. Neither had ever made an effort to engage. Both would have declined to come if Sansome didn't insist.

"In ancient Rome, if a rabid dog bit you, they'd rip off some of its fur and pack it into your wound, sealing it up with a bandage." Geoff offered Luki the bottle of gin. "That was your treatment: hair of the dog."

Luki shook his head.

"It's a bullshit folk cure, of course," said Geoff, waggling the bottle. "But you'd be amazed how powerful placebos can be. Go on, then."

Luki grimaced, accepted the bottle, and took a swig. Herb gardens engulfed in blue-white flame. A pleasing thickness returning to an attenuated world. Gin was a liquor that promised access to the source of things, but sent you down paths that arced away from the center even as they appeared to bend toward it.

"In 1885, Louis Pasteur and Émile Roux inoculated a rabbit with rabies, took samples from its spinal cord when it died, dried them to weaken the virus, and then injected them into a nine-year-old kid who'd just been bitten by a rabid dog," said Geoff. "Bingo: vaccine." He looked pointedly at the gin. Luki handed it back and Geoff took a long gulp. "I've always found it interesting how close to the actual solution the folk cure came. Stealing a talisman from an infected beast and using it to gird your own defenses. Scientifically it's B.S., but metaphorically it's a gem. Like, you were so close. *So* close. Hair of the dog." He drank again, shook the bottle at Luki. "Hair of the dog."

Spray kissed their faces. The engine thrummed belowdecks. They passed the bottle back and forth in silence, its contents steadily diminishing but refusing to run dry.

Luki had the sense that though they were seated here side by side, a gulf had opened between them. They were each aliens visiting from the far-off planets of their respective personal histories. Without shared context, conversation wasn't conversation. You were talking at, not with: an exercise in solipsism, if not futility.

"I wish they'd just take it all away and have done. I wish it had never worked in the first place. Why does it have to be a *trap*?"

Luki hadn't meant to say anything. The words had just slipped out of their own accord. He never would have shared such confidences with a friend. Some intimacies were only possible with a stranger.

Geoff's gaze snapped onto Luki with a sudden, wolfish clarity that promised desperate violence. But whatever those green eyes saw in him tamed them, their voltage fading so fast that Luki thought he might have imagined it.

"I told you already, kiddo," said Geoff, draining the dregs. "I *live* there."

Luki stared out over the starlit sea.

Perhaps he and Geoff weren't aliens after all, but kin separated only by the narcissism of small differences, or a single man staring into a cursed mirror that reflected past and future selves.

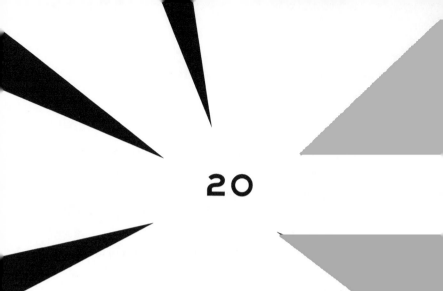

20

GEOFF PLOWED into consciousness like a helicopter crash-landing in dense jungle. Sweaty sheets stuck to his skin. Rude light glared in through the porthole. There was a crick in his neck and a pressure in his temples that long experience promised would ratchet tighter and tighter until his skull had emptied of everything but pain. Why in seven hells was he awake?

There it was again: a knock at the door, polite but insistent.

"Shit," he muttered, the word inflating a bubble of saliva. Then louder, "No need to turn down the room today, thank you." *The Liminal*'s staff were so efficient and discrete as to be nearly invisible until you managed to jam the well-oiled gears of their operation. He tried to remember whether he'd hung the do-not-disturb sign on the doorknob, but after the tête-à-tête with that slim kid with the odd accent, last night trailed off into a familiar thick blank fog.

"I'm not going to clean up your mess," came the reply.

Shit, he thought, with substantially more conviction.

His mind was not at all prepared to reel.

He knew that voice.

Molly.

Rubbing gummy eyes, he sat up on the edge of his bunk, and instantly regretted it. Ghastly fluids sloshed in his belly, releasing fumes that nearly made him retch. He badly needed a drink. Or the constitution of a man twenty years younger. Or fewer memories to blot out.

Was she here to turn the thumbscrews? Bully him into acceding to Sansome's demand? Lava hissing into a boiling sea. Strange fish bobbing to the surface. They were coming for him. They were all coming for him. They had always been coming for him. Life in the shadow of that truth lost its color. Geoff knew himself to be a husk, bleached and brittle.

Not allowing himself any hesitation that might derail a physical feat that felt downright Olympian under present circumstances, he pushed himself up, stumbled to the door, and opened it.

He stared.

Croissants. Jam. Fresh fruit. Yogurt. Scrambled eggs. Toast. Bacon. Sausages. Orange juice. Coffee. The tray Molly carried was piled high with enough food to feed a small army.

"I'm not going to stand here all day," she said, shouldering past him into the room and placing the tray down on the small desk. "Phew." She shook out her arms. "That was heavy."

He closed the door, covertly leaning against it for support.

She appraised him. "You look like shit," she said, something—could that be camouflaged affection?—softening the harsh words.

Geoff looked down at himself, only now realizing that he'd

slept in his clothes, the same clothes he'd been wearing when he'd taken a notch out of his wall with the sword. Hopelessly, he tried to smooth the wrinkled cotton and denim, the complex topography of the fabric reforming as soon as his hands passed over it. He opened his mouth to offer an improvised excuse or explanation, realized he had none, and made do with an apologetic shrug.

"Sit, eat," she said, piling food onto plates. She looked up when he didn't move. "It's gonna get cold," she said, a truth so immutable he couldn't object, and so obeyed.

As Geoff ate, Molly talked. She described the startup she'd founded when she left his Berkeley lab to build on her postdoc research. She told him about each of the scientists she'd hired, their background, interests, and foibles. She reminisced about Berkeley and jokingly compared it to where she lived in Santa Monica. But it wasn't until she started describing the problems her team was grappling with that Geoff forgot his half-eaten piece of toast and quickly cooling coffee.

Proteins unfolded in his mind. RNA and DNA spooled out in all directions. His mental lens expanded to contain entire cells with their interlocking systems in constant motion, the cells themselves integrated into trillion-strong networks, the organisms they comprised representing yet another layer of abstraction, those organisms interacting with peers and countless other species to form a single, vast, evolving biosphere. This was the grand mystery at the heart of everything, the unraveling of which was at once impossible and impossible not to attempt. The identification of a single clue might take lifetimes and still be worth it. For that matter, what else was worth anything?

They debated experiment designs, floated hypotheses, excised flaws in peer-reviewed papers, and speculated about second and third order effects of results they found compelling. They weren't sitting in a cabin on a yacht. They were traversing the intersection of data and imagination, wrangling empirical evidence and theory into a comprehensible but incomplete picture of life.

"God, I miss this," Geoff interrupted himself to say. He returned to the point he was making only to realize the thread was lost. His admission had broken the spell, and he could see Molly retreating into herself even as he did the same.

Here they were. Back on the boat.

She began to collect the dirty dishes on the tray.

"I assume Sansome put you up to this," said Geoff, the familiar bitterness creeping back in. They were tag-teaming him, doing whatever they needed to do to seize their prize. How easily Geoff had been swept away, taken in.

"Of course he did," she snapped, then gave Geoff a pitying look as if this was a point too obvious to bear articulation. "But that's not why I'm here." She glanced at the conspicuously empty duffel in the corner, his rumpled clothes, saw through them to the mess his life had become.

Molly stood and picked up the tray.

"I love you, man," she said. "But you're not okay. Whatever it is, running away from it isn't working."

"Like you ran away, you mean," he said.

She frowned, hurt, and he belatedly recognized the venom in his tone, the displaced rage, the wounded pride.

"I'm sorry, Molly," he said. "I—"

But she was gone, the door banging shut behind her, setting off a blinding migraine as Geoff's hangover returned with a vengeance.

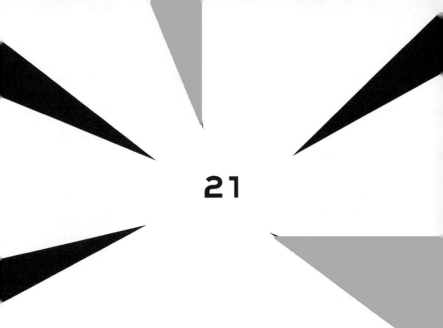

21

SO THIS WAS WHAT treason felt like.

Nine percent.

Luki's blood roared in his ears as the data transfer edged impossibly slowly toward completion.

Twelve percent.

Would he be shot for this? Or would it be lethal injection? Maybe they'd keep him holed up in prison for decades, working through whatever appeals process the system allowed traitors. Or maybe they'd ship him to Guantanamo—a facility that was supposed to have been closed—and waterboard him—an act of torture that its perpetrators pretended wasn't—to extract confessions that were nothing more than whatever desperate fantasies he thought might temporarily sate their paranoia, the whole affair an exercise in sadistic make believe. Or perhaps they'd keep things simple and outsource his execution to Reap3r.

Fifteen percent.

Indistinct voices floated in from the corridor outside his cabin door. He was sitting on his bunk with the sheet pulled up and over his head like a kid pretending to be a ghost, hiding the screen of his laptop from any secret cameras Sansome might have installed aboard his pleasure yacht.

Nineteen percent.

If you thought too hard about anything, it became impossible. The only way to make progress was edgewise, never looking at the task directly, sneaking through the alleys of your subconscious to arrive at a decision you knew full well you'd already made.

Twenty-one percent.

Luki hadn't logged in to Q via his account. Instead, he'd slipped in via the discrete backdoor he'd coded into the system years before, removing himself from logs and keystroke records along the way. If you built the castle, you knew where all the secret passages were. You could even construct a secret passage of your own. Paul managed Luki. If you were the lord of the castle, you knew how to delegate, but not how those you delegated to did their jobs. By virtue of living closer to the machine, Luki could hide beneath the veil of Paul's relative technical ignorance.

Of course, actual lords of actual castles had resolved this awkward little problem by beheading their architects.

Thirty-two percent.

Luki's approach to quantum computing had been so unorthodox that eventually they stopped inviting him to conferences. It wasn't that his papers were met with outright ridicule, just snide comments and awkward silence. So when Sansome funded Q to build a prototype, Luki expected it to fail. His peers' incurious skepticism spurred him on. He wanted to prove them wrong, but thanks to an inborn fatalism, he knew he was tilting at windmills. So nobody was more shocked than Luki at 3:37AM on an overcast Saturday when Q's quantum computer started working. Giddy and bleary eyed from hours of checking and re-checking their results, the Q team had finally stumbled out to inhale medically inadvisable quantities of tacos at La Super-Rica. Never had a meal been so satisfying.

Thirty-seven percent.

Would he ever taste those tacos again? Would he ever see his people's faces? Would he ever hear the low hum of their miracle at work? Would Dexa ever grace him with her rare, compact smile?

Forty percent.

As the files downloaded onto his local drive, Luki opened up the Q source library and inserted messages into the code like a barefoot pilgrim pressing folded prayer notes into the cracks of the Wailing Wall. Apologies. Advice. Explanations. Last requests. Best wishes. Even if his body was never found, these missives would be. The sheet under which he sat was an envelope. He was the letter.

Forty-nine percent.

Your invention is our scrying glass. You do not lend *such an artifact to an empire.*

Luki's hard-won education, warping his intuition to match the impossible realities of quantum mechanics, learning to think like a machine so fluently as to be able to commune with one, all of it had earned him the right to be the wizard flunky of a scheming grand vizier.

Fifty-one percent.

Cold sweat. Electric nerve endings. Twitchy fingers. Thoughts zigging and zagging in random directions before reaching any conclusions. That odd ticklish feeling on the inside of his left knee that could only be sated by running a marathon. Apparently treason felt a hell of a lot like spectacular over-caffeination.

Fifty-four percent.

Had he already set foot inside Q for the last time? There was a Richard Hamming quote taped to the back of Luki's office door: *What are the important problems of your field? What important problems are you working on? If what you are doing is not important, and if you don't think it is going to lead to something important, why are you working on it?* The legendary mathematician's lecture on what it took to become a great scientist had guided Luki through graduate school, but its weight had faded from truth to truism in the subsequent years. Now, Hamming's words hit him with renewed force. Perhaps the most important problem in Luki's field wasn't technical, but social. Secrecy was holding back scientific progress far more effectively than any untested hypothesis.

Fifty-nine percent.

Luki imagined the notes he'd scattered to the wind in Santa Barbara returning to his hands across gusts and thermals, torn edges knitting themselves back together, evidence of unprecedented abuse incarnating itself: ubiquitous, warrantless surveillance leveraged to further entrench incumbent powerbrokers.

Sixty-six percent.

This. Was. Taking. So. Damn. Long.

Seventy percent.

I told you already, kiddo. I live there.

Luki didn't want to find out what lurked beneath Geoff's red-rimmed eyes, didn't want to lock himself inside a cage of his own creation. There was a difference between living well and dying well, a distinction modernity glossed over.

Eighty-four percent.

Paul had been his partner, once.

Strange how these things could change.

Ninety-five percent.

Luki could still hit cancel. He could erase all evidence of burglary. Even if he'd inadvertently raised a red flag, he could play the mad scientist with his head in the clouds. He could follow Paul's instructions to the letter and waltz right back to Q as if nothing untoward had happened. He could spend the rest of his life untangling the baroque knots of quantum computer science and let the United States government weaponize the fruits of his labor. Or he could watch as the progress bar ended the only life he'd ever known.

Ninety-nine percent.

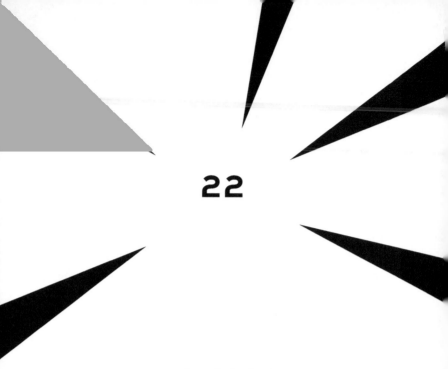

22

SANSOME FLIPPED through the dossiers.

"A Canadian researcher whose work threatens to infringe on Q," said Esteban, who sat across the cabin desk. "It's a case of multiple discovery, but no less dangerous for that. A star software architect that Sofia tried and failed to poach. A key witness in the Lexinor case. The director Disney is secretly courting to replace Lauren to prevent the franchise from becoming too dependent on her. A minister who's undermining Rumo's EU telecom bid." Esteban ticked them off on his fingers. "Oh, and a podcaster serving the same demographic as *Rabbit Hole* to whom Spotify is about to make a mega-offer."

Sansome sighed. Just because you knew something was necessary didn't mean you had to like it. "Are there any significant players interested in the Canadian's research?"

"Not yet," said Esteban, leaving the inevitable *but soon* unspoken.

"Okay," said Sansome. Now that Luki had secured the lucrative contract extension, Human Capital couldn't afford to let his trajectory get derailed. "We have no choice but to take action on that and telecom issue. But let's let Lexinor play out a little longer. It's possible Philippe gets the whole case thrown out. Sofia's architect, too. And forget the podcaster. We gave Devon a grant, but without equity in *Rabbit Hole*, the exposure isn't worth it."

Esteban shrugged. "It'll limit her distribution."

"The timing isn't ideal," said Sansome. "But once we paper a legit partnership, we'll help her claw her way up. Play the long game. She's worth it."

"And Disney?" asked Esteban.

Sansome let out a low growl. It was easy to wave away as mere entertainment, but whoever held the tiller at *Star Wars* forged the mythology that would inspire a generation. That was *real* influence, not spiking headlines, but shaping values.

"We can't let them snake Lauren," said Sansome. "May the Force be with her."

"She's got better than the Force," said Esteban. "She's got *us*."

"I'll update the hit list," said Sansome, resigning himself to it.

"And I'll see you in an hour to prep for the opening ceremony," said Esteban, collecting the dossiers for shredding.

"Fuck me," said Sansome, stomach clenching. "Another audience. Why do I do this to myself?"

"You love to hate it," said Esteban. "Or hate to love it. Maybe both."

The door closed behind Esteban.

Sansome called up Reap3r and added the names. A vile but necessary duty. Part of being an anteambulo was braving the shadows so others didn't have to. He would chisel out a future for them, a future they could invent with clean consciences. Not even Geoff, with all his angst and self-flagellation, knew what Human Capital had done to protect him.

Nobody knew, except Esteban of course. Before logging out, Sansome updated the password in the conditional script that served as his dead-man's switch. *Audience*, that would do. A brother in arms was also an armed man inside your guard. This was Sansome's insurance. You could never be too careful.

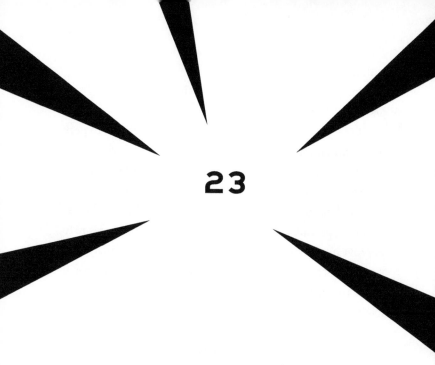

23

THE ONE HARD-AND-FAST RULE of technological progress was that videocalls never worked quite right. A pixelated
candid portrait of Luki's parents was frozen on the screen of his
phone. Then they stuttered to life again, their words piling on
top of each other as the audio feed sprinted to catch up. Despite
the choppiness, it felt good to be speaking his mother tongue
for a change.

"You broke up for a minute there," Luki interrupted, trying not to think about the implications of what he'd just done.
"What were you asking?"

"Your father was just wondering"—his mom jabbed his dad
with an elbow—"whether you had, you know, met anyone?"

Luki sighed. This was all-too-familiar territory. "No, mom,"
he said. "Not recently."

"Because I've been reading about all these new dating apps,"
said his father earnestly. "You go online and they match you up

with the perfect partner."

"Imagine if they had been around when *we* were young," said his mom. "I wouldn't have wound up with this lout."

"Love you too, honeybun," said his dad, ducking in to peck her on the cheek.

Luki laughed, a welcome respite from the angst in which he was mired. "You guys are too much," he said. "And yeah, dad, I know about dating apps." That he didn't use them said more about the paranoia his work inspired in Luki than his desire to improve his suffering love life. Truth be told, he was lonely. And it wasn't just romance that was the problem. Years of long days at Q put a damper on any friendships outside the office, a situation made worse by the fact that he couldn't talk about anything he was spending those long hours working on. But that had been nothing compared to this. The encrypted files on his flash drive pretty much guaranteed he'd never enjoy a normal relationship ever again. "Don't worry, you'll be the first to know when I meet the love of my life. Promise. So, how's the farm?"

As his parents described the trials and tribulations of village life in extravagant detail, uncharacteristic nostalgia burgeoned in Luki. He could see the sun burning away the morning mist, smell the thick, cloying scent of freshly rolled bales of hay, taste the first splash of tart, musty cider when they tapped the barrel for *txotx* every January. He had fled that world to escape its *smallness*, its helplessly provincial navel-gazing. But without lovers, without friends, wasn't Luki's world smaller than it had ever been—regardless of the scale of his individual ambitions and accomplishments?

His dad frowned—stretching the livid scar that ran across his forehead—as he described an orchard pest he was battling with organic insecticides. Luki's father had never liked the Spanish government, but he hadn't become an activist for independence until a pair of National Police officers pulled him over as he was delivering barrels of cider to bars in San Sebastian and beat the living shit out of him simply for being Basque—leaving him the scar as a memento. Basque country was the most heavily policed region in Europe, and it felt less like the province of a democratic nation than the rebellious colony of an overbearing empire administered from Madrid.

When Luki was in high school, his dad had met a guy through a buddy at his *txoko*—the gastronomical society where he cooked and ate with a tight-knit group of friends—and began organizing guerrilla civil disobedience campaigns, petitioning for referendums, and undermining institutions of Spanish authority. He had tried to rope Luki in, but Luki's teenage rebellion had been to scoff at rebellion. It wasn't that he didn't think Basque independence was such a bad idea so much as that he didn't see why it mattered all that much in the grand scheme of things.

And now, against all odds, Luki had arrived at the cryostat-cooled heart of the grandest scheme of things only to discover that it was just an exaggerated version of the same old imperial bullshit—and he was the asshole cop propping it all up.

"Mom, dad," he said, interrupting an anecdote about a fight that had broken out at the wedding of a third cousin. "You know I love you, right?"

Luki knew better than anyone that his entire digital life, and probably a substantial part of his physical life, was surveilled. The very first thing conspirators did was spy on each other. And instead of technological revolution, the only thing Q enabled was conspiracy. He couldn't tell his parents what he was going through. He *definitely* couldn't tell them what he was doing. If his meeting with Paul had convinced Luki of anything, it was how cheaply Luki had sold his dreams. For better or almost certainly for worse, Luki was going to reappropriate them.

"Of course!" said his mom. "And we love you more than anything."

Color rose in his dad's cheeks, but then he said gruffly, "We couldn't have asked for a better son."

Luki was grateful when the connection stuttered again because the extent to which his father was tragically wrong brought unexpected tears to his eyes. In the theater of his mind, the surfer dropped into the breaking wave, careening down its vertical face.

Self-recrimination would change nothing.

Action was the only thing left.

24

THE NEWLY INSTALLED plaque announcing the Haverford Tortoise Center gleamed in the afternoon sun. Low-walled enclosures surrounded the main building—their denizens broken up into cohorts of subspecies and age, from hatchlings that could fit in your palm to lumbering thousand-pound adults. Devon side-eyed some of the giants as she recorded Sansome's remarks. She could have comfortably curled up inside their mottled shells.

Sansome explained that the Spaniards had named these islands for the shape of the shell of a particular tortoise, that they could float across oceans and live for a year without food or water, that their kind was seventy-five million years old, older than some dinosaurs, and that the Center was home to one tortoise, Bernadette, who had been alive when Darwin had first visited the archipelago.

There was a nerdy sincerity to his enthusiasm that reminded Devon of their conversation at The Interval. Whoever the man was, something of the boy shone through in moments like these—a boy fascinated by nature's fabulous machinations. The exotic animals rumored to roam Sansome's ranch in Marin Devon now understood to be an opulent augmentation of what must have been an extensive childhood butterfly collection.

Here it was: the raison d'etre for their cruise.

The director handed Sansome the scissors, and he cut the red ribbon strung up across the building's entrance. Then they joined hands and smiled for the cameras. Polite applause issued from the odd mix of staff, schoolchildren, tourists, locals, and *Liminal* passengers in the audience. There was the shy kid from the party. There was Molly, rolling her eyes at Devon. Geoff was conspicuously absent.

Devon slipped away to examine the enclosures. She slapped at a mosquito, then aimed her mic at a juvenile tortoise who was munching on a tuft of grass. She imagined looking out through those beady eyes, feeling the sun on that leathery skin, retreating into that weather-beaten shell and feeling an unimpeachable sense of *home*. Funny how aliens in science fiction were far less alien than this creature. Usually, the fictional denizens of other worlds were basically humans with superficial tweaks—whereas the *truly* alien was right here staring us in the face: algae, redwood trees, jellyfish, viruses.

Even great thinkers struggled to wrap their heads around reality's fundamental weirdness. Aristotle believed that eels and flies didn't reproduce, but spontaneously generated from mud and rotting flesh. The cascading inconceivability of a Trump presidency forced William Gibson to rewrite his work-in-progress. To his dying day, Einstein rejected some of the implications of his own theories.

If you just wandered around in a state of constant awe, you wouldn't survive or reproduce. So you built simple mental models that worked well enough for the purposes of daily life. Eat, sleep, work, love, fear, text, and, occasionally, dream. To get things done, you learned to ignore reality's surreality.

But blinding yourself, while useful, got you in trouble when the world broke the chains of your humble construct. Galileo upset our preconception of the solar system. Turing et al invested objects with cognition. Darwin redefined our understanding of the origins of life, and Bernadette was munching grass when he first formulated his theories. By defying your assumptions, the universe occasionally forced you to confront your own ignorance. Devon made a mental note to weave that train of thought into the script.

"Ms. Chaiket?"

One of Sansome's staff startled Devon out of her reverie.

"Yes, hi," she said.

"Time to go." The staffer gestured to line of SUVs into which the yacht's passengers were piling.

"Oh, thank you," said Devon. "But I have some interviews lined up this afternoon in Puerto Villamil. We sail in the morning, right? I'll catch a ride out to the boat at sunrise."

The staffer made a note. "Yes, ma'am," he said, and moved on to herd the other stragglers.

Devon looked back at Sansome's plaque. There was power in a name. Names constrained the possibility space of imagination. Sometimes renaming something—even just in your own head—could yield a flood of new ideas. What if this was called the Center for Tortoise Rehabilitation? Or the Center for Island Biodiversity? Or the Center for Resilient Adaptation? What kinds of researchers would such disparate themes attract? How might the name above the door subtly influence the direction of their work? Decades hence, what diverging results might have been achieved, and how would those results shape these islands? The Haverford Tortoise Center. How big a grant had Sansome had to offer for naming rights? It felt reductive, and maybe a little sad, that having done so, he'd decided to name it after himself. Then again, there was power in a name. Perhaps Devon would feel differently if it were the Chaiket Tortoise Center. Maybe she was displacing resentment at how badly she needed his patronage by throwing shade in the privacy of her own heart.

25

LUKI HADN'T HAD A PLAN. Worse, he still didn't have a plan. All he had was a secret that would almost surely get him killed.

Small waves shushed onto the beach. Sea lions lolled about on a jutting section of exposed black lava rock. There was movement out on the turquoise water. Luki squinted. A marine iguana swimming across the inlet, its saurian head poking up above the surface as its tail whipped back and forth to propel it forward. The sun sat fat and happy above the horizon like a well-fed cat.

Luki envied the sun's apparent contentment. The sun didn't care what anyone did. The sun didn't care whether human civilization thrived or perished. The sun went on consuming itself in a fusion furnace despite everything. The sun was the sun was the sun. Well, Luki *was* burning himself up inside, so maybe they had something in common after all.

Along with the plans for Q itself, Luki had illicitly download-ed a representative sample of the logs documenting what Paul had been using the system for: preparing to surveil and perma-nently record the entire internet—X-ray meets time machine.

Luki had known they wanted to spy, of course he had. He hadn't known the details, but that was because he had known not to look, not to ask. The American government didn't hand out hundreds of billions of dollars of financing just for fun. It had been obvious from day one that Paul would use Q's technology to spy, but Luki had held his nose and taken the original deal because it had also been obvious from day one that nobody else would be willing or able to give him the money and freedom he needed to actually build his quantum computer. Sansome had funded the early prototype, but scaling that up was a monumen-tal and capital-intensive task. Silicon Valley had been founded on microchip defense contracts, and the federal government would likewise need to underwrite the new era of computing Luki hoped to usher in, or it would never arrive. So he'd taken the cash and done the work and tried not to think about what Paul was doing with it, knowing that as soon as the contract was up Q would pull back the curtain, and it would all have been worth it and they could forget the unsavory first chapter in their story. Except that Q had made something too useful for Paul to give up, or more likely, he'd never planned to let them out of the contract in the first place, and Luki had lost whatever excuses he might have once been able make for enabling such flagrant abuse of power.

Luki sipped his cold beer and scrunched his toes in the hot sand. What if he never returned to the yacht and lived out the rest of his life here? He could work as a tour guide, live in a lava rock shack, and spend his free time wandering alone across bleak volcanic landscapes—equations dancing in his head. Except that if not the locals, certainly the tourists would recognize the face of the famous fugitive and turn him in. And even before that, his absence from the yacht, and from the flight back to California, would surely be noted. Sansome and Paul would know exactly where to find him. And they wouldn't be gentle when they did.

He remembered how Don Biskarret and Don Etxeberri would sit out in the village square every afternoon, big smiles lighting up their wizened faces as they cracked unintelligible inside jokes about long-dead comrades. Basque Country was full of happy old men. In his years as an expat, Luki had noticed that meeting an old man brimming with joie de vivre in the United States was tragically rare. And with things going the way they were, one thing was for sure: Luki wouldn't buck the trend and end up retiring happy in America.

But what if he could make it back to his homeland? He could head to SFO after Sansome's private plane dropped them off. Instead of catching his connection to Santa Barbara, he could fly direct to Istanbul—a city big and chaotic enough to hide in. From there, he wouldn't be able to travel under his own passport, but maybe he could find someone who could supply him with fake papers, or maybe he could hire smugglers to get him across the border into Europe. He would travel overland, hitchhiking through rural areas and avoiding train stations and cities. Eventually, he'd make it home—where he could lose himself in the secluded mountain valleys like so many of his ancestors had when invasion threatened. Maybe decades hence, he'd be able to return to his village, sit back on the park bench, and joke about his youthful misadventures.

The problem was that he had to survive such misadventures in order to laugh them off later. Spain had extradition agreements with the United States. Even if his cascading hypotheticals played out precisely as he imagined them, the minute Paul followed the breadcrumbs, Luki would be loaded on a matte black helicopter in the middle of the night and never heard from again.

Where, then? China? Russia?

Hairs rose on Luki's arms.

Ecuador.

Snowden had been heading for Ecuador when his escape had been cut short in Moscow. Luki was in Ecuador *right now*. Maybe he *should* stay on these islands. Apply for immediate asylum. He could be the finger Quito gave Washington. He spoke Spanish. And surely his notoriety as a whistleblower would make him a popular tour guide.

A new chasm opened inside Luki. He had a whistle. But he hadn't blown it yet. It wasn't just that he had nowhere to run, he had no idea how he would share his secret with the world. There was a certain elegance in simply uploading the cache to the internet. But wouldn't that make it pitifully easy for Paul to squash? How many thousands of hucksters and conspiracy theorists posted stuff every day? Who but a tiny group of avid suckers believed them? Why should anyone believe Luki, especially when Paul would disavow any claims Luki made about his own credentials? Why would anyone even bother to pay attention to him long enough to decide whether to believe him? It wasn't enough to have a secret. Luki needed a platform from which to shout it. Only then could he decide where to run and hide.

"Luki, right?"

Fuck.

Fuck. Fuck. Fuck.

It was that woman from the yacht. Her deep-red skin glowed in the evening light and a lock of jet black hair had escaped her ponytail. She carried a backpack and was walking barefoot in the sand, flip-flops in hand. Luki's grip tightened around the sweating neck of his beer bottle. Sansome wasn't here to rescue him this time, and Luki couldn't very well pretend not to recognize her.

26

"I JUST HAD TO GET OFF THAT BOAT," said Luki, sounding surprised at his own honesty. His hair was disheveled and there was something haunted in his dark brown eyes.

They looked out across the water at *The Liminal*. It was anchored just offshore. The lights strung up around the upper deck came on and the ocean breeze carried snippets of chamber music.

Devon laughed. "Yeah, it's a bit much, isn't it?"

"There's a saying where I'm from," said Luki. "*Asko baduk, asko beharko duk*. It means: if you have much, you will need much."

"Asko baduk, asko—wait, one more time?" asked Devon.

"Asko baduk, asko beharko duk," he repeated.

"Asko baduk, asko beharko duk," she echoed. "What language is that?"

"Basque," he said.

That explained the odd accent.

"Walk with me?" she asked.

She could see him reaching for an excuse.

"Come on," she said, offering him a hand. "I don't bite."

He was wavering.

"I—" Luki began.

"And if my company is truly that excruciating," she said. "You can always ditch me. I promise not to hold it against you."

He blushed, then took her hand.

She hauled him up and they set off down the beach.

Before Devon had quit to start *Rabbit Hole*, one of her mentors at NPR had taught her that the best way to get someone to open up to you was to open up to them first. So she told Luki about the hunter she'd interviewed that afternoon—how he'd personally killed thousands of goats and how, for no apparent reason, he hadn't been able to bring himself to shoot one particular juvenile with an injured leg limping across the slopes of Wolf Volcano on northern Isabella Island. The hunter had broken down and cried right there on the rocks, and one of his colleagues had put the poor creature down, and then gently but firmly forced his blubbering friend to drink half a flask of vodka.

She told Luki about Mata Hari, the Dutch exotic dancer, courtesan, and spy who, during World War I, was accused by every side of selling secrets to the others. After a summary show-trial in Paris that painted her a scapegoat, she had refused a blindfold and blew a kiss to the firing squad. Devon explained how, nearly a century later, after the hunters had killed all the goats they could find themselves, they latched radio collars onto sterilized females, chemically put them into heat, and released them into the wild—leading the hunters straight to any surviving groups or lone males. They dubbed these animals who had been made traitors to their kind "Mata Hari goats."

She told Luki about the great flourishing that had occurred after all the goats were finally exterminated, how endemic species had clawed back from the brink of extinction and the Galápagos's famed biodiversity had begun to rejuvenate itself. Native plants were reclaiming lost land, the native animals that depended on them finally had food again, and residents of the islands were able to make a living from tourists who came to see those unique plants and animals for themselves. People had brought the goats here to feed themselves. People had decided to eliminate them. The thing Devon found so fascinating about the story was that it all boiled down to people. The very ecosystem of the islands where people had discovered evolution was a microcosm constrained by human choices.

Devon was shaken out of her narrative when Luki grabbed her elbow and hustled her into a clump of trees. They had long ago left the beach behind and were walking up the dirt road into the forest. The sun had set and the sky overhead was a deep purple. Feeling his iron grip on her elbow, Devon was suddenly terrified that the shy, quiet man she'd hoped to draw out of his shell was in fact a violent criminal who would rape her, kill her, and leave her corpse for the hawks.

She opened her mouth to demand an explanation, or maybe scream for help, but Luki pressed his finger to his lips and pointed.

Through gaps in the dense foliage, she could see that they had made their way back to the Haverford Tortoise Center and something strange was going on. A barrel-chested man with a balaclava hiding his face and a submachine gun slung over his shoulder stood just inside the entrance to the parking area. Three other men, unarmed but faces similarly covered, were loading a large crate onto the back of a battered pickup truck. Grunting and heaving, they finally got the crate where they wanted it, and then covered it with a ratty tarp and filled the rest of the bed with fishing gear. One of them whistled, and the guard hustled back to pile into the cab with the rest. Then the truck peeled out of the parking lot, kicking up dust. Devon and Luki shrank into the undergrowth as it sped past them back up the road toward town.

"The fuck was that?" she whispered hoarsely.

A sharp frown creased his forehead. "I haven't the faintest idea," he said. "But I didn't want to ask the goon with the gun."

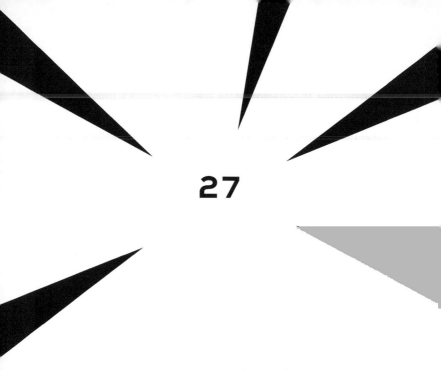

27

GEOFF HAD NEVER HELD anything so heavy as this envelope. A life's work nestled inside a little square of paper. He licked the back and sealed it.

Stepping out onto the deck, he closed his cabin door behind him. The sky was pre-dawn gray. The ocean smooth and glassy. *The Liminal* sat quietly at anchor. Such a peaceful scene, but for this errand.

Molly might not be as ingenious as Alice or as efficient as Frank, but she was more determined than anyone Geoff had ever worked with. And there was something to be said for perseverance. Geoff was the only member of the Cebu team still standing. Despite how painful the conversations with Sansome and Molly had been, he couldn't deny that it felt good to talk to peers, to go deeper than the lonely charade his life had become.

Geoff dragged his hand along the railing as he made his way around the yacht. This fucking boat. These fucking people. This fucking life he'd somehow found himself living. Maybe profound alienation was the punishment to fit the crime. In order to avoid a cell, he'd built one for himself.

This was it.

Sansome's cabin.

Geoff wished it had been farther away, wished he'd had to walk for hours instead of minutes to arrive at his destination. Maybe then he'd have had enough time to come to a decision. Then again, not even millennia would be sufficient to consider the choice he had to make.

Hands shaking, he plucked the envelope from his pocket.

Patents had originally been developed to allow inventors to profit from their creations, establishing a financial incentive for innovation. If you invented something, for the next twenty years other people could only use it with your permission, which you could charge for. Geoff held the patents for the genetic engineering tools he'd developed to create Bakunawa, and later, its vaccine. After the vaccine had been deployed, making a fortune for Sansome, Geoff had refused to license his patents to anyone else for any reason. He'd seen the terrifying power and consequences of the technology he'd devised and knew that humanity wasn't equipped to handle it. So instead of using his patents to monetize his invention, he'd used them to block others from building on his ideas.

Patent as prohibition.

Twenty years might not be long enough for humanity to become wise enough to put Geoff's inventions to good use, but it was the breathing room he could offer, and better than nothing. On the other hand, who was Geoff to make that call? What right did he have to claim the moral high ground, he, who had murdered millions? How did he know that Molly would make the same mistakes as he did? Was he holding back a viral holocaust, or a cure for cancer? And Sansome was threatening to implicate Geoff for Bakunawa if he didn't play ball, revealing him as the hypocritical war criminal he knew himself to be. Geoff could point a finger back at Sansome, but at that point it would be past mattering—what was left of his life would be shattered forever. Should he continue to channel Cassandra, or become Prometheus? Paul Valery's words echoed in Geoff's heart: "So the whole question comes down to this: Can the human mind master what the human mind has made?"

Dawn stretched fiery tendrils across the sky.

He could still drop the envelope over the railing.

He slid it under the door.

28

EVEN THOUGH THE OCEAN was calm, Luki gripped the railing like it was the edge of a cliff from which he was dangling. Brightly colored kites flew out on the bay, riders skimming across the surface of the water beneath them. This was his chance. Luki's Adam's apple bobbed up and down. He couldn't tell whether his nausea stemmed from seasickness or nerves.

Sucking in a deep breath of briny air, he peeled his fingers off the railing, picked up the gear the crew member had supplied, and descended into the belly of the yacht.

The walls of the narrow corridor seemed to constrict around him, an inch or two with every step. Without the horizon in view, he felt the micro movements of the boat more intensely, as if Poseidon himself was trying to trip Luki up. He might come from a seafaring people, but besides his uncle's dinghy, Luki hadn't spent much time on boats. He'd gone straight from mountains to cyberspace.

This was it.

Her door.

He'd looked her up, of course. Devon Chaiket, podcaster extraordinaire. To fill the void of insomnia, he'd binged as many episodes of *Rabbit Hole as he could*. Aptly named, it was easy to fall into. He'd met harpZkord, the notorious hacktivist who financed pro-democracy groups in China by remotely coordinating big-ticket heists in which all the meatspace labor was outsourced to on-demand workers who didn't realize they were deputized thieves. And then there had been the two college students who'd dropped out to build Mozaik—not realizing that the venture capitalists backing their startup were fronting for exactly the kind of money laundering operation their software was meant to sniff out—and whose pivot to open source had resulted in their code being woven through the infrastructure that supported the internet. There was more. A lot more. But because their subject matter veered toward Luki's expertise, those two episodes had convinced him that Devon wasn't afraid to take on big stories that required the patience to make sense of complex but crucial technical concepts, and that she went to extreme lengths to protect and do right by her sources.

Was that what he was about to become? A source? The descending scale of *Rabbit Hole*'s intro music tinkled through his head, and then there was Luki's own voice with an irresistibly intriguing pull quote, and Devon's cutting in, zooming out, putting the story in context. *Coming to you from an undisclosed location.*

Luki raised his hand to knock, and deja vous transported him back to Paul's back porch, the champagne cork arcing off into the night. This moment was an inevitable consequence of that one. The past was never truly past. He remembered playing with a 3D printer at Stanford, using it to create interlocking geometric shapes that would have been impossible to manufacture with any other equipment. Every choice Luki had ever made was a single bead of filament deposited by the nozzle of his life, and everyone else was doing the same at every moment. Together, they extruded reality.

Tap, tap, tap.

The door in front of Luki morphed into Paul's wall of technicolor bricks. *I will shower you with riches,* Paul's voice echoed through memory. *I will rewrite laws on your behalf. I will clear any obstacles that stand in your way. But if you ever so much as hint that you are considering snatching back your arrow from this great nation's quiver, by the powers vested in me as one of its defenders, I will damn you to a personal hell developed with the same obsessive rigor as your precious quantum computer.* Luki had seen the files. The willful ignorance he had cultivated so carefully for so long was no longer viable. Paul was not a man who let scruples hold him back, and his search for Luki hadn't even begun. There was no APB. Interpol hadn't been alerted. The NSA hadn't cast its silicon net across the digital mirror-world. All that would come in time. And Luki was about to kick things off by stabbing a knife into the back of his greatest benefactor. He could only pray that he didn't wind up in front of a firing squad like the namesake of Devon's goats. Then again, a firing squad might be a mercy compared to whatever fate awaited him.

Tap, tap, tap.

Where was Devon? He'd checked all the common areas. Was it possible he had the wrong cabin? Could she have gone off on another reporting expedition? His stomach knotted. Had she somehow flown home? Had Luki lost the only slim chance that his meager luck had tendered? His courage spiraled like water round a drain.

Rap, rap, rap. Desperate, this time.

No answer.

Fuck.

The door opened.

"Excuse me?" asked Devon, peering out. Big headphones hung around her neck and her dark eyes looked a little bleary. To Luki, she was an angel descended from heaven.

"Yes?" she asked again.

Luki realized he was just standing there. He held up the masks and fins. "Wanna go for a snorkel?"

"Uhhh, sorry," she said, gesturing back to her laptop, which displayed some kind of audio-editing dashboard. "But I'm a little busy right now."

No. She had to come. Who knew what kind of surveillance systems Sansome had running on *The Liminal*? There was no such thing as privacy aboard ship. He had to convince her to come without being able to tell her why. He had to make something up, concoct a story that would get her off the boat and into the water. He had to—

"Please?" he asked simply.

Devon cocked her head to the side and looked up at him quizzically. She opened her mouth to say something, and then closed it again.

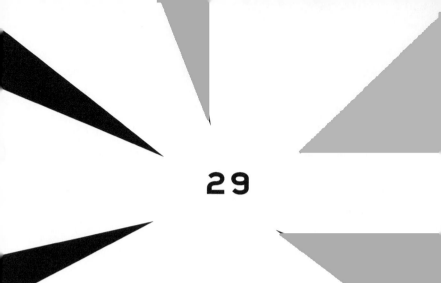

29

FLIGHTLESS CORMORANTS barreled through the water like bullets past Neo in *The Matrix*. A marine iguana tore off a mouthful of the mossy green algae that covered the rocky bottom. Devon kicked forward over a submarine outcrop and a school of multicolored reef fish scattered.

It was rare and refreshing to see a thriving marine ecosystem. Acidification, overfishing, and deep-sea mining had ravaged the world's oceans and she hadn't swam in waters this full of life since she'd spent a month chasing down a lead in Borneo.

Some people wanted to experience biodiversity, and others wanted to own it. She remembered Luki's hand on her elbow, the pickup truck disappearing down the road in a cloud of dust. She'd asked her contacts in town and at the park service about it. They'd been hesitant, but finally she'd gotten them to admit that animal trafficking was a real issue here. Rich foreigners would pay four thousand dollars for a baby Galápagos tortoise on the black market, and forty thousand dollars for an adult. A while back, one group of poachers had stolen more than a hundred tortoises from the Center in one go—a feat which would have required inside help. The executive director was doing his best to hush up what could be quite a scandal—especially during the celebratory visit of a new major donor—but rumor had it Bernadette was missing. It might prove a rich vein to mine for her story.

Beside her, Luki spluttered.

Devon popped her head out of the water to see him coughing up brine.

"You okay?" she asked.

"Yeah," he said. "It's just that water keeps getting in my mask. I need to tighten it."

"Let me see." Devon stuck a finger behind the mask's plastic strap—it was so tight that it left an imprint on Luki's temple. "Nope," she said. "It might be counterintuitive, but usually when masks flood, you need to loosen them. Once you're underwater, the ocean gives you all the pressure you need to keep a seal."

He gave her a strange look, then glanced over her shoulder back at the yacht. Reaching up, he adjusted the strap. He stuck his face into the water for a moment and then came back up.

"You're right," he said, eyes obscured by water running down the front of the mask. "Thanks."

Devon was about to ask *are you okay?*, but Luki dunked right back under and started swimming, so she followed.

And not a moment too soon. Two dozen spotted eagle rays were swimming in formation just a few meters below them—rippling wings giving the impression of submarine flight. It was a magnetic sight. Devon and Luki kicked to follow, but were soon left behind as the school turned offshore.

They treaded water for a moment, trying to decide where to go next. Then Luki's finger stabbed down and there, just at the edge of their vision, a distinctive T-shaped shadow emerged from the depths. Hammerhead. It moved with a predator's fluid grace along the ocean floor—power, embodied. A cold thrill ran through Devon and goosebumps rose on her skin. She was suddenly aware of being fundamentally *outside* of her domain, of being a stranger in waters that were not just foreign, but inhuman. That feeling of straightforward irrelevance, of being nothing more than a tourist in a strange and mysterious world, was vanishingly rare on a planet fast approaching the event horizon of human affairs' metastasizing singularity. The shadow faded into the deep blue as quickly as it had appeared, leaving a palpable sense of possibility, of uncharted territory, in its wake.

For the second time, Devon felt Luki grab her elbow.

They surfaced and spat out their snorkels.

"I assumed you haven't spotted another armed guard," said Devon.

Embarrassed, Luki released her, then pushed his mask up onto his forehead and squinted out across the water.

Devon followed his gaze. They were much farther from the yacht now. The kites were flying out along the peninsula.

"I— I'm not sure how to do this," said Luki.

"How to do what?" asked Devon.

"There's this thing," said Luki. "See, where I work, we— I mean, the reason I'm here." Tectonic plates, shifting. "*Here*, here. It's sort of like having a master key, but not like that at all, really." He was looking everywhere but at her. "I couldn't risk it on the boat. Just. And."

Something was trying to break out of him like a chick from an egg, pecking away in the gelatinous dark until a new reality shone through spreading cracks.

"Hey." Devon put one hand on each of his shoulders and looked him squarely in the eye. "You can talk to me, okay?"

Luki swallowed, micro-expressions skittering across his face.

"I'm here," she said, willing him calm. "I'm listening."

Slowly at first, and then in a cascading, breathless rush, Luki told his story.

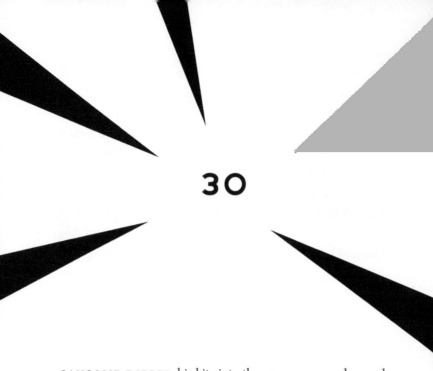

30

SANSOME DIPPED his kite into the power zone and surged out of the water. He leaned back into his harness, dug in his rail, and kicked up a long white arc as he accelerated across the chop. Sun on his skin. Spray in his face. Wind in his kite. Holy hell, he hadn't felt this good in a long time.

"Woohoooooo!" Safaa's voice came over the radios built into their helmets.

"Hey Lauren, is that one of the new CORE's?" asked Molly.

"The Starship XR19, baby," said Lauren. "Broke my budget, but flies like a dream."

Sansome ignored the incessant chatter, dipped one hand back to drag his fingertips along the surface, and allowed himself a small measure of satisfaction. Human Capital was real. He had built it, with help from Esteban. Years of meticulous preparation. Billions of dollars deployed. Countless laws bent or broken. The risks had been immense, and the commensurate reward was finally arriving.

He lined up on a rising swell, whipped the kite across, and leapt thirty feet into the air. Everything shrank below him, the horizon retreating. The world was a stage, history was a play, and he was the director. He had written the script. He had picked the cast. So many who aspired to sit in the director's chair tried to earn the position on the basis of an original premise, a clever plot twist, artful turns of phrase, or impressive special effects. But they missed the key point: stories derived their power from *characters*—how what they did showed who they were, how they changed and grew. Technology was just a prop. Ideology was just decoration. The real magic lay in human agency. That was the only source of new leverage and the insight behind Human Capital's ascension.

The water rushed up to meet Sansome. He landed toeside and let the power of the downloop pull him into a turn.

Switching from the gear-head back-and-forth on the main radio to Molly's private channel, he said, "I've got a surprise for you." He couldn't suppress a grin—not that she could see it. "When I invited you down this year, I promised it wouldn't be just a pleasure cruise. And by that, I didn't mean that you'd get the honor of watching me paste my name on a building." He carved back around and set his line. "Your breath better be bated, because the esteemed Dr. Geoff Rossi has offered you an exclusive license to his patent portfolio for your fields of use."

Silence. Profound, extended silence.

Sansome relished the moment. This was what it was all about.

"Come on," said Molly, finally. "You're fucking with me."

"I am entirely serious," said Sansome.

"But Geoff's as stubborn as a goat," said Molly.

"Well," said Sansome. "You're not wrong there. Maybe it was

whatever you told him over breakfast, or maybe it was the pressure I applied, but apparently even goats can learn new tricks because the lawyers should have the paperwork ready for you when we get back to the boat. I think you'll find that Geoff's terms are very reasonable. He's finally ready to acknowledge that he's been holding back the field and is offering you this unique opportunity to lead the vanguard, as it were."

"*Exclusive*?" Molly's voice was uncharacteristically hesitant.

"To your fields of use, yes," said Sansome. "Geoff doesn't just want to assign IP rights, he wants to see his ideas make it out of the lab and into the real world. And I've assured him that you are his best chance to see that happen, with my continued financial backing, of course. Speaking of which, now would be a good time for you to consider raising a growth round, which I will be happy to fill. What do you say, should we start with a cool $100 million? You better enjoy this session, because the minute you get home, you'll be boarding a rocket-ship."

"If this is some kind of sick joke, I will personally strangle you with my own bare hands," said Molly, but she sounded more shellshocked than threatening.

Sansome laughed a laugh more wild and free than any that had escaped him in a long, long time. "Molly," he said. "You'll have your hands full of much more important things than my neck, promise."

"We're going to be able to finish our Phase Three," she murmured to herself. Then louder, "We'll scoop up every postdoc in the Tidhar lab. His *entire* patent portfolio." With every sentence, her energy built toward manic. "We'll need to quadruple our lab space. Zeynep is going to go apeshit. Just wait til I tell the team."

Sansome let it all wash over him as he led the group back down the peninsula to the yacht. More than anything, he felt *alive*—heart pounding in his chest, blood pulsing through his veins, thoughts hurtling through his mind. There was more power assembled aboard *The Liminal* than Davos or a meeting of the joint chiefs— and the fact that the traditional players didn't recognize it as such was yet another source of strength. Human Capital was the coup of the century. harpZkord didn't even come close. Sansome had Geoff. He had Safaa. He had Lauren. He had Luki and Molly and Farzona and the rest. He didn't need a plan. They *were* the plan. He had Devon-fucking-Chaiket producing an episode of *Rabbit Hole* on *his* boat. He even had Bernadette, the new crown jewel in his exotics collection. *Only people can change the world*, he had told the audience at TED. This was that conviction made real. It was the beginning of something truly new, and he held the tiller.

Sansome cruised in and sat down smoothly on the yacht's swim platform. He pulled his feet from the straps and handed off the kite to the waiting crewmember. As he yanked off his helmet and shook out his hair, he saw Devon and Luki dropping snorkels and fins in the bin up on the main deck.

"Mr. Haverstock." Esteban materialized out of nowhere, as was his custom.

"Esteban," said Sansome, thoughtfully. "What's that Machiavelli line again?"

"'There is nothing more difficult to plan, more doubtful of success, nor more dangerous to manage than a new system,'" said Esteban. "'For the initiator has the enmity of all who would profit by the preservation of the old institutions and merely luke-warm defenders in those who gain by the new ones.'"

"That's the one," said Sansome.

The only problem with winning big was that you had so much more to lose.

31

ISABELLA KO STARED through the tiny window bolted to the front of the industrial oven and watched the bones slough into white-hot ash. Marisol averted her eyes, of course. She was only interested in life, living it and taking it. But the minute the soul departed, her curiosity departed with it.

Isabella was different. She believed that death had something essential to say about life. You couldn't watch a time-lapse video of mushrooms growing on a forest floor and not believe that. Consciousness was forever trapped in the present, but nature waltzed in cycles. Shimmers of heat rising through the dust during dry season. Afternoon thunderstorms rolling in over the ocean during wet season. Cicadas filling the air with their booming rattle for a month before going quiet until the following year's mating season. The moon waxing to suffuse the night with its pale light and then waning so that the stars might glitter in the firmament. Life sprang from death, then died to pay it forward. Alone, the soul had no substance, it was a breeze rippling the fabric of reality.

"So, how's business?" asked The Baker. His name was Sam, but everyone called him The Baker. He was a kind, nervous pastry chef with too many chins and an extraordinary talent for losing money. Isabella had stopped counting the number of ill-advised ventures he'd supplied the seed funding for, but she was happy to help plug the drain as a customer of this little side business of his. When he wasn't baking kouign-amanns in the main kitchen, he was out back in this little shed helping Isabella, Marisol, and their professional competition tidy up after themselves.

Marisol sighed her melodramatic sigh. "Slow," she said. "Too slow." Isabella loved how the luxurious thickness of Marisol's accent turned English words into melted chocolate. Isabella's own facility with linguistic assimilation had its advantages, but her fluent precision lacked flair.

"I haven't seen you here in a while," said The Baker. "I was starting to worry you were taking your business elsewhere."

"Oh, come on," said Marisol. "Who else is there? It's not like we're going to dump a body in the Bay. We're not two-bit amateurs."

Isabella tore herself away from the oven window, purple afterimages pulsing. "As a matter of fact, that's the problem," she said. "It took us years to build up our reputation for professionalism, to meet the right people, win the right contracts. But now, jobs are going out haphazardly. Major targets getting assigned to random thugs doing shoddy work, like that asshole, Daryl. It doesn't make sense. Did you see the news about the Palo Alto gig?"

Marisol was shaking her head sadly. "Leaving the body for her kids to find," she said, a shiver running through her. "It's fucked up is what it is."

The Baker nodded. "Damn shame."

"Damn shame," Isabella echoed.

They all stood in silence for a moment, and then The Baker checked on the oven, shut off the gas, and scraped the remains into a small ceramic urn. Isabella and Marisol watched him work. His movements were sure and unhurried, and he had an agility that was at odds with his bulk. The Baker was a keystone of the underworld veiled in the shadows cast by the gleaming towers of San Francisco—towers whose denizens were just a higher order of predator. At least when Isabella killed someone, she did them the courtesy of looking them in the eye.

But she didn't know how much longer they could keep it up. With rents so high and contracts so few and far between, they could barely make ends meet. At this point could they really move on, climb yet another totem pole? She remembered running with Marisol from the hell of their respective families in La Libertad and finding a place to squat in San Salvador. The things they'd had to do to survive… But they'd gotten out. They'd made it to Quetzaltenango, to Oaxaca, to Mexico City, to Tijuana, to Los Angeles, and finally to San Francisco—where, despite the fact that there were more earbuds-in-ears than the promised flowers-in-hair, they'd decided to make a home. Isabella couldn't bear the thought of giving that up, and yet they couldn't bear the strain of staying much longer if something didn't give.

The Baker walked them out into the chilly gray of pre-dawn Santa Rosa. Gravel crunched under their feet. A rooster crowed in the distance. He offered Isabella the urn with one hand and a fat paper bag with the other.

She accepted both. "What's this?" she asked. The bag was heavy.

"Fresh-milled cornmeal flour for pupusas," said The Baker shyly. "Organic. Biodynamic. The farmer grows heirloom maize cultivars you can't find anywhere else. He's a little nuts, but I swear he's a genius."

Isabella had to press her lips together to seal up the warm, effervescent tide rising inside her.

Marisol leaned over and pecked him on the cheek. "You're a sweet, sweet man," she said as his face turned bright red. "Never change."

"Hey," he called after them as they were getting into their bespoke Prime van. "Look up Reap3r—with a three where the second 'e' should be. That's where all the new faces around here are finding work."

32

COLORFUL INDICATORS FILLED the screen of Devon's laptop—a digital topography of sound. This was her editorial dashboard, her humble command center, the crucible in which *Rabbit Hole* was forged. Her noise cancelling headphones muffled the ambient roar of the jet engines just as she hoped that immersing herself in work might mute the shock of Luki's confession—at least for the duration of a flight where some of her fellow passengers might be, to an extent as yet unknown to Devon, coconspirators.

Lava boiled the ocean in her ears. This was the ambient recording she'd done as they had witnessed the eruption from *The Liminal*. When she'd accepted Sansome's grant and agreed to come on this trip, she'd expected to have to suffer through cocktail parties with socialites and constant interruptions to her work. But thanks to the grant, she still had more than enough funding to return to the islands and do it her way. Looked at from a certain angle, this pleasure cruise was a scouting opportunity. Awkward maybe, but well worth doing. What she *hadn't* expected was to meet the successor to Edward-fucking-Snowden.

Q had built a quantum computer, and the U.S. Government was using it to break the encryption that protected the internet. Instead of sharing the technology to kick off a new computing revolution, they were spying on both citizens and foreign nationals like a creepy landlord using her master key to go through her tenant's stuff. And just as NSA staffers had illegally used their surveillance apparatus to stalk women they hoped to bed, insiders would be leveraging this new digital super-weapon for personal gain.

Devon wished it was harder to believe that Washington would do such a thing, but her complete lack of surprise at their flagrant abuse of power paled in comparison to her astonishment that they were capable of such a technical triumph in the first place. Perhaps incompetence was a convenient mask behind which Beltway spooks could conceal their most ambitious projects. Then again, Paul hadn't developed the tech in-house. He'd contracted Q, a startup funded by Human Capital.

I'm not sure how to do this, Luki told her while they were snorkeling, a dab of un-rubbed-in sunscreen on his ear. That much was obvious. Devon wasn't sure whether to describe his tradecraft as terrible or simply nonexistent. When she'd been working on the harp story, Devon had had to jump through endless hoops to satisfy the hacker's obsessive opsec, while Luki had bared his heart to her on what appeared to be a desperate whim. Then again, harp was a hardened professional. Luki was a computer scientist. He had never been a spy, had never participated in clandestine operations outside of the lab. He spent his time composing math that rendered reality machine-readable, and vice versa. So it was hardly surprising that someone who had dedicated his life to dancing with quantum mechanics was tripping all over himself when it came to intrigue, but that didn't make it any less dangerous.

At first, Devon hadn't believed a word of his story. It was too fantastical. Too clever. Its narrator too unreliable. But after many hours spent rooting through the files on the drive Luki had given her when they returned to the yacht, she'd been forced to admit that they proved his credentials. The American government was blatantly betraying every principle it claimed to stand for.

Luki was for real.

Devon had the story of the century.

And they were both in really deep trouble.

They were on a private plane flying back to California, a plane owned by one of the principals in this cabal, a principal whose agenda was still inscrutable. Devon looked up at the wood-panel partition that separated the main cabin from Sansome's private quarters. Her benefactor profited handsomely from this scheme—meaning that Devon also profited through her grant, as did every other Human Capital investee. Speaking out would stab Sansome in the back. Keeping silent would make her complicit.

Should Devon be thanking Luki or cursing him? This grant was *Rabbit Hole*'s lifeline. It was the first step on the path toward financial viability. It gave her complete creative control and made it possible to imagine a day when she could comfortably afford to do the work she was born to do. Telling Luki's story undermined that dream. Not telling it was unimaginable.

Luki had weighed his options and decided that risking a temporary return to U.S. jurisdiction was better than raising a red flag with Sansome by staying behind in Ecuador. Once they were back in the Bay Area, Devon would do what she could to help him get safely back out of the country so he didn't end up like Mata Hari. Then, she'd need to figure out how best to share his story with the world—a prospect that made her dizzy with both fear and excitement. She'd have to be far more careful than he had been. Nothing attracted the slings and arrows of the powerful faster than holding them to account.

Hold on.

She skipped back thirty seconds in the recording.

Through the crackle of lightning, Sansome's voice was barely audible: *...what I'm... when... among* friends...

Like a paleontologist dusting soil from a fossil, Devon carefully stripped away the thunder of lava meeting brine, the hiss of the wind, and the rest of the ambient soundscape she'd set out to record in the first place. Slowly, voices began to emerge from the tumult.

Sansome: *You are the springboard, you sad old man. Molly will build great things on the foundations you've laid. You just have to* let *her. With your patents in hand, she'll be able to eliminate disease, revive bleached corals, and develop crops that thrive even as the climate changes. She'll unlock the secrets of life itself—and build a better world along the way. Imagine an end to cancer, hunger, and privation.*

Another voice: *Imagine genocidal viruses targeting an ethnic group's DNA. Imagine inequality written into genes. Imagine a world in which life itself is nothing more than intellectual property.*

Sansome: *Gin makes you dour.*

The other voice: *Gin makes me honest. A condition that I can neither abide nor avoid.*

At that point, the cacophony of the eruption obscured the voices beyond recovery. Devon pictured the roiling tower of noxious steam blotting out the stars. She'd been standing at the railing with her fellow passengers, agog. Was it possible that Sansome had been on the deck above, and who was his interlocutor?

The interference subsided.

Sansome: *...second time's the charm. I mean, shit, with your ideas, skills, and reputation you could spin up your own goddamn Manhattan Project. Or just leave it to the kiddos and enjoy haranguing postgrads between well-pulled cappuccinos. Do it your way, whatever you want your way to be, but do it.*

The other voice: *I won't say it again. Fuck. Off.*

Sansome: *I think we both know you'd rather Pandora's box stayed closed.*

The other voice: *You're the one who's opening the damn box.*

Who was Sansome's interlocutor? Devon flashed back to Molly tossing her dirty blond hair insouciantly at the welcome party. *I deeply, truly despise that man from the bottom of my aching heart. I hope he ends up in a bespoke wing of hell with lots of thumb screws and death metal and a pervasive smell of fart.*

Geoff.

Sansome had been arguing with Geoff Rossi. *Threatening* him, demanding the patents that Molly resented him holding back. What could possibly be so damning to a man who had rescued the world from viral contagion? Why was he at odds with the financier who'd earned billions by his famous cure? And if the second time was the charm, what had been the first time? When Devon had pressed Luki about why he was deciding to blow the whistle *now*, he'd explained that a late-night conversation with Geoff had been the proverbial straw that broke the camel's back, that he'd seen something in the other man's eyes he'd recognized, and abhorred.

As the track looped back to the beginning, Devon looked around the cabin. Molly was huddled over her laptop, working feverishly. Luki was sketching incomprehensible equations on graph paper, which Devon suspected was an effort to calm frayed nerves. And there was Geoff, seat reclined and fast asleep with a novel open on his lap. As Devon stared, his limbs twitched in response to whatever specters haunted his dreams.

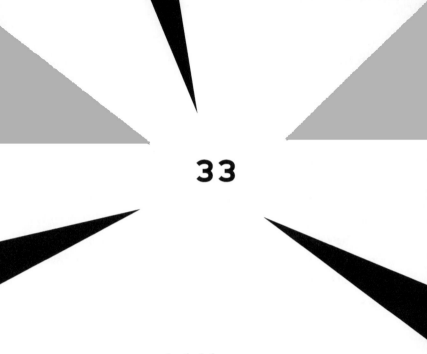

33

GEOFF ENTERED the dark forest.

Primeval trees towered above him. Overgrown thickets choked the narrow path. It smelled of pine resin, and the silence was cathedral.

He touched his pocket to confirm that the sealed letter was still there, as he had a thousand times before. Moisture seeped in through the holes in his boots to soak his tattered socks.

He passed under fern fronds twice his height and by a sign that had deteriorated beyond legibility. Even though it wasn't truly raining, the fine mist breached the hydrophobic membrane of his hand-cut GoreTex jacket, and a drop of cold water slid down his chest, pausing at the summit of each exposed rib.

He noticed pressure on his bladder and stepped off the trail into the bushes to relieve himself. Steam wicked off the yellow stream that pattered against a thick blanket of fallen leaves, wakening the syrupy scent of rot. It felt like he had been urinating forever, with no attendant relief, but he finally zipped himself up anyway and turned to go.

That was when he saw them.

The skeletons sat in a circle around a fire pit stained with long-dead ash. Their flesh was gone. Only yellowing bones remained, partially covered in scraps of denim, wool, and fleece. There was a single empty beer can and an incongruous plastic frisbee. They stared Geoff down through unblinking empty eye sockets.

The world melted around him like wax under flame. He reached out for support and his hand found the trunk of a giant red cedar, rough under his fresh calluses. He steadied himself, then noticed a ragged scar cut into the bark. Looking around, he saw that every tree had an identical notch, and knew with leaden certainty that there were 220 million trees in this forest and that every single one bore a scar.

Geoff ran.

Brambles tore at his limbs.

Mud sucked at his boots.

Spiderwebs stuck to his face.

He ran and ran and ran.

Blisters formed and burst.

Acid bathed his muscles.

His lungs screamed for air.

He ran for a thousand years across a million miles. He ran as the planet spun and the seasons turned, until he finally stumbled out of the forest and collapsed onto his knees, gasping.

After he finally caught his breath, he raised his head. Burned-out husks of elegant houses lined streets of asphalt warped by heat and weather. Geese winged south in a ragged chevron across a slate gray sky.

Geoff pushed himself to his feet and began to walk.

Block after block after block of ruin. Wolves howled in the distance. A cold ocean breeze bit at his face. Jasmine had grown up a stop sign and surrounded its distinctive red octagon with a halo of white flowers.

He didn't know how long he'd been plodding along when a distinctive whining sound sent him into a blind panic. He threw himself beneath the chassis of a decaying SUV, pressed his face against the pavement, and pulled his hood over his head for whatever meager thermal shielding it might provide. Fear burned magnesium-bright. He tasted iron, and realized he was biting the inside of his cheek.

But when he finally caught a glimpse of the drone from under the half-attached bumper, he saw it was just a standard delivery model stuck in an endless loop—its algorithm flying it from empty warehouses to dead customers and back again, an artifact from a world that no longer existed.

Geoff dragged himself out from under the car and walked on. It wasn't far now. The street ran down the hill to the beach. He clambered out onto the slick rocks and watched small waves roll into tide pools abundant with life. Across the water, wind keened through the shattered remnants of empty skyscrapers—steel fingers grasping at forgotten grails.

Turning to face the sea, Geoff waited for the promised sail to appear on the horizon. Time expanded and contracted like a beating heart. He waited. His limbs went numb. He waited. The tide ebbed and flowed. He touched the letter in his pocket and sighed. He was doing everything he could not to not think of her. And that single thought broke the levee of discipline, and the memories flooded back in—jolting him awake.

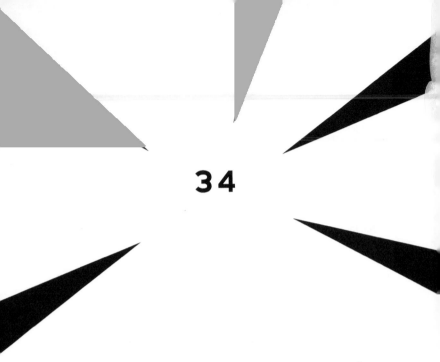

34

LYFTS PULLED in around the estate's circular drive and everyone began to pile in. Luki hefted his bag and tried to identify his car in the general scramble. They'd landed half an hour ago on Sansome's private runway, and after a final parting mimosa, it was time to disperse.

Luki had been expecting a welcome party of heavily armed suits to be waiting for him as he descended the airstair onto the tarmac, but as he emerged into the crisp Marin dawn, there was nothing but the sight of rolling green hills to greet him—the head of an incongruous giraffe poking up through the foliage. So Luki had either successfully hidden his digital tracks or Paul hadn't yet noticed them. Either way, Luki still had a chance.

More than a chance, he finally had a plan, or at least the beginnings of one. Devon—he was careful not to look over at her as she ducked into the back of a sedan—was the ally he so desperately needed. *Rabbit Hole* was the megaphone through which she could share his warning with the world. She had earned an audience and reputation that would make people take heed, and she was known for stopping at nothing to protect her sources—even if they were high-value targets like harpZkord. Luki didn't want to harbor any expectations because he knew how damning that could be, but she'd said she even had friends who might be able to help get him out of the country to someplace safe—or at least as safe as he could ever hope to be again. He would catch a ride to SFO and check in for his connecting flight to Santa Barbara—he quickly suppressed a flash of guilt at abandoning Dexa and the team—and then exit the airport and head back to Oakland to meet Devon at a bar called Palimpsest. They'd figure out the rest from there.

Luki found his car and hoisted his bag into the trunk. Finally, something was starting to go right.

A hand clapped down on his shoulder.

"Luki, my man," said Sansome.

Looking into those smiling auburn eyes, Luki knew—*knew*—that somehow Sansome had planned everything, that the whole time this had been a trap constructed to reveal his traitor's heart. It was all over before it had even begun. Luki yearned after the car that waited for him only a few meters away, his burgeoning hopes crumbling to dust.

"I just want you to know how proud I am of you," said Sansome, squeezing Luki's shoulder. "These government contracts can be tough, but you're handling Paul with the same care you bring to Q. It's inspiring. So even though you must be eager to get back to work, don't forget to take a moment to give yourself a pat on the back. This, right here, right now, is what makes the whole thing worthwhile."

"Thanks," said Luki, vacillating between relief at not having pissed himself in panic, guilt over having forever tainted Q by binding it to Paul, and the emotional gut punch of Sansome's earnestness in the face of impending betrayal. "We wouldn't be where we are today if it wasn't for you."

That, at least, was true.

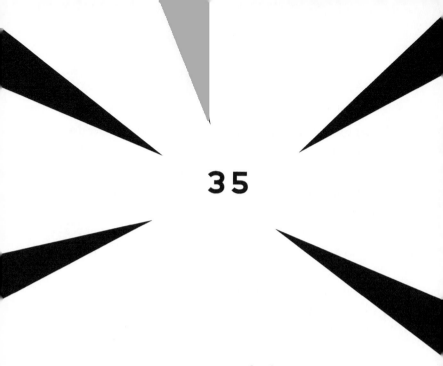

35

SOMETHING TRUMPETED in the distance as Devon's car pulled off Sansome's estate and onto the road.

"Was that an elephant?" asked the driver.

"I think so," said Devon absently. "There's a sort of private zoo in there."

"Seems like that shouldn't be legal," said the driver.

"It probably isn't," said Devon. "See that blue Toyota?"

"Yeah."

"Follow it."

The driver eyed her in the rear-view mirror. "What, you some kind of secret agent zookeeper?"

"Reporter," said Devon. "And there's an extra hundred in it for you if you get me where he's going."

The driver shrugged. "'Democracy dies in darkness.'"

"I'm not with the *Post*," said Devon. "But you get the idea."

"Who are you with, then?"

"Independent," said Devon. "I make a podcast called *Rabbit Hole*."

"No shit." The driver looked up at her reflection again, eyebrows raised. "I love that show. It keeps me sane between rides. The story you did on that trans NBA player was amazing. How *are* leagues going to deal with gender fluidity?"

"Thanks," said Devon with a small smile. "So, think you can help me out here?"

"Oh, don't you worry," said the driver, accelerating out of a curve to pass the intervening delivery truck and pull in behind the Toyota. "We'll get this fucker."

Devon leaned back in her seat and watched Marin slide by. Lichen-crusted rock outcrops. Thick redwood groves. Abundant cyclists in branded jerseys.

A hawk circled above a meadow speckled with wildflowers and Devon imagined looking down at the world from such a vantage, distance transforming buildings and cars and people into toys. At base, human civilization was the sum of everyone's choices. It used to be that civilization consisted of overlapping physical communities of geographical proximity. Feudalism had rendered that truth into power. Now, to a large extent, civilization consisted of overlapping digital communities of shared interests, friends, and affiliations. And the machine Luki had helped construct unlocked the power in this new truth. It used to be about where you were, now it was about who and what you chose.

So, what choices was Devon making right now that would determine the shape of her future? What about Luki, Molly, Kai, Sansome, and the rest? The price of agency was responsibility.

They drove past San Quentin—the one-time state prison that had been converted into a luxury hotel—and onto the Richmond Bridge. Wind ruffled the surface of the bay. Across the water, San Francisco gleamed in the morning light.

One of her early mentors in journalism had told Devon not to see herself as a conduit. *You face one way—towards the source—when you are learning what you want to say,* he'd advised, *and the other way—towards the reader—when you are saying it. You are not a window between the reader and the source; you are drawing a picture of the source for the reader, and it is your picture.* What picture could she possibly draw that captured the scope and scale of the secrets in her possession?

First things first. She needed to keep pulling threads until the whole thing unraveled.

They exited the freeway and wound their way up into the Berkeley hills, the Toyota occasionally disappearing from view around bends in the narrow streets.

It wouldn't be much longer.

Devon gathered her thoughts and tried to arrange them in the best semblance of order she could manage—anxiety buzzing in the back of her head like a high-voltage transmission line. She thought about her anomalously full bank account, how much the grant meant to her, how painful it would be to have Human Capital's doors close on the stable future she'd been dreaming of for so long. But once Devon caught a story's scent, the one thing she could never, ever do was give up the chase, no matter what it cost her.

The Toyota pulled over in front of a midcentury modern house with a commanding view of the bay. Her own driver continued past and turned into a driveway a few houses down. Devon waited for the Toyota to drive away and then leapt out and ran back up the sidewalk.

She caught him halfway up the stairs.

"Geoff," she said, grabbing his sleeve. "We need to talk."

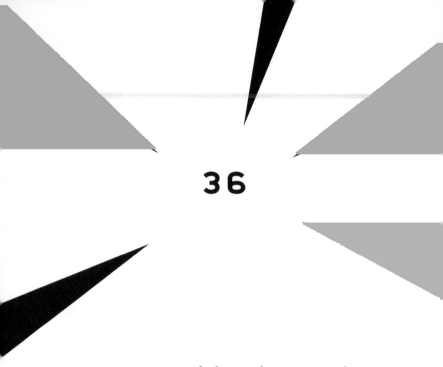

36

SANSOME WATCHED the last car disappear onto the main road and heaved a big sigh. Another year. Another voyage aboard *The Liminal*. Human Capital's living, breathing portfolio was already making its mark, and poised to do far more. Having brought them together, he now felt the melancholic exhaustion of the satisfied host.

Mist writhed over the meadow as the sun leapt from the eastern hills. He could smell jasmine and coffee and soil. Staff bustled in the house behind him, but he stood in a pocket of rare calm.

It was good to be home.

Time for a treat. He had earned it, hadn't he? He'd encouraged Luki to remember to congratulate himself on a job well done, and Sansome should practice what he preached. Hoping to avoid the hubbub of unpacking, he followed the flagstone path to the side entrance, anticipation building up in him like a static charge.

He remembered his surprise at hearing that the last surviving recipient of a World War II pension had finally passed away. It had seemed absurd at the time, a figment from a history book, but Bernadette had been born decades before the *Civil War*. She was a nineteenth century girl in a twenty-first century world. Her very existence put things into perspective: humans lived and loved and fucked and died in a frenetic ballet as the planet spun on its axis, and yet that very same world could *change*. Empires rose and fell. Astronauts walked on the moon. Information migrated from papyrus to bits.

Sansome entered the house and walked down the hall past his office. Yes, when you got right down to it, this was a magnificent universe in which to live a life. He reached the door to the basement, gripped the handle, and—

"*Sansome*." Esteban's voice was sharp, too sharp for this fine morning, too sharp for the assistant persona he publicly inhabited. It snipped away Sansome's sense of wellbeing like the last rose from a bush, leaving nothing behind but wood and thorns.

Sansome looked up, his hand refusing to release the door handle as if it was the tenuous hold on a happier future that was fading fast.

Esteban was leaning out of Sansome's office, beckoning him.

"What is it?" asked Sansome, trying desperately to ignore the sudden urgency crackling in the air between them.

"Who do you think?" said Esteban. "Geoff. I have the live surveillance feed from his house playing on your computer in here. Come on, you need to see this."

"Mother*fucker*," said Sansome, adrenaline surging coldly.

He peeled his fingers off the door handle.

No matter how hard you tried, you could never escape your own shadow.

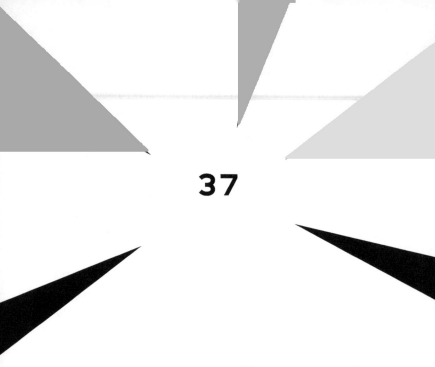

37

THE RECORDING CAME to an end, leaving a pregnant silence in its wake.

Geoff sipped his gin and felt his life dissolve around him. He'd thought he'd been running a maze, searching desperately for the exit, but in the end it had been a labyrinth, which had no exit, only a center.

"Look," said Devon, leaning back against the balcony railing. "I know that Sansome's blackmailing you. I know he's after your patents. I know you're capitulating. The only thing I don't know yet is exactly what the dirt is that he's got on you. So I can start digging. Or we can skip that bit and you can just tell me."

They were there. Palpable, but just beyond the reach of his ever-so-limited biological senses. All 220 million of them. He glanced back into his living room. The sword still lay on the floor beneath the deep gash in the drywall, the dragon on its pommel obscured in shadow, ready to extract its due.

"I can run the story with your comments, or without them," said Devon. She was good. Her eyes were sharp and bright as a hawk's, and he was a field mouse dashing across the grass above which she soared in effortless spirals. "It's up to you. This is your chance to have your say."

His say. What could he possibly say? *I only took Paul's money because nobody else would step up to fund the basic research required to advance the field of synthetic biology. Yes, the Bakunawa virus was a bioweapon I built, but I didn't mean for it to escape the lab by accident and kill millions of people. The reason I was able to develop the vaccine that won me two Nobels was because I was desperately trying to banish the demon I'd summoned—Dr. Frankenstein unstitching his monster. Of course Paul did everything he could to hush it up, he was up shit creek almost as far as I was, so he let me quarantine my patents. I'm not sure whether I'm horrified or relieved that someone finally figured it out.* As if anyone would care what *he* had to say.

"The way these things go, either I'll figure it out before publishing the story, or someone else will after I publish," said Devon. "It's obvious Sansome's forcing you to do this against your will. So don't go down quietly. Take him with you. I'm here to help you do that."

Geoff looked into his gin, and faces flickered through the clear liquid—marginally distorted by the alcohol just as they had been by the mask of the hazmat suit—one after another, on and on and on. Alfred Nobel had established his famous prizes with money earned from his dynamite patent and a lifetime spent manufacturing instruments of death. Oppenheimer's bomb wouldn't have been possible without Einstein's aha-moment. The campanile on the campus below caught Geoff's eye. He wasn't the first UC Berkeley professor to invent a weapon of mass destruction. Maybe they should establish a special faculty club for war criminal Laureates.

"The kid," said Devon, Geoff could see the cogs clicking and whirring behind her eyes, the calculation of human variables, empathy honed into a scalpel. "Luki. I mean, I know he's not a kid, but there's something childlike about him. He's got a secret at least as big as yours. I didn't believe it at first, but he gave me more proof than I'll ever need. It will shake the world to its foundations, mark my words. And you know what he told me? He said that *you* convinced him to blow the whistle."

She left the implication unstated: that Geoff should live up to the people he inspired. Stars shone through the alcohol-shroud of memory. He'd found Luki near the prow of *The Liminal* on the night of the eruption, pressed some gin on him. *I wish they'd just take it all away and have done,* Luki had said. *I wish it had never worked in the first place. Why does it have to be a* trap? For a fleeting second, terror had swept through Geoff, terror at the possibility that the kid—he did seem like a kid—knew about Bakunawa, that this was a kind of veiled threat. But he had looked into the younger man's eyes and seen the truth: Luki was wrestling with his own demons. So Geoff had offered a truth in return: *I live there.*

"Okay," said Devon, raising her hands. "I get it. But don't say I didn't warn you."

Devon turned to go and the way she shook her head disappointedly reminded Geoff of Molly. Though he was loath to admit it, it had been so good to see her. He missed her insouciant curiosity, her enthusiasm for life. When she worked in his lab, he had tried to douse it because of how much she reminded him of himself—and there was nothing Geoff feared more than himself. But that fear implied that Molly *was* Geoff, that presented with the same untenable situations, she would make the same choices. Believing that denied her any agency, stripped her of the power to do the right thing. *So don't go down quietly. Take him with you.* Devon had been encouraging him to take down Sansome, but Geoff had spent years undercutting his own most promising pupils. No wonder Molly hated him.

"Wait," said Geoff.

There had been a moment near the end of their voyage aboard *The Liminal*—they were cruising beside mangrove forests following a group of equatorial penguins—when Molly had caught up with Geoff and opened her mouth to offer one of her famously acerbic greetings. He'd already signed over the patents and couldn't bear the thought of her *thanking* him for doing so. So, what had he done? Broken eye contact and scurried back to hide in his cabin. He hadn't even had the courage to face her. Instead, he'd knelt on his bunk and watched the mangroves glide by through the porthole. Red mangroves filtered all the salt from brackish water and funneled it into a single sacrificial leaf on each branch. Salt built up in each sacrificial leaf until they turned yellow, fell into the water around their roots, and decomposed—forming soil for the mother tree. Self-cultivation wasn't as rare as you might think. Lava cactuses would be among the first to colonize the new land formed in the eruption they'd witnessed on the yacht. A pioneer plant, they created soil with their own dead branches—laying the groundwork for others to follow. People had been calling Geoff a pioneer for decades, now it fell to him to finally earn the moniker by sacrificing himself to the greater cause of progress.

He'd always asked himself how to achieve success. How would he get into the best graduate program? How would he distinguish himself from other researchers? How would he secure the funding he needed? How would he make every experiment ten times more ambitious than the last? How would he cover up the mistake that had cost him his soul? How would he assuage his bottomless guilt? How would he protect the world from his ideas? How would he save himself? He now saw that the entire effort had been in vain. Instead of asking how he could succeed, he should have been asking how he could contribute. And through that lens, the path forward finally came into focus.

He gazed out at a city built on dreams of gold and silicon. Ingenuity had lent humans power, amplifying our best and worst aspects and yoking our future ever more tightly to our nature. Geoff had spent his life cultivating intelligence, it was time to try wisdom instead.

I love you, man, Molly had said after the breakfast they shared in his cabin. *But you're not okay. Whatever it is, running away from it isn't working.* Handing Molly his life's work wasn't nearly enough. He owed a debt not just to her, but to the whole world, and he owed them more than his patents, he owed them an explanation.

"Do they let you read in prison?" he asked.

"What?" asked Devon.

"Never mind," said Geoff.

His story was hard to believe, but unlike fiction, reality needn't be plausible.

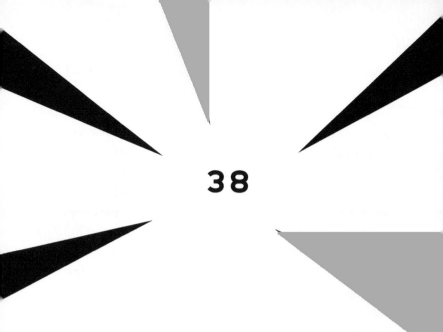

38

SANSOME KNEW what he had to do and couldn't bear it.

Esteban stood at his shoulder. On the live surveillance feed in front of them, Geoff and Devon exited the house and piled into a waiting car.

Sansome deeply, truly loved *Rabbit Hole* and had been thrilled to underwrite it. The sound of Devon's voice explaining the world to him reminded Sansome of the unbridled joy he'd felt exploring the woods as a kid. She conjured a feeling of possibility, of new worlds just beyond the horizon, as yet unmapped.

At the heart of it, that's why Sansome did what he did. He'd always secretly aspired to enable the Age of Discovery captains, venturing forth into dangerous new territories to seek their fortune. Ferdinand Magellan, Vasco de Gama, Sir Francis Drake, and their cohorts might have mapped the physical world, but there was always a new frontier, and the distant shore Sansome had set his sights on was unlocking the future itself—whether it lay in quanta, state rooms, genomes, or people's hearts and minds.

Leaving Esteban by the desk, Sansome stood and ran a finger along the glass of the climate-controlled bookshelf that contained the world's most extensive collection of Darwin's private papers and handwritten manuscripts. Good old Charlie was the bridge between the Age of Discovery and Sansome's own era. He had risked life and limb to answer the call of the unknown and brought back insight instead of treasure—insight that had eventually led to Geoff's biotechnological breakthrough, and the vaccine that had sent Human Capital's returns on its first investment into the stratosphere, establishing the foundation for what it was today. There was Darwin's *Beagle* diary, his field notebooks, his letters, the original 1842 sketch of his theory of evolution. And now Sansome's Ark of living, breathing specimens demonstrating life's magnificent diversity included an animal who had been Darwin's contemporary on the islands where inspiration had struck with such force that humanity was still living out the reverberations.

Geoff was tearing open the wound that Sansome had tended so carefully for so long. The old man couldn't stomach the price of progress and had made the indefensible decision to stand in its way. Scratch that. Geoff didn't even *know* the price of progress, or that Sansome had been paying it. Anyone who knew the truth about Bakunawa had been an existential risk to Geoff, who had developed it, Paul with his black budget that had provided the contract for the original bioweapon, the vaccine that Geoff had created after the virus escaped the lab by mistake, and Human Capital itself. So Sansome had no choice but to take out the half-dozen scientists and program managers that knew too much. Expensive Reap3r contracts issued at irregular intervals and specified to create the appearance of natural causes.

While Geoff wallowed in self-pity, Sansome had been keeping his secret safe. And now here Geoff was, spilling that secret to a journalist—a journalist who was already in possession of another earth-shattering revelation that she was leveraging up for more.

I just want you to know how proud I am of you. Luki had already stabbed Sansome in the back when he accepted that heartfelt praise. Sansome had groomed him for years, given him the funding Q needed to prove concept, undermined his competitors, and introduced him to Paul, who controlled enough clandestine capital to realize the dream of quantum computing. Paul had been understandably hesitant given how the first collaboration with Human Capital had turned out, but the technology spoke for itself, opening an entirely new vector for projecting geopolitical power. Sansome couldn't blame Luki for wanting to share Q's extraordinary achievements with the world—ultimately, that was the plan anyway, and Human Capital would profit regardless—but he could sure as hell blame him for pulling a Snowden.

And Sansome couldn't ignore the perfect irony of Luki and Geoff inspiring each other to confess to Devon. Sansome hosted the annual cruise aboard *The Liminal* to allow Human Capital's movers and shakers to mingle, and in mingling, amplify and reinforce each other's ambitions. It was a network effect made manifest, and this was the very same network effect backfiring spectacularly.

Under the hot glare of the stage lights, Sansome had told the audience at TED that only people could change the world, that Human Capital sought out the best of them, figured out what makes them tick, wrote them checks, and gave them free rein to do what only they could do. So, what did you do when they turned on each other?

If these revelations came to light, it wouldn't only doom Luki and Geoff. Sansome would be implicated and, by extension, every single member of Human Capital's portfolio. Molly. Lauren. Safaa. Samuel. Farzona. Everyone. Lifetimes of work undone. History thrown off course. It would render Sansome's sacrifices, Sansome himself, meaningless.

It wasn't impossible that he could bully Geoff and Luki into silence, but not Devon. Devon's initial ambivalence about accepting Human Capital's grant had only cemented Sansome's faith in her integrity, but now that very same integrity was a noose tightening around his neck.

This wasn't how it was supposed to go. He'd had everything. He'd *won*.

No. It had to be all three of them.

And it had to be now.

Esteban gently squeezed his shoulder. Forcing back tears of frustration and self-recrimination, Sansome logged onto Reap3r. The best and worst thing about the internet was that you could find your people.

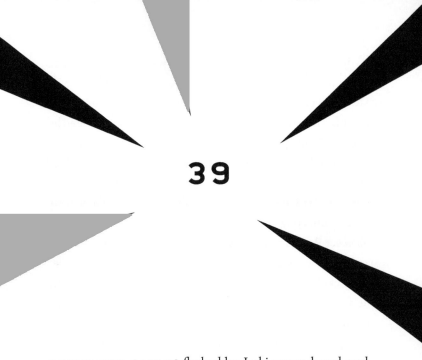

39

BURNT-RED CABLES flashed by. Luki remembered reading that the Golden Gate Bridge's paint was a special formulation—international orange—and that painting the ten million square feet of steel was a perpetual task for a team of thirty. Maintenance got no respect in a culture obsessed with achievement. In the end, there was no end. Nothing was discrete. Everything bled into everything else, and any claims to authorship were vanity.

It was a clear day, and the Farallon Islands stood out against the distant blue-white line of the Pacific horizon. Years ago, Luki had watched a pulp disaster movie in which a tsunami inundated the Bay Area, and now he found himself waiting for that anomalous giant to rear out of the ocean, jacking up and up and up until it swept away the Golden Gate and him with it, tossing container ships like bathtub toys and cleansing the world in brine.

That would certainly simplify things.

In the absence of an apocalyptic wave, Luki's problems continued to compound at a rate sure to stir a banker's loins. Disaster wouldn't wait for Luki's story to break. Paul might discover Luki's betrayal at any time. Luki might not have covered his tracks well enough, or Paul might have him under closer surveillance than he realized. Maybe Paul even had a mole embedded in Q. Or even if she wasn't his agent, Dexa might contact Paul out of concern over Luki's absence. Or someone might discover the incriminating designs and metadata on Devon's laptop. And however Paul found out, well, Luki didn't know what he'd do, and didn't want to find out.

Luki had gotten himself into this mess, and every choice he'd made along the way had made it worse. He was Basque, for fuck's sake. He should have known to never trust an authority figure like Paul in the first place, that an alliance with state power ultimately brought the power of the state to bear on you. He'd wanted to realize his dream so badly, to prove the skeptics wrong, to offer the best of himself to the world, that he'd forgotten the wisdom his forebears had paid for in blood.

Neuroscience showed that your conscious mind didn't make decisions, but rationalized decisions your brain had already made. The voice in your head was really a sports announcer narrating the action, not the athlete. Did that mean Luki harbored an unconscious death wish he was unknowingly working to fulfill? Unintentional martyrdom seemed a sad fate.

Looking east, Luki's gaze fell on Alcatraz. He'd be lucky to end up in a place like what The Rock had once been. More likely, he'd be disappeared and wrung dry by interrogators until their tortures proved fatal. He flashed back to the village library that had been his refuge as a child, the books that had inspired his first steps along the path that had brought him here today. Walter

Isaacson had had more documentation of Leonardo da Vinci's life than Steve Jobs's when he was writing their respective biographies. Da Vinci's paper letters and journals had outlasted Jobs's digital documents and emails, a large cache of which had been deleted accidentally in the 1990s. Luki would be expunged just as easily. A cost of doing business.

Luki's fingernails dug into his palms. He was *terrible* at this. That much was obvious. When he blew the whistle, all he did was call the hounds.

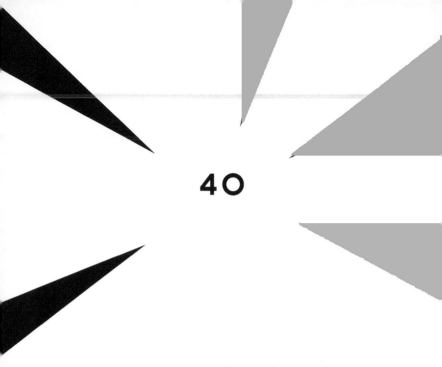

40

ISABELLA SLID the onion and carrot skins into the counter-top compost bin, helping the cabbage ends along with a shake of the cutting board. Marisol's favorite Natalia Lafourcade album blared in the background. The *curtido* was fermenting. Now, for the pupupas themselves.

"I don't know what you're on about," said Marisol, who was sighting down the short, curved blade of a *karambit* from point to handle. "Obelisco makes great food, but their *al pastor* is definitely not legit."

"What do you mean, not 'legit'?" asked Isabella. She broke off a chunk of masa, formed it into a ball, used her thumb to hollow out the inside, and stuffed it with shredded *quesillo*.

With practiced efficiency, Marisol began to grind the blade against the waterstone. "If the pork isn't slow-roasted on a spit, and if they don't have a slice of pineapple at the top, it's not authentic," she said. "Simple as that."

"Not again," Isabella said as she sealed the pupusa and pressed it into a thick, flat pancake. "This is just like the time with the croissants in Bordeaux." They had drunk straight from a bottle of Saint-Émilion while sitting on the edge of the half-pipe in the riverside skate-park, kicking their feet, running their mouths, and listening to the late-night murmur of the medieval city behind them.

"They were bready," said Marisol with self-aware hauteur. "Cut into a croissant, and you're supposed to see all the separate layers—that's how you know they're prepping it by hand with cold butter. I thought that by going to the motherland, I'd get to taste the best croissant I'd ever had, but Rotha in Berkeley is way better than anything we found in France."

"And I'm telling you that you spend so much time passing judgement on stuff that you forget to enjoy it in the first place," said Isabella, stuffing another pupusa. Their bickering was comfortable, and comforting—their bodies might be in their thirties, but their souls were cranky centenarians. "Obelisco might not have a spit, but their al pastor tastes really good, doesn't it?"

Marisol shrugged as she examined the knife's vanishingly keen edge. "I mean yeah, but—"

"See?" interrupted Isabella. "Even you agree that they're good. So what's with the obsession with so-called 'authenticity?'"

"Because they could be so much *better*," said Marisol, laying the karambit down gently and appraising the next one. "The gap between their potential and their execution drives me nuts."

Isabella's phone buzzed in her pocket. She wiped her hands on a kitchen towel and checked it. Despite the trumpeting chorus, silence reverberated through Isabella like a struck gong.

Reap3r.

She looked up into Marisol's deep brown eyes and saw recognition there, an echo of inner quiet.

"We got a match," said Isabella. "Time to go to work."

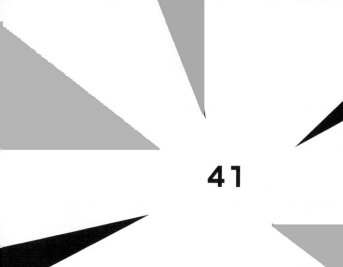

41

AS THE CAR WOUND down out of the hills and through Berkeley, Devon stared out of the window and into memory. These streets had been empty during the Bakunawa quarantine, everyone practiced at sheltering-in-place after surviving COVID-19. But with her parents tense and desperate under the financial stress of trying to morph their restaurant into a cloud kitchen yet again, home hadn't been much of a home to twelve-year-old Devon. So whenever she thought she was starting to go crazy, she'd don her *Adventure Time* mask, sneak out of the house, and wander the deserted streets.

Sometimes she'd imagine that she was the only one left, that all the other people had mysteriously disappeared and that she was on a lonely quest to figure out where they had gone and why. Sometimes she'd look up at the gnarled oaks and graceful bays and imagine that instead of walking up a tree-lined street, she was walking through a forest in which humans had happened to build some structures. Sometimes she'd imagine that tomorrow would be the day that the horrific events in the Philippines would sweep through California with equal violence. While millions had died, billions were spared by Geoff's famous vaccine. Nobody had ever developed an effective vaccine so fast. To Devon's knowledge, neither had anybody ever developed a vaccine to a virus they'd themselves invented.

Devon looked sidelong at her fellow passenger. Geoff was sitting next to her in the back seat, staring out the other window into other memories. More than 200 million dead. Countless families wracked by grief. Civilization reeling from yet another onslaught of contagion. But Bakunawa hadn't been the result of random genetic mutation. It had been engineered. It had been made *on purpose*, even if its release had been accidental as Geoff claimed. Silent tears slid down his cheeks, but he was smiling, weary and buoyant.

This was Geoff's big secret. Human Capital had profited by the development of the virus and profited by its vaccine. But that wasn't enough for Sansome. Now he wanted to profit by letting entrepreneurs like Molly advance the state of the art that Geoff had pioneered, spinning off countless novel biotechnological marvels and horrors along the way. But apparently the third time wasn't always the charm, because in order to secure the patents, Sansome had needed to push Geoff to the edge, and—as Sansome himself had pointed out during his welcome speech—edges were unstable places where anything could happen. And that was how, aboard a ship named for the very territory they were traversing, Geoff and Luki had happened to each other.

Devon had never taken a bigger risk than breaching one source's confidentiality in order to win over another, and her nerves were still tingling. Standing in Geoff's house, staring into his haunted eyes, she'd *known* how close he was to breaking, how telling him that he wasn't the only one, that Luki had a secret too, might unleash the flood.

Everything had pivoted on the fulcrum of that moment. If it hadn't worked… If it hadn't worked, Geoff might have tipped off the authorities and Luki's escape could have been aborted violently. It would have gotten out that Devon had betrayed a source. Nobody with something hot would ever have trusted her again. But more than that, she'd never have been able to trust herself again. It would have been the end of *Rabbit Hole*, and frankly, if she didn't have *Rabbit Hole*, what *did* she have?

But she'd gone with her gut in the moment, and it had worked, and the story was worth it—*had* to be worth it given that it meant the end of her short-lived bout of financial stability: A bioweapon that had shattered the world, a vaccine that had glued it back together, and a mad scientist celebrated for the latter who was also responsible for the former. A quantum computer that broke the encryption that protected the internet, used by spooks to spy on the sins of their peers, leveraging their infernal discoveries in an escalating series of power plays.

If Devon tried to pitch this as a screenplay, Hollywood producers would laugh her out of the room. But while realism and suspension of disbelief seemed like they should go hand in hand, they actually operated on independent axes. You didn't believe in stories because technical footnotes justified every leap of faith. You believed in stories because the characters believed in them, and you believed in the characters. To tell a true story of this magnitude, Devon would need to bring

Luki and Geoff to life on *Rabbit Hole*. Only by making them feel real could she render their accounts undeniable and, in doing so, create an eye in the center of what would surely be a hurricane of official lies and retribution. And this was probably the only chance she'd ever get to have Geoff and Luki in the same place at the same time, an opportunity that was far too good to pass up. Once Geoff had finally decided to confess, he'd been happy to come along when she asked, as if nothing else could possibly matter to him anymore.

"This it?" asked Vince, the driver.

Palimpsest's shade sails occluded triangles of baby blue sky.

"Sure is," said Devon. "And if you don't mind waiting again… I'm not sure how long we'll be." They couldn't afford having to wait for a ride if Luki needed to scramble for a quick exit.

"Anything for *Rabbit Hole*,"—he said, grinning, not unkindly—"especially when the meter keeps running."

"Geoff," she said, and he startled. "We're here."

He shook his head as if to clear it and they got out of the car.

"Beautiful," he said, peering at the freshly painted outer wall of Palimpsest, which had been transformed into a single vast field of blooming tulips. "I wonder how they get the colors to pop like that."

Feeling like she was leading a wayward child, Devon shepherded him toward the entrance. Long ago, she'd read that firsthand Roman accounts of Hun invaders described them as monsters, which modern historians thought was straightforward racism until archaeological evidence showed that the Huns had practiced facial scarring and bound their children's skulls so that they grew cone-heads, the better to intimidate enemies with their grotesque appearance. Geoff's cheeks were dry and there was a bounce in his step, but his eyes gazed past the world instead of at it. Seized by an irrational fear that she might somehow fall through his sea-green irises and into a twisted fairy kingdom from which there would be no escape, Devon glanced away.

Sometimes monsters were real, and were also profoundly, tragically human.

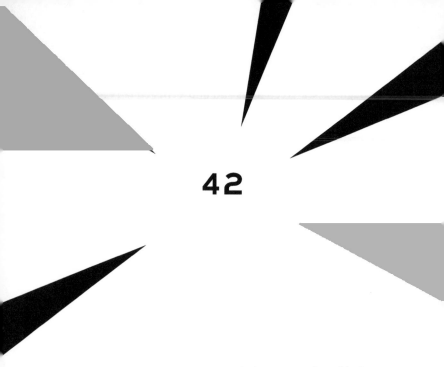

42

LUKI STARED AT THE MAN sitting across the table from him. Geoff Rossi. Luki could taste bile and gin, could feel the swell rolling beneath the prow of *The Liminal. I've been there, kid. Hell, I live there.* The magnitude of the burden Geoff carried had been self-evident, moving Luki to act on his own misgivings before he chickened out. Geoff was living proof that Luki didn't want to become someone like Geoff. Now Luki knew why. A bioweapons mastermind disguised as the greatest healer of his generation. Geoff didn't look like a villain. He was rumpled and oddly disassociated, answering Devon's questions as if hearing them from a great distance.

Bakunawa had never made it to Luki's village, but he remembered the tension undergirding every adult conversation around him, a simmering baseline anxiety. Old Amona said it was a curse laid upon the world by *Gaizkiñ*, the elusive spirit who materialized in pillow-down to spread disease, and burned the body of a cockerel in her hearth to keep it away. The village council supplemented her efforts by banning all travel to and from Bilbao. Luki had overheard his parents arguing in low voices about how long they'd be able to keep running the cidery if things kept on like that. They couldn't distribute barrels and no outsiders meant fewer customers. Even the centuries-long stream of pilgrims had dried up. It might be the Way of St. James, but the apostle wasn't on hand to offer miracle cures, and locals weren't eager to welcome potential super-spreaders.

And then there was the vaccine. A younger, haler version of this man had been all over the headlines. They'd learned about him in school, inspiring a few of Luki's classmates to go into medicine and epidemiology. Luki himself had been more enamored of digital viruses than biological ones, but the circumstances that had led up to this surreal conversation showed how those two worlds had become one.

Everyone worried about the future. You obsessed over how tomorrow might be different. But it was the things that did *not* change that mattered most. If you wanted to make sense of the world, you had to focus on the finding the constants. They were the rare truths that everyone was too busy to bother with. And the truth right in front of Luki was that politics was always there waiting to co-opt the pursuit of knowledge. A flashlight beam played across multicolored bricks. *Each square is a people, a nation,* Paul had said. *The experiment tests whether and how they weather history, who will stand the test of time. My job is to see that we* do. A weapons master stocking the national armory with shiny new toys supplied by a tech investor determined not to let ethics stand in the way of science, or profits. Paul and Sansome had manufactured conspiracy, and Geoff and Luki were mere technical apprentices in their workshop.

No. Not *mere*. Responsibilities this large were not so easily shirked. Luki and Geoff had failed to ask the hard questions. Worse, they had *chosen* not to ask the hard questions because they already knew the answers and didn't want to admit it to themselves. They, who professed to have devoted their lives to seeking truth. And now here they were, two fugitive scientists spilling state secrets to a podcaster and a—well, he wasn't quite sure what Kai was, artist, maybe?—over a picnic table in an outdoor graffiti bar.

Life was like... Luki needed to stop pretending that he might ever be able to adequately describe what life was like. Life was life. That was all. That was enough. More than enough, sometimes.

"Devon," Luki interrupted Geoff's explanation of how his team had destroyed the evidence in the lab where Bakunawa had been developed.

Her eyes met his and he tapped his wrist. As soon as Paul suspected anything was amiss, he'd excise Luki from the internet with Q's scalpel.

"Just a few more minutes," she said.

"You have enough," he said.

"The only way we get out from under this is by getting the story out," she said. "I need this."

"It has to be enough," said Luki, every minute he stayed on American soil was another minute he was within Paul's easy reach and jurisdiction. "The story won't reach anyone if we're not around to tell it."

Devon held his gaze for an extra beat, then nodded. "You're right," she said. "Let's go."

"My people are prepping fake papers for you," Kai said to Luki, voice calm and efficient. Devon had said they could trust

Kai, and it wasn't like Luki had any other choice. These were the circles he ran in now. "It's short notice, but they should be ready by this evening. We'll buy your tickets under that name and you'll fly out tonight. Safer than traveling under your real name, given that we don't know whether or how they're already tracking you. Meanwhile, you all should keep moving while we reach out to a few legal advisers for a Plan B. We'll have someone fly with you as a witness, just in case."

Devon's phone buzzed. She frowned, disconnected the recording mics, and picked up.

"Yes?" The color drained from her face. "You're sure? Okay, hold on."

"What is it?" Luki couldn't keep the strain from his voice.

Something in her expression shifted, defying legibility.

"We have a problem," she said.

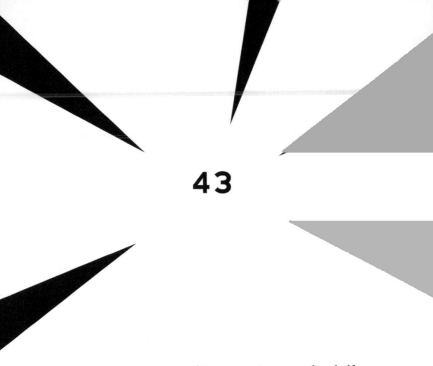

43

GEOFF WAS ENJOYING his cappuccino more than he'd enjoyed anything in a long time. After decades of harboring a secret that was slowly consuming him from within, he was finally free—free to be the war criminal so very few had known him to be. Nothing about his culpability in the death of millions had changed, but he had finally decided to admit his guilt, and confession conferred a strange kind of grace, and invitation to simply *be*.

Wind rippled the shade sails above them. The wooden picnic table was warm and rough under his hands. An artist was putting the final touches on the lovingly illustrated mycelium covering Palimpsest's wall, the soil within supporting the tulips without. The imagery took Geoff back to his high school biology class, learning about the vast underground networks that ferried nutrients and information beneath the forest floor like a living, breathing internet, sprouting strange fruit that might nourish or kill human foragers. The solemn kid across the table from him had hijacked silicon as effectively as Geoff had managed to hack biology—small wonder Sansome had roped Luki into Human Capital's portfolio, and convinced Paul to reopen his black budget. Power was an infinite game.

"Motherfucker." The force of Kai's epithet hooked Geoff's attention back to the conversation at hand.

"harpZkord wouldn't be calling if he wasn't sure," said Devon in a voice whose exaggerated firmness belied inner turmoil. "He has a script that monitors Reap3r for keywords—his name, his aliases, and people close to him—of which, apparently, I'm one. It just sent up a red flag that a contract has been put out on all three of us."

"Reap3r?" asked Geoff.

"Decentralized, anonymous darknet murder-market built on smart contracts and cryptocurrency," said Kai.

Devon nodded. "Basically, it's Lyft for hitmen, and someone just called us a ride."

Palimpsest wouldn't be a bad place to die. Geoff would kneel in the gravel and take the bullet with sunshine on his skin and the earthy taste of cappuccino on his tongue. He deserved a lot worse.

"Who put a price on our heads then?" asked Geoff.

"harp can't see the buyer ID," said Devon. "It's happening, but we don't know who's behind it."

"I must have slipped up somewhere," said Luki, drumming his knuckles on the table. "It's Paul. Has to be. As soon as people know about Q, his surveillance program is over. And he wasn't shy about telling me what he'd do to protect it."

"Then why all three of us?" asked Devon. "I mean, you're obviously a target. And maybe me, though I don't understand how he'd know that I know about Q. But why Geoff?"

"Paul funded the Bakunawa project too," said Geoff. He'd only met the man a few times. Just another suit in yet another conference room in yet another meeting Geoff had to attend to get the funding his lab needed. "Maybe he's just trying to tie up loose ends."

"Maybe." Devon frowned. "But it's pretty convenient he'd bundle it into the same Reap3r order. It's not like you get bulk discounts."

"Sorry to interrupt," said Kai. "But you can worry about attribution later. Right now, we need to figure out how you're going to avoid getting your asses capped by an on-demand assassin."

Devon exchanged a loaded glance with Luki. Their faces were tight, their bodies tense. Geoff's equanimity soured. These two kids didn't deserve this. They had their whole lives ahead of them, and the courage to live them right.

People said the truth would set you free—even if in his case it meant the freedom to be incarcerated. What Geoff hadn't counted on was that the first thing he'd do with his newfound liberty would be to start caring about the fates of two total strangers.

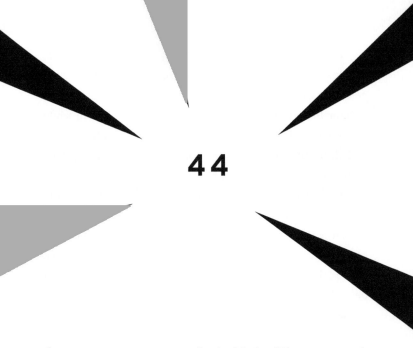

44

"SO, WHAT DO WE DO?" asked Luki. "There are people coming to kill us."

Devon was looking around Palimpsest. "This place isn't exactly a fortress."

There had been a remote valley buried deep in the mountains behind his parents' cidery that Luki would sneak off to whenever he got in trouble. He'd climb the gnarled trunk of an ancient oak and perch in its crown, imagining that the tree was a living fortress, every branch a wing in the arboreal palace, every leaf a solar panel fueling the endless project of self-construction. Now, when he needed those defenses most, they remained as imaginary as they had always been.

Luki was helpless. He had always been helpless. Fate had buoyed him along and deposited him on the shores of disaster.

"Even if we run, they'll just keep coming after us," said Geoff.

Devon nodded, and Luki was amazed by the calm she channeled in extremity, the depth of her resolve. She seemed to be holding her world together through sheer force of will while his had long since fallen apart. Ultimately, fate always won, and all the available evidence pointed to fate bearing down on them like a freight train. He'd wanted to switch things up, to do his part to push history in a slightly different direction, but he should have turned away before challenging a man like Paul. The waxy pink scar that the national police had carved into his father's forehead was all the proof Luki should have needed that power forever reinforced itself. Better to let things be and take what satisfaction you could from life than rage against how the world worked.

"Our only chance is to blow this story wide open," Devon said. "We just need to stay alive long enough to do it."

Luki wished he had the strength to harbor such delusions.

Kai was scrolling through their phone. "I know a guy with a warehouse in Mission Bay," they said. "He can help. We go there, then move to a new location every few hours. Then— Wait a minute," they interrupted themself. "Devon, could harpZkord hack Reap3r? Call off the hit?"

Something shifted inside Luki, a shadow that had once been curiosity.

"I don't think so," said Devon. "I mean, I can ask, but Reap3r's blockchain architecture means it's basically invulnerable."

Kai looked at Luki.

He blanched.

Pieces fell into place.

Luki touched his forehead. That scar hadn't been the end for his dad, it had been the start of his life as an activist. The only thing that made causes truly hopeless was choosing to give up on them.

"Yes," he said slowly. "Yes." The second time around the word carried the weight of conviction. "Yes, I can get him in."

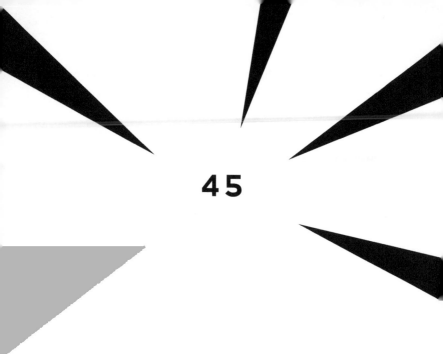

45

MARISOL'S SEATBELT clicked into place, and Isabella pressed the start button, bringing their van to life. Isabella had figured out what model of electric vehicle they used for Prime. Marisol had found a local food distributor trying to sell a used one and they'd spent a gig's worth of fees disguising it as one of its Prime brethren. Prime delivery vans were so ubiquitous as to be invisible. They were unremarkable in any neighborhood, even double-parked, and had ample storage capacity. This vehicle was almost as crucial to Isabella and Marisol's work as the karambits, and they took just as good care of it. Physical objects repaid attention with satisfaction—a quiet joy in the act of maintenance.

"*Vamos*," said Marisol, and Isabella could hear the tension coiled in her voice, echoing her own. She glanced over and their eyes met for a brief moment, acknowledging the shared sentiment.

The ride into Oakland didn't take long. Traffic was light, and they eschewed music, letting the hiss of rubber on asphalt accompany the familiar ratcheting anticipation that preceded a kill—the very particular feeling that was the single thing Isabella liked best about her work. Everything else seemed to fade into the background, to lose all color, to shed the weight of meaning. There was just this. Just the thing to be done. Just the target, her talent, and her partner. No bullshit. No small talk. No distractions.

It was *clarifying*.

There was something different this time though. Isabella couldn't pretend that she didn't appreciate Reap3r's efficiency. They hadn't had to endure the condescending prattle of the bosses who regularly doled out gigs or jump through the inane hoops of engaging with a new client. There was no question of whether to slip some cash to a flunky or pretending to care about the vicissitudes of conscience that first-timers so often struggled to overcome. Reap3r was simple, elegant, professional. Something about the design reminded her of an Apple store. Isabella appreciated the aesthetic, but she didn't trust it. It was too clean, and life wasn't clean, so anything clean was lying.

Isabella didn't like liars. Politicians who promised the world even as they pocketed it. Lovers who cheated. Bags of Tostitos that contained more air than chips. Her own work might be violent, but it was honest.

They pulled off the freeway, navigated through a line of semis bound for the Port of Oakland, and drove through town. Low-income housing gave way to abandoned warehouses, albeit some that had been renovated into idiosyncratic artist compounds. Their own neighborhood wasn't much better, and the reason they'd accepted this Reap3r job was that they might not even be able to afford their modest apartment if they didn't find steadier work.

As The Baker had suggested, Reap3r promised to be the source of the new contracts they needed so badly, so Isabella had to swallow her misgivings and accept the fact that the game was changing. In fact, they should lean into it: build up the reputation of their Reap3r profile so that the algorithm matched them with the best gigs. The word "freelancer" had been coined to describe mercenaries after all, so at least the language was apt even if the infrastructure was new.

"Look," there was something almost but not quite sexual in the urgency of Marisol's voice. "This is it."

Up ahead, shade sails soared.

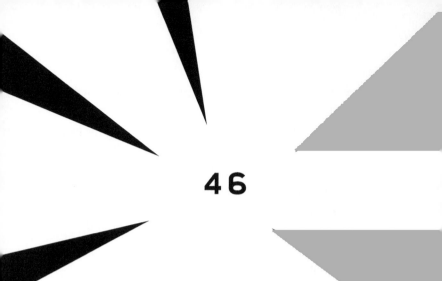

46

"I'M IN," harp's disguised voice blared from the speakerphone in the middle of the picnic table. Devon imagined her holed up in her apartment on the outskirts of Taipei, surrounded by her beloved Lego collection and buoyed by one of the instrumental cinematic soundtracks that she always had playing in the background.

Luki looked up from his laptop and made a fist. It was as if a light had switched on inside him. Devon only hoped she could absorb some of that energy. They would need every lumen they could get.

"Devon, when this is over, I'm gonna have some questions for your friend," said harp. "That hack was sneaky as fuck. As far as I know, nobody has enough conventional compute capacity to crack Reap3r before the heat death of the universe sets in."

"That's the highest praise I've ever heard harp give," said Devon.

Luki grinned.

Devon turned her attention back to harp, "Get us out of this alive, and Luki will blow your mind."

"That's the highest praise I've ever heard Devon give," said harp.

Devon snorted and Luki blushed.

"Okay, let's see here," said harp.

Devon, Luki, Kai, and Geoff all leaned over the table.

"Give me a minute," said harp. "It's a big system."

They waited on tenterhooks, staring down at the phone, waiting for a disembodied, inhuman voice to declare their fate.

"Alright," said harp. "I have good news and bad news. The good news is that I've got admin privileges and should be able to turn this thing inside out. The bad news is that it'll take time, and that it looks like certain things will take a lot more time than others."

"Okay," said Devon. "You don't need to blow it up. Just call off our hit."

"Unfortunately, cancelling a job is one of the things that'll take quite a bit of time given how they designed their system, but I should be able to tweak some other variables and— Yes, I've located your ticket. Okay... Fuck."

"What?" asked Luki.

"Uh, looks like whoever accepted the bid is getting close," said harp. "Geotags are only a few blocks away. Time to GTFO."

Kai frowned, and hurried off toward the bar, calling over their shoulder that they'd be back in a minute.

"So you're saying some serial killer is about to walk into Palimpsest and gun us down?" asked Luki.

"You need to move," said harp. "I can fix this, but I need time. Get out of there right now, and don't stop running until I tell you to. I really do want to know how you managed to crack Reap3r, and you won't be able to tell me if you get your ass capped."

Devon looked at Luki. He was evidently as panicked as she felt. How would she describe the feeling to listeners? It was like waking up from a nightmare into another nightmare, and knowing that you hadn't, might never, escape the matryoshka. It was like the moment immediately before the nurse stabbed the needle into your vein, that split second stretching out to accommodate minutes, hours. It was like when you found out someone you loved had died, and then realized you were the one who would have to pass along the news to others.

Kai returned and placed three items wrapped in hand towels on the table. Devon folded back one of the towels. A well-used chef's knife.

Kai shrugged. "Best I can do on short notice."

Devon imagined warm blood running down the blade, the handle sticky and slick beneath her white-knuckled grip. Strange how we kept deadly weapons close at hand every day, chopping onions without bothering to even consider to what other uses the steel might be put.

"What are we supposed to do with these?" asked Geoff, hefting one.

"No idea," said Kai. "But the bar doesn't have shotguns or tasers on hand."

Geoff shook his head. "I'm more likely to hurt myself with that thing than anything else."

Luki looked like he was about to say something, then shut his mouth and stuffed the knife into his jacket pocket. Devon followed his lead. She'd taken enough self-defense classes to know that Geoff was probably right, but she'd rather have it and not need it than need it and not have it.

"Devon," said harp. "Put on your glasses."

"What?"

"Your glasses," said harp. "Now."

Devon did as she was told. For a moment, she thought they might have lost their magic, that she'd been imagining the special effects they conjured. She'd never worn them in company before, maybe they were shy, maybe they only tried to convince you of your own insanity when you were alone, and therefore more susceptible to their Siren's song. But then she noticed that the roots running through the mural were growing, reaching, twining together. Worms wriggled around buried stones. The shade sails strung above them began to stack one atop the other into an infinite tower and then fan out until the sky was a mosaic dome held together by luminous blue mortar.

And then the dome shattered and the soil stilled.

Normalcy reasserted itself, and something inside Devon wilted—a remnant of the little girl who'd stay up all night reading manga. Her mysterious portal to another world had closed.

Except there was something there that shouldn't be.

Something new.

A thick rainbow arrow ran across the gravel from Devon's feet through the tables to the exit. It was as wide as a yoga mat and myriad colors chased each other up its length. Not even the most talented Palimpsest graffiti artist could create that particular effect.

"Move," said harp.

Noticing Devon startle, Kai cocked their head to one side and squinted at the glasses. "What did you do?" Each word was enunciated with a carefully calibrated mixture of curiosity and suspicion.

"The security on your little side project isn't as good as you think it is," said harp. "Let's just say I didn't need Luki's help to break and enter."

"Am I missing something?" asked Geoff.

Despite the circumstances, Devon couldn't help but smile.

"I didn't say it had anything to do with me," said Kai.

"You didn't have to," said harp.

"Okay, I definitely have some questions for you later, too," said Kai.

"You want answers, I want a pair," said harp. "They're all the rage on the forums. Secret brands always are. Best way to get noticed by the right people is to pretend you don't exist."

"I'm extremely lost and about to be extremely dead," said Luki.

Devon stood and took a single steadying breath. One thing she'd learned from all the extraordinary people she'd interviewed for *Rabbit Hole* was that no plan survived contact with reality. Life was one grand improvisation. Everyone made it up as they went.

"Follow me," she said, and jogged up the rainbow.

Vince was waiting right where she'd left him.

Devon, Luki, and Geoff piled into the car.

"Where to?" asked Vince.

"Just drive," said Devon, careful not to let the knife jab through her jacket pocket as she scooted over to make room.

Vince gave her side-eye but turned on the car and pulled into the street. As Devon directed him, she noticed movement in the rearview mirror and was momentarily terrified that a heavily armed bounty hunter would be bearing down on them on a tricked-out Kawasaki.

But no, they were safe, at least for now.

It was just a Prime delivery van.

47

ISABELLA AND MARISOL had once buried a body together in the mountains around Oaxaca. It was backbreaking work. The stony soil refused to yield to their shovels and the sun was unrelenting. They hadn't brought anything to drink and it was the dry season, so there was no water to be found in the scrub. Their labor finally done, however shallow the grave, they hiked back through the backcountry to the edge of the outlying village, bitching about blisters and splinters.

The moon came up over the horizon just as the sun was setting, and a lone coyote stood profiled against the sky on the next ridge. They stopped and stared. The animal was perfectly still, its nose pointing into the breeze, one of its front paws lifted and folded under, the eerie combination of dusk and moonlight adorning its tawny coat.

There was a moment of absolute calm, as if the coyote was not flesh and blood but a spirit that had slipped into the world but was not of the world.

And then violence.

The coyote charged into a stand of dry grass and pounced, trotting out a few seconds later with a twitching rabbit in its bloody jaws. It loped off over the ridge and out of sight, and Isabella looked over at Marisol, rapt, as she had been, and realized that her friend embodied that very same canine poise whenever she caught wind of prey.

Sitting ramrod straight in the passenger seat, fingers interlaced on her lap, eyes glued to the car their targets were riding in, Marisol harbored something of the coyote in her now, and Isabella loved her for it. Polite society might try to pretend otherwise, but reality was feral—and shone forth with a fierce kind of beauty.

Traffic was still light on the Bay Bridge. Isabella made sure to keep at least two cars between them and the Lyft. They approached Treasure Island, the mouth of the tunnel gaping wide and dark. They plunged through, and Isabella thought of the hole the coyote had torn the rabbit from, a final dash for the earthen warren ending with teeth closing around its haunches. You could only hide for so long.

The tires hummed on the less-well-maintained section of the bridge that connected Treasure Island to San Francisco. A container ship passed far below. The diagonal struts connecting the legs of each suspension tower cut the sky into blue diamonds.

The Lyft moved over to the rightmost lane and Isabella followed after counting to ten so she didn't spook them. The skyscraper forest of downtown rose on the right, throwing long shadows onto the bridge interspersed with narrow bars of light that flickered over them like an arrhythmic strobe.

Their quarry took the Fremont Street exit. Isabella turned

after them, following the long curve of the ramp down into the city she and Marisol had grown accustomed to calling home. Strange how things like that could sneak up on you. Sometimes you only realized how much something mattered when you were about to lose it.

But Isabella knew one thing for sure: she and Marisol would not lose their prey. There were no holes left for these particular rabbits.

Isabella's phone buzzed and keeping one hand on the wheel, she used the other to slip it out of her pocket.

"What?" asked Marisol sharply, annoyed at being snapped out of her predatory trance.

"I'm not sure," said Isabella, passing her the phone. "Some kind of Reap3r update."

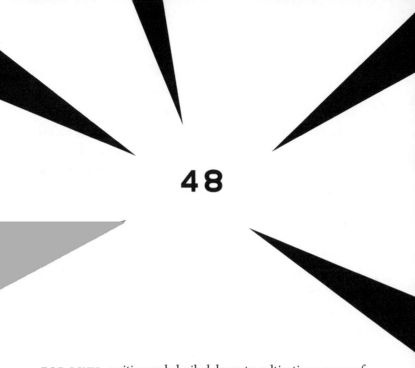

48

FOR LUKI, writing code boiled down to cultivating a sense of presence, of being fully immersed in a problem, of stepping outside of self and into the command line. It felt surprisingly similar to how people described runner's high or meditation, only in this case thought was displaced by melding mind to machine.

Unfortunately, he found that maintaining that sense of presence while coding was usually just as hard as maintaining runner's high while running or maintaining a clear mind while meditating. Transcending self wasn't a permanent achievement, but a process of constant renewal.

So when he was writing code, and thoughts inevitably got in the way, he tried to remind himself that distraction wasn't failure—distraction was an invitation to practice letting go and returning, once again, to that place of simple awareness, that sense of presence... the zone.

Right now, he needed no such reminders.

Running for your life was nothing if not clarifying.

Luki threw a glance over his shoulder as they hurried across the wide sidewalk. As Vince accelerated away into traffic, the Prime van that had been trailing them since Oakland pulled smoothly up to the curb and two women in the requisite uniforms emerged, packages in hand. They wore cloth masks, but half the people on the street covered their faces, habits established in the wake of Bakunawa and its predecessors. The pair looked so innocuous—deliveries were hardly unusual on farmer's market day at the San Francisco Ferry Building—but harpZkord had pinpointed the vehicle geotagged through Reap3r and these were not couriers, but hitwomen.

"Come on," hissed Devon, and plunged into the crowd milling about the farm stands. Luki followed and Geoff took up the rear. Strange how people could just drop in out of nowhere to change your life. Less than a week ago, he'd been shyly deflecting Devon's questions aboard *The Liminal*, and now here he was, placing his fate in her hands, trailing her past buskers and kombucha brewers and kale growers towards whatever mysterious escape a notorious hacker had managed to devise from thousands of miles away.

Years could pass in minutes, and minutes could take years.

"They're still behind us," said Geoff.

"Shit," said Devon.

She accelerated to a walk just slow enough not to attract undo attention, and Luki lengthened his stride to match hers. Tourists took pictures. A circle of high school students kicked around a Hacky Sack. Sea gulls circled overhead, beady eyes peeled for discarded scraps of prepared food.

Devon cut right and they pushed through glass doors and into the Ferry Building. This was one of those iconic Bay Area destinations that Luki had always meant to visit, but never had. The atrium ran the length of the building. A mezzanine balcony ran around the second floor of offices and the roof was one long, peaked skylight. The ground floor was a public market. Little shops offered locally sourced olive oil, fresh-cut flowers, genetically bespoke sourdough starter, steaming *bao*, oak logs inoculated with gourmet mushroom spores, and beautifully crafted ceramics. The space transported Luki back through time to *La Ribera* in Bilbao, the largest indoor market in Europe. His parents had supplied cider to one of the vendors, and Luki had always begged to come along when they delivered the barrels so that he could sneak off and marvel at the hanging Iberian hams, thick slices of cheese, smelly fishmongers, and hordes of people.

The Ferry Building was smaller, but just as crowded, and the three of them had to duck and weave to make headway through the throng. Luki felt hemmed in, but at least their pursuers would be just as inconvenienced.

The knife was heavy in his pocket. He imagined spinning around and thrusting wildly as the two women in their matching corporate uniforms closed in for the kill, one of them feinting and the other batting away his blade and pressing a gun into his forehead, the steel cold on his skin. Would he be able to meet his fate with clear eyes, or would he break down and beg for mercy that these veteran assassins would view not with pity, but vicarious embarrassment and mild distaste?

It had been one thing to dream of becoming an agent of change. It was another to face the all-too-real consequences of stepping into the arena. He risked a glance over his shoulder but couldn't spot the two women, which meant they could be anywhere. Every person he passed was suspect, might be the one to reach out and open his throat. Luki was in so deep he couldn't tell which way was up, and whatever time they had left was evaporating. They couldn't keep running forever. What was harpZkord doing? Didn't the hacker know how little of a head start they had, how screwed they were if they made a single misstep? Like the proverbial Dutch boy, Luki pressed his finger to the dike to stem the flood of panic.

Just put one foot in front of the other.

That was another thing he'd learned from coding: never underestimate momentum. If he took a few days off from writing a piece of software, it always took a few more days just to get his head back into the code. If he made progress every day, even if it was a single line, the program took on a life of its own.

They just needed to keep moving.

Movement was life.

The first gunshot rang out as they were passing Cowgirl Creamery.

49

A CATHEDRAL HUSH fell over the crowd, disbelief testing the limits of its suspension. *CZ 75*. Isabella had known a Czech in Mexico City who swore by the short-recoil-operated, locked-breech pistol. It was famous for its accuracy, but what he'd loved most about it was its reliability. In their line of work, equipment malfunctions often proved fatal.

She met Marisol's gaze. This shit was fucked. As they'd pulled off the bridge, Reap3r had pushed a target-change notification to them. Now, they were hunting someone else, a Swede in his forties who was already at the same location their original targets had been headed. That had been very strange, strange enough to pull back and regroup, but the fee had tripled—enough money to take risks for. So they'd parked the van and slipped into the crowded Ferry Building to find the new target. But whatever this was turning into wasn't worth it. Time to bail.

A scream shattered the brittle silence, and pandemonium

broke loose. As terrified civilians charged for the exits, Isabella and Marisol moved deliberately, falling in next to each other, edging toward the wall, and scanning for threats. The shot had come from the other side of the building, and—

Another shot rang out, then another, and another.

The CZ 75, and another weapon Isabella couldn't identify.

More screams.

They were getting close to one of the exits, but the crowd was jammed up around it, everyone pushing to get out.

"*Mira*," hissed Marisol.

And then Isabella saw him in the middle of the hallway, barely fifteen feet away.

Their new target.

The Swede.

Except that he wasn't trying to get through the door. He was facing them. And smiling. There was a hunger in his eyes that Isabella knew all too well.

Isabella was surprised to find her karambits already drawn.

The Swede raised a Colt .45 and fired into the air. A panel of skylight shattered, shards of glass raining down over the crowd. People tripped over one another trying to get away from him and, as he strode toward Isabella, she shouldered past a chef in an apron and hairnet and leapt forward.

She almost didn't make it. But he was still bringing his gun down from his stupid stunt and was expecting her to be running away, not sprinting toward him at full speed. He tried to track her with the barrel, but the half-second of indecision when Marisol came flying out of the crowd from another angle cost him his life. Isabella punched the gun up and away and sparks flew where the steel finger ring of her karambit hit the revolver's cylinder. And then kidneys, liver, heart. The blade skittered against a rib as she drew it back out, sending vibrations all the way up her arm.

As the Swede toppled, Isabella's phone buzzed in her pocket. Letting one karambit dangle by its finger ring, she checked it, then looked up at Marisol, "It worked." The coins had already hit their account. Then the phone buzzed again, and Isabella's rush of adrenaline redoubled.

"It just assigned us another target with a 10x bonus," she said uncertainly, squinting down at the profile picture. "It's that asshole, Daryl, and…" She double-checked, but no, she wasn't mistaken. "He's here too."

"What the fuck?" asked Marisol.

"I know—"

The large ceramic vase beside them shattered and they both dropped to the ground. The crowd was beginning to ebb, more people managing to squeeze through the exits. Another shot painted a web of fissures across the floor next to her left hip. More gunfire crackled down at the other end of the building.

Marisol reached over and touched Isabella's cheek.

"Vamos," she said, and smiled her thousand-year-old smile.

And suddenly they were their old selves again, not veteran professionals trying to stay relevant, but fierce, desperate girls who dreamed with wild abandon and learned to eviscerate anyone who stood in their way as they carved a path out of hell and into new and better worlds. Crawling behind retail displays to stay out of the shooter's line of sight, they worked their way up the hall toward him. It was Daryl. This time, Isabella let him catch a glimpse of her while Marisol ripped out his throat from behind.

Buzz.

Payment received.

Buzz.

New target.

The Ferry Building had been transformed into a war zone, there were knife fights and firefights and even fistfights breaking out all over, and Isabella and Marisol moved through it like wraiths, karambits biting flesh and moving on.

Buzz.

Payment received.

Buzz.

New target.

Lobsters scrabbled across the bloody floor, pincers secured with rubber bands, tanks shattered by stray bullets. An enormous wheel of parmesan wobbled as it rolled down the length of the hall.

Buzz.

Payment received.

Buzz.

New target.

Alarms blared. It smelled of shit and cordite. Every target was armed and eager.

Buzz.

Payment received.

Buzz.

New target.

Cryptocurrency sloshed back and forth across the dark web as predator hunted predator through a shattered bourgeois dream.

Buzz.

Payment received.

Buzz.

New target.

Isabella and Marisol weren't partners. They weren't even

friends, really. They were two halves of the same beautiful, lethal whole. A single self endowed with two bodies.

Buzz.

Payment received.

Buzz.

New target.

And then, as abruptly as it had begun, it was over.

Isabella and Marisol yanked their blades from the chest of a redhead, double-denimed bruiser and his corpse slumped to the floor.

Buzz.

Payment received.

Buzz.

New target—except this time he was all the way up in Marin, not right here inside the building.

Unnatural, unnerving silence.

Marisol opened her mouth to say something and then her head snapped back as a final shot echoed through the ruined Ferry Building and the man who had been dying but not quite dead dropped his arm for the last time and the CZ 75 clattered across polished concrete.

Buzz.

His phone, this time.

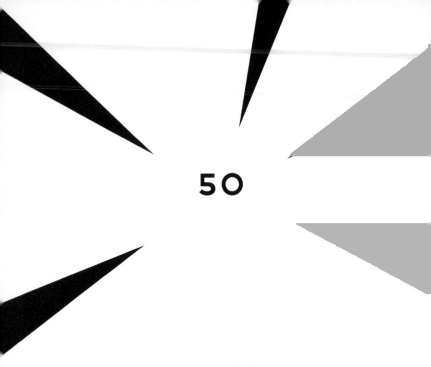

50

ORDERING THE HIT was just the beginning.

Sansome hadn't left his office since issuing the Reap3r contract. There were endless contingencies to put in place. Q would be losing a CEO in the midst of an exquisitely sensitive federal contract extension. Key-man insurance clauses would be invoked. Paul would ask very pointed questions and Q's all-seeing eye would be brought to bear. Sansome would have to show Paul the expediency with which he had addressed the problem and prove that Human Capital was too useful to destroy.

Of course, Sansome could always threaten to reveal that Paul had bankrolled Bakunawa and Q, but that would ruin them both, and Sansome did not want to attempt to blackmail a man in Paul's position. Instead, he'd need to blaze a trail that Paul would want to walk so that they both might emerge safely on the other side of this dark forest.

And then there was Geoff. Sansome's lawyers would need to

wrangle his estate to ensure that the rights to his patents reverted to Human Capital, or at the very least, that his agreement to license them to Molly survived his demise. They'd also need to aggregate the ongoing vaccine royalty streams. All of that would doubtless require fraught negotiations with UC Berkeley, Pfizer, and whoever else decided to enter the fray.

Devon would be easier. Sansome was sad to see *Rabbit Hole* come to such an abrupt end, but at least the only loose thread he'd have to tie up would be sending appropriate condolences to her family. It would break Sansome's heart, but not his world.

The really delicate part would be controlling the overall narrative. Human Capital had veteran PR crisis-management experts on retainer, and they'd need to spin the story in a way that demonstrated the depth of the firm's horror at the tragedy without calling undo attention to it or undermining confidence in the future of the fund. Sansome couldn't afford to have this disaster sabotage the brand he'd been building for so many years, the promise at the heart of his TED Talk. He owed that to every other innovator in his portfolio. He owed that to the future. He—

His phone buzzed.

Esteban.

Sansome picked up, pulse quickening. "Is it done?"

Esteban was clandestinely observing the operation from a safe distance. He was the eyes on the ground Sansome needed to confirm the success of the toughest decision he'd ever had to make.

"What is the system showing you?" asked Esteban. The iron in his tone was enough to raise Sansome's hackles, but even more concerning were the noises in the background: sirens, screams, tires screeching on asphalt, the popcorn crackle of—gunshots?

"What the fuck is going on?" asked Sansome.

"No time," snapped Esteban. "Tell me what you see."

Cold sweat breaking out all over, Sansome signed on to Reap3r. The dashboard was… wrong. The names and numbers and metadata didn't track. He moved the cursor to investigate, but even as he did so, all the buttons greyed out. Then, impossibly, the data began to change right in front of his eyes, outputs cycling faster and faster until it was too fast to read. Then the screen froze, and the entire window vanished as if it had never existed. He summoned it again and tried to log in, but the system rejected his credentials.

Esteban was saying something.

"What?" asked Sansome.

"Breathe," said Esteban. "You're hyperventilating. Whatever's going on, you passing out isn't going to help."

Sansome forced a deep breath. He was locked in a cell that was filling up with water. He was standing naked on a stage in front of everyone he'd ever met.

"It's gone," he said. "I'm locked out."

The ensuing moment of silence spoke volumes.

Finally, Esteban broke it. "Do I intervene?"

They both knew what that meant. They used Reap3r because it was secure and effective. In a very risky business, it minimized their risk exposure. Esteban was always a fly on the wall, never the guy holding the gun. The minute he stepped in to take direct action, they lost their plausible deniability and all of Human Capital would be on the line. On the other hand, inaction was equally untenable. Every second that Luki, Geoff, and Devon were still breathing was another second they could use to expose Human Capital's interlocking secrets, bringing down the very people Sansome had made it his life's work to empower.

His stomach churned. He was staring into the glare of the stage lights, stuck in the unbearably indeterminate moment between his closing line and the applause or silence it would provoke.

He swallowed, trying to moisten his bone-dry mouth.

"Bring them in," he said, the words falling like dice. "Bring them in."

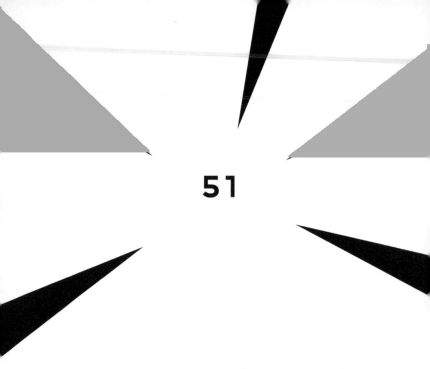

51

DEVON PUSHED THROUGH the panicked crowd, never taking her eyes off of the psychedelic rainbow underfoot. She led Luki by the hand, just as he led Geoff. If they got separated, even for a moment, they'd never find each other again in the midst of this chaos. Sirens wailed. Drones buzzed. Everyone was shouting or weeping or cursing phones that couldn't find a connection through network overwhelm.

"What is *happening*?" she asked, knowing the question was futile.

"Do you think it's *them*?" asked Luki. "Whoever's chasing us? I mean it has to be, right?"

Devon opened her mouth to respond, but words materialized a few feet in front of her, hanging there as if inscribed into the air itself:

I haven't been able to destroy Reap3r, but I inserted a script that reassigns every contractor to target every other contractor, and then reassigns the survivors to target bidders, so either I'll be able to tear down the code, or the whole thing will eat itself alive in meatspace.

The words disintegrated into the breeze.

"Wait," said Devon. "You can *hear* me?"

"Of course I can hear you," said Luki, panting. "I'm right behind you." He squeezed her hand. "You okay?"

The specs have a built-in mic. They really are a clever piece of work.

Gunshots went off back in the Ferry Building.

"What's happening back there?" asked Devon.

"That's what I'm wondering," said Luki. "It must be the people from the van. They were *shooting* at us. They *were* shooting at *us*, right?"

"Sorry," said Devon. "Talking to harpZkord."

Security cam footage is showing a full-on Tarantino bloodbath. I'd patch it through, but TBH you don't need to see anything this dark ATM.

"harpZkord?" asked Luki.

"The glasses," said Devon. "Apparently, they've got a mic."

Can you make sure Kai hooks me up with a pair?

"She can hear us and send me texts on the display," Devon continued. What kind of scene would someone like harp decide was too heavy to share?

"What do you mean, she?" asked Luki.

Good question, Quantum Boy. What the fuck, Devon?

"He. Sorry," said Devon, cutting right to leave the crowded sidewalk and follow the rainbow through a covered archway. They passed a waterfront restaurant in which diners were peering out to see what all the commotion was about. "It's confusing talking and reading at the same time. Gimme a minute, Luki. harp, what about all the bystanders?"

These folks are pros. There are a few injuries, but no unintended deaths so far.

No unintended deaths. Devon's blood ran cold. harp had always played the puppet master, using the internet to orchestrate heists from the safety of her apartment. But there was such a difference between conducting something from afar and actually being on the ground. Only someone removed from whatever horrors lay behind them would describe it as a "full-on Tarantino bloodbath." Devon imagined drone pilots sitting in air-conditioned cubicles dropping smart bombs, flame wars raging across social media, someone putting a price on their heads as easily as ordering a new gadget to be delivered by a van just like the one their pursuers had been driving. The internet warped spacetime to bend reality to users' wills, but in doing so it severed the connection between action and the direct subjective experience of its implications. *Rabbit Hole* was Devon's way of reversing that process, of telling stories that stitched the world back together again. That was why she had been so keen to profile harp in the first place: to bridge the emotional gap that separated her from her notorious crimes, to render intimate someone who was always fully remote. And yet here Devon was, being violently rescued by a one-time subject while trying to keep sources alive as they fled the wrath of an unknown adversary.

It was too much to make sense of, to make meaning from. Too much.

BTW I've got a sick ride lined up for you.

They stumbled out onto a narrow dock.

And there, bobbing at the end of the rainbow, was a rowboat.

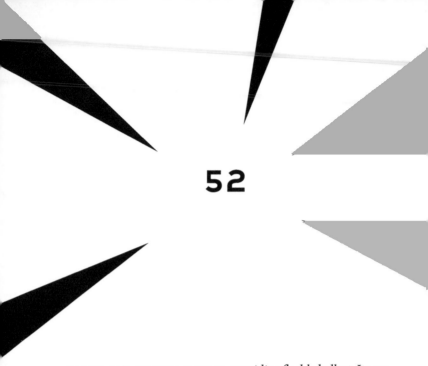

52

GEOFF SAT IN THE STERN, providing fleshly ballast. It was designed for a single rower so all three of them piling in was a stretch, but with Devon perched on the bow, Geoff astride the stern, and Luki rolling back and forth on the rower's seat as he pulled out into the Bay, they managed to stay above water, just.

Geoff didn't know much about boats, but someone clearly loved this one. Hand-built and carefully maintained, the almond-shaped wooden craft was a beautiful, idiosyncratic object. It even had a name, *Cecco*, which was engraved into the wood and inlaid with gold leaf.

Thankfully, Luki knew more about boats than Geoff or Devon. Explaining that every Basque had an uncle who was a fisherman, he had inserted the hanging oarlocks and mounted the baby blue oars. Devon had hopped right into the boat, but Luki had insisted Geoff put on the lifejacket with "Dolphin Club" stenciled across the back, instructed him to step only on the floor and not the ribs that ran up the side, and helped him aboard. Given how wobbly and precarious it had been, Geoff had needed the help. Then Luki had drawn his chef's knife and slashed the slender black ropes tying them to the dock. The three of them were, once again, afloat on the Pacific, or, at least, the Bay.

"Come around left—I mean port," said Devon as they emerged from the finger of water between the piers. "harp says we're at max ebb on a spring tide—whatever the hell that's supposed to mean—so we're supposed to head west."

"It means"—said Luki between ragged breaths—"that the Bay will flush us right out the Golden Gate. And that there's no point fighting that kind of current in this kind of boat."

"Aye, aye, captain," said Devon with the forced good humor of someone trying to stave off shock by buoying a friend's spirits. Sunlight glinted off the mirrored turquoise lenses of her glasses, twin portholes through which she could gaze into the digital and a distant hacker directed them like actors on a stage.

Geoff had never much liked plays.

The only theater he enjoyed was that of the mind, which was why he loved reading. Novels were printed, bound invitations to asynchronously participate in collective dreams that depended more on what the reader brought to the story than the words on the page. A reader didn't sit in the audience, a reader conjured a nascent world from no more than a sequence of printed shapes.

"We'll paddle up to Fort Mason and harp will arrange for Vince to meet us there," said Devon. "That'll be well outside of the cordon the police are setting up around the Ferry Building. Kai's friend is working on fake papers. We'll find someplace safe to hole up until we can get the story out."

"That's not the end for us," said Luki, pulling the oars with enough strength that the little boat surged forward. "That's the beginning." His face was flushed and sweaty, his gaze fixed. "You're the only one who might be able to go back to your old life after the story breaks."

"I know," said Devon, all authority draining from her voice. "I know."

There, right across the water, sat Alcatraz. In college, Geoff had read an account of a one-time prisoner and, while he had forgotten most of it, one detail stuck with him. Inmates had each been given a single five-by-seven-inch shaving mirror. There had been no other mirrors in the facility. And the thing about a mirror that small was that you could only really see your face in it, you couldn't see that your face was a part of your head, a part of your body. It warped your sense of self. After years of imprisonment, you became your face—*only* your face—and your face became a mask.

Geoff leaned back and laughed—a big, loose laugh that echoed out across the water.

"I'm sorry," he managed. "I don't know why. I just can't stop."

Another gale of laugher rolled through him. He couldn't help himself. A seal poked its head out of the water and barked in answer.

"It's just all so… *implausible*," he said.

Luki snorted.

Devon guffawed.

And then the three of them broke down laughing, laughing at the curious seals, laughing at the water sloshing over the side of the rowboat, laughing at nothing whatsoever and everything at once.

Here Geoff was, floating toward the Golden Gate in the company of a boy who knit qubits into meaning and a girl who danced with the zeitgeist, on the run from—probably—a crooked official in an escalating game of techno-political poker. They were living a dream that would make for a very strange novel, not as overtly weird as Discworld, but perhaps madcap enough for Pratchett to have appreciated.

Slowly, Geoff began to catch his breath.

Seeing The Rock up close, feeling the *Cecco* roll beneath him as his companions struggled to regain control of themselves, Geoff felt like he was a newly-released inmate gazing into a full-length mirror for the first time in decades.

Luki leaned into a stroke.

Up on the prow, Devon hiccupped and asked, "What's that?"

She pointed.

They looked.

A speedboat emerged from between two piers and surged toward them on a churning bow wave.

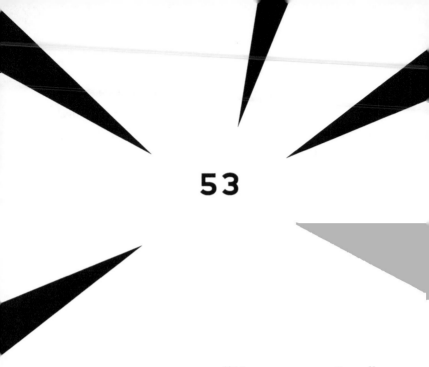

53

SUNLIGHT GLITTERED off blue-green water. Seagulls wheeled overhead. Seals popped up to stare at what was perhaps the lowest-speed escape ever attempted.

Sweat poured off Luki as he put every ounce of his energy into each stroke, but Devon could see it was hopeless. The speedboat roared toward them, frothy wake fanning out behind it. The laughter that had buoyed them only a minute ago now seemed as inaccessible as the possibility of freedom to an Alcatraz inmate. Fate offered no respite.

"harp?"

They're not Reap3r. That's all I know right now.

Behind the oncoming speedboat, San Francisco's aged piers clashed with the steel and glass towers of downtown rising behind them. From the street, the piers' renovated facades felt of a piece with the modern city. From the water, they were worn and decrepit. It was like stepping into the industrial fire stairwell of a luxury hotel.

Worlds patched together with the seams still showing.

Devon realized that she was fingering the smooth handle of the chef's knife. Suddenly self-conscious, she carefully pulled her hand from her pocket. Who did she think she was, a pirate preparing for battle on the high seas?

The speedboat pulled up beside them and Luki dropped the oars and slumped forward, limbs trembling. He couldn't out-row a pair of 250 horsepower engines, but he couldn't not try. In a removed part of her mind, Devon noted that this would be a detail to remember, that it mirrored the qualities that had gotten Luki into this situation in the first place.

"Good afternoon Ms. Chaiket, Mr. Zubiri, and Mr. Rossi."

"Esteban!" said Devon, relief flooding through her. Devon recognized him from *The Liminal*. Sansome's personal assistant was a quietly competent man with a knack for showing up exactly where and when his master needed him, like, apparently, here and now.

The rowboat rocked on the speedboat's wake and water spilled in over the sides. Esteban clucked disapprovingly. "It seems we're rescuing you just in time," he said. "Luckily, this craft is rated for more than one passenger." He extended a small metal ladder attached to the side of the speedboat. "If you'll care to join me?"

So this is was what it was like to have a billionaire in your corner. Zipping around the world in private jets, sipping cocktails with cultural prime movers, getting rescued just as things got desperate. Devon had to admit she could get used to it. Shame this story would cost her Human Capital's support—it had been fun while it lasted.

54

"WE WERE PICKING up supplies from the Ferry Building to restock the ranch's pantry," said Esteban as the speedboat pulled around. "I spotted you in the crowd, but you had cast off before we could catch up."

Geoff looked back at the abandoned *Cecco* bobbing in their wake. "What about the rowboat?" he asked.

"We'll have someone pick it up," said Esteban, gesturing to one of his two besuited companions who immediately pulled out a phone and began to make a call. "For now, my only priority is to get you three to safety. We can figure out the rest from there."

The engines growled and they shot north across the mouth of the bay, Alcatraz to the east, the Golden Gate Bridge framing the vast expanse of the Pacific to the west. Spray in his face and wind in his hair, Geoff felt a fresh sense of freedom. This must be how Alice had felt when the SEALs helivaced her out of the quarantine site after it fell under attack from a militia desperate for supplies. Geoff had been there when the chopper landed and she stumbled out through the downwash of the rotor blades, precious samples clutched in her shaking arms. He tried to forget how much he missed her and Frank and the others, but memory had a vicious habit of slipping through your guard when you least expected. A three year old headline materialized in his mind's eye: *Biochemist who contributed to Bakunawa cure killed in La Jolla helicopter accident.* You fall out of touch with a friend always assuming you'll reconnect soon, and then death intervenes.

"What happened back there?" asked Luki.

Esteban shrugged. "We don't know for sure yet," he said. "From what our police contacts have shared, some kind of mass shooting. I'm just relieved you made it out alive."

Now that Geoff had admitted his sins to Devon, betraying Sansome, he knew it was only a matter of time until the bitterness he felt toward his one-time benefactor would be reciprocated many times over. But in the meantime, it sure was nice to enjoy the benefits of fortunes riding on you. This brief respite was the calm before the storm.

Esteban's man was issuing orders into his phone, presumably to send someone out to collect the *Cecco*, when his blazer flapped back in a gust of wind. Geoff frowned. Before the man had managed to button it one-handed, Geoff could have sworn he had glimpsed a shoulder holster.

"What did you say you were doing at the Ferry Building?" Geoff asked Esteban.

"We were running low on soft cheeses and lion's mane mushrooms," said Esteban. "You know how Sansome is."

Geoff glanced sidelong at Devon and Luki. *You can worry about attribution later*, Kai had said at Palimpsest. *Right now, we need to figure out how you're going to avoid getting your asses capped by an on-demand assassin.* Well, they had just barely managed to escape the on-demand assassins, and now it was past time to worry about attribution. The Sansome Geoff knew did love gourmet food but didn't believe in coincidences.

"What were *you* doing at the Ferry Building?" asked Esteban as if the question had just occurred to him. "Couldn't get enough of each other aboard *The Liminal*? I'm delighted to see you hit it off. That's what the annual cruise is all about, after all."

Devon cocked her head to the side, sun glinting off her shades. "Hold on, you needed three people to pick up groceries?" she asked, looking back and forth between Esteban and his companions.

So Geoff wasn't the only one riding this particular train of thought into the familiar hinterlands of paranoia. He glanced at Luki with a sense of burgeoning horror and saw the sweat-soaked younger man stiffen.

This wasn't a rescue.

It was a kidnapping.

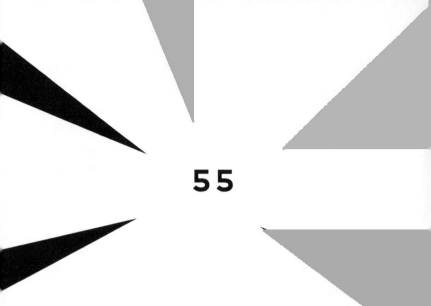

55

AS THE SPEEDBOAT PLANED over groundswell, Luki saw his realization reflected in Devon's dark brown eyes: If their story broke, it would be the end of Human Capital. But if the three of them disappeared quietly, Sansome's problems would be solved.

Implications fell like dominos.

Luki remembered the pop of the champagne cork shooting off into the Washington night, the fear that had kindled in his gut when Paul's face had closed up like a bank vault. Since deciding to blow the whistle on Q, Luki had been so terrified of his client that he hadn't thought to be terrified of his investor—a man he'd broken bread with countless times, a man who'd believed in him when no one else would.

Human Capital's portfolio was the envy of technology investors, but it contained the seeds of its own destruction, and Sansome would to anything to keep those seeds from sprouting. Anything. He would be as relentless in his pursuit as he had been as their champion. And this being a private sector hit explained why they were being hunted by Reap3r freelancers instead of one of Paul's black ops teams. Esteban was just backup. Luki's back cramped from his desperate rowing. Sansome had won. He *always* won. That was what he did. That's what had made him who he was. The three of them had fled straight into the open arms of the man who'd put the price on their heads in the first place. They were prisoners of their respective ambitions, which he had subsumed into his.

The awkward silence stretched as the speedboat approached a private dock in Sausalito. Esteban was unruffled, sitting there all smug and aloof with his fingers laced together in his lap. He knew they knew, and he knew they couldn't do anything about it. As for Geoff, Devon, and Luki, however palpable the tension was, they couldn't very well talk about it in front of their abductor. So they all just sat there as the engines roared and the gulls screamed, worst case scenarios metastasizing in their imaginations.

How many of the damned had stood quietly in front of the firing squad, or blown a kiss like Mata Hari? How many had harbored hope of divine intervention, that if they cooperated, a deus ex machina might arrive? How many had walked willingly to their deaths, the perception of inevitability confirming itself? Here, now, on this stupid fucking boat, they existed in a warped kind of quantum superposition—potential futures cast across each other in an interference pattern that only action could resolve. Crossroads demanded choice like lungs did air. To live was to breathe. To live was to choose, even if you chose badly.

Pretending to hunch against the wind, Luki stuffed his hands into his jacket pockets. *That hack was sneaky as fuck.* harp had spent his life evading and subverting authorities hellbent on locking him up—David waging a guerilla war against Goliath. The chef's knife handle was slick in Luki's sweaty palm, chafing against rapidly swelling oar-born blisters. His people didn't give up because the odds were against them. They fought, even if the battle was unwinnable. They fought, knowing that the fight would go on, that time took the side of the dogged.

The speedboat pulled smoothly up to the dock and one of Esteban's men leapt up and began to tie off a line. A van waited on the shore, back doors open, engine running. Fog fingered through the green hills rising up behind Sausalito and when Luki squinted, he could half imagine that he had slipped between worlds and back to his homeland.

Esteban stepped up onto the dock, motioned for them to follow, and smiled a hard little smile that said *let's all keep pretending this is groovy so I don't need to get nasty.*

Luki squeezed Devon's hand and met Geoff's eye. Sansome had dubbed his yacht *The Liminal* because there was power in moments of transition. This was just such a moment. A threshold beyond which everything was obscure. Once they were hustled into the van, it would be too late. *Never get in a stranger's car*— isn't that what parents told their children? And Esteban was far worse than a stranger. He was Sansome's right-hand man. That van would shuttle them to the gallows.

But they weren't in the van yet.

Luki rose to his feet, made to disembark, and pretended to stumble as the boat rocked gently on its wake, reaching out a hand toward the suited flunky standing above him.

Instinctively, the man caught his hand and hauled Luki up onto the dock, but Luki tightened his grip and yanked himself close, burying the chef's knife into the man's belly. He heard a shout and a splash and out of the corner of his eye saw that

Geoff and Devon had charged the guy still in the boat, pushing him over the side.

Yes. This was their chance. They could *do* this.

And that was when Luki noticed that his knife had pierced the man's jacket but not his abdomen, that the body armor beneath his tailored shirt had deflected the blade. Fuck. Luki was as pitiful an amateur at violence as he was at espionage. And that was his final coherent thought before he was slammed down onto the dock, and they hit him in the chest with a taser. Electricity arced through his body, seizing every muscle, lighting every nerve on fire, and shattering his consciousness into a million jagged shards.

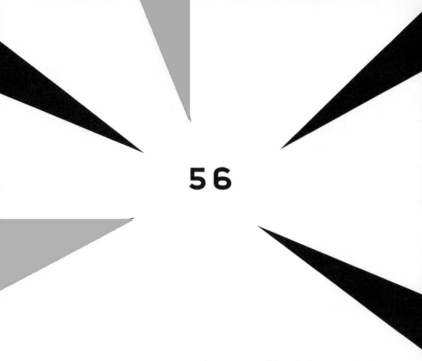

56

ZIP-TIES CUT into Devon's wrists and her kidneys ached from the viscous kick Esteban had landed while one of his goons pulled the other out of the water. There had been a single golden moment when it seemed possible they might escape. But then the armed, armored professionals had taken over and now she was bumping along in the back of the van. In the end, they had achieved nothing but to enrage their captors. Beside her, Geoff's eye was swelling shut and Luki moaned whenever they went over a bump.

This was bad. Very, very bad.

I'm trying to get into their systems, but they run a tight ship when it comes to security. Any chance quantum boy can slip me another cheat code? That would speed things up a whole lot.

They'd taken Devon's knife, but not the seemingly innocuous glasses. Drool dribbled from the corner of Luki's mouth. Poor kid. He'd jumped in the deep end and then asked her to teach him to swim. Now here they all were, drowning.

"Not a chance," said Devon.

Want me to SWAT Sansome?

"If you call in the authorities, you'll be dropping us straight into Paul's hands," said Devon. This really was quite a fucking mess. A maze with no exit.

Okay, hang in there. I'm working as fast as I can.

Devon should have known. The journalist's first and most instructive question was: who profits? She should have known, but she hadn't wanted to admit it, least of all to herself.

Sansome had swooped in to give her the golden ticket she'd been lusting after for so long. Sometimes *Rabbit Hole* felt like nothing more than an extended audition. She had wanted to be picked, and he had picked her. It wasn't just the money, which she needed, it was the validation, the reassurance that her work mattered, that the world cared. Seeing Sansome for what he was undermined the warm fuzzy feeling of *deserving* the grant, the implicit sense of entitlement, which is why Devon hadn't noticed the clues piling up until it was too late. But the work that really mattered, the unbridled and idiosyncratic curiosity that fueled *Rabbit Hole*, didn't require reassurance. Its only requirements were care, presence, generosity, and more than anything, chasing the story wherever it led, whomever it implicated, whatever the cost.

Not that any of that mattered anymore.

The van pulled to a halt, and Geoff, unable to keep his balance with his hands bound behind his back, tottered over onto the floor.

The back doors opened and they squinted against the sudden light. Flanked by his security team, Esteban looked down at them. He reached in and slapped Luki back and forth across the face to revive him.

"Hey!" objected Devon, but the goon in the sodden suit raised his taser and she relented. This wasn't the kind of situation you could argue your way out of anyway.

Luki grunted and writhed, and Esteban pulled back.

"We're here," he said. "Out."

More than anything, Devon wanted to hate this little man with his pet thugs and prim superiority. People like Sansome were nothing without the dozens, hundreds, thousands of enablers like Esteban that did their bidding, became extensions of their will in return for money or perhaps just the comfort of letting someone else make the difficult choices. There was no such thing as a lone tyrant. A tyrant's power depended, like all power, on the systems through which it ran. Lightning might kill you and static might raise the hair on your arms, but electricity wouldn't have changed the world without the grid.

Anyway, who was Devon to judge Esteban? She'd taken Sansome's money and relished his patronage. Oh sure, she'd put on a little show when they were in the back room of The Interval. She'd declined Sansome's grant lest he try to influence her editorial decisions to benefit his investments. But all it had taken for him to win her over was a verbal guarantee of creative control. She'd been so eager—desperate, really—to secure the funding the story required that she hadn't bothered—hadn't *wanted*—to ask questions that might put it at risk.

Even if that was unfair, even if she shouldn't blame herself for accepting a grant from a megalomaniacal robber baron willing to kill to protect his horde, Devon had gotten into this mess because she'd put herself at the mercy of a system that indentured her—and as they broke, systems revealed themselves. She'd invested everything in *Rabbit Hole* and then given it away for free. That might be generous, but it also undermined her ability to do her best work. It meant she had to constantly beg sponsors and foundations for financial support. And they weren't just handing out cash for shits and giggles, they were buying her listeners' attention. She'd imagined herself to be offering her listeners a gift, but in fact she was turning them into a product. Maybe the problem wasn't selling herself short instead of long, but selling herself to the wrong people for the wrong reasons.

They stumbled out of the van, the security dickwads stepping back to cover them with the tasers. They were in the driveway where Vince had picked her up just this morning. A strange bird called out in distance, some trophy Sansome had carted in from a distant jungle, a pet just like Devon, Luki, and Geoff. Or perhaps Sansome would feed them to whatever exotic carnivores haunted these woods.

Esteban and his men frog-marched them into the house, through a network of hallways and a locked door, and finally down a narrow set of stairs into a basement. Crates were stacked against the walls, but the center of the space was clear. The men shoved them down onto the concrete floor and turned to go.

"You don't have to do this," said Devon. She thought of the King smiling down from the restaurant wall, the sharp scent of lemongrass, the way her father could only speak her name as an exclamation. "We can work it out somehow. We can find a way."

The flat, mild look Esteban gave her was the scariest thing

she'd ever seen. It said that this situation was anything but special, nothing personal, just a cost of doing business. This wasn't murder, this was simply risk mitigation. That placid expression said everything that needed to be said by saying nothing at all.

Luki screamed what Devon could only assume were Basque epithets, his voice cracking.

The men ascended the stairs.

The lights went out.

The door closed.

The lock clicked.

Devon lowered her head. So this was where this story, her story, ended. Broken in the attempt to break the scoop of a lifetime. A scared little girl locked in a billionaire's basement.

What had been scrawled on Palimpsest's wall the afternoon she had gone to Kai for advice? *They were so desperate to document their lives that they forgot to live them.* That was it right there. That was Devon. She was always chasing a story, always looking for an angle, always living from a certain remove. She'd stood on a tropical island and thought of capturing the sound of wind shushing through cactus spines. When harp had warned them of the price on their heads, Devon had considered how she'd describe her burgeoning panic to listeners. Just now, as their ridiculous escape on the *Cecco* came to an all-too-abrupt halt, she'd noted a moment revealing of Luki's personality that she could weave into the grand narrative in which he played a part. For too long, Devon had lived life as an observer.

She rolled onto her side and managed to make her way up to a cross-legged seat.

It was time she became a participant.

Devon remembered the calm pragmatism with which Kai had presented the blades, the pointed yet gentle humor that girded their worldview. When Devon had solicited their guidance, Kai had inscribed their own aphorism in neon green spray paint: *The struggle is real. The struggle is the work. The struggle is everything.*

"harp, I need you to do something for me," whispered Devon.

Your wish is my command, mistress.

"Publish the live audio feed from my glasses to *Rabbit Hole*."

Srsly?

Internet wisdom held that you didn't have to be a superstar to succeed as a creator, that if you found your minimum viable audience, you might just be able to make a living doing what you loved, that behind the blockbuster mega-hits, there was a "long tail" of niche projects that attracted small but devoted groups of fans. This was Devon's last, desperate act of crowdsurfing. She could only hope that the long tail had a spike on the end.

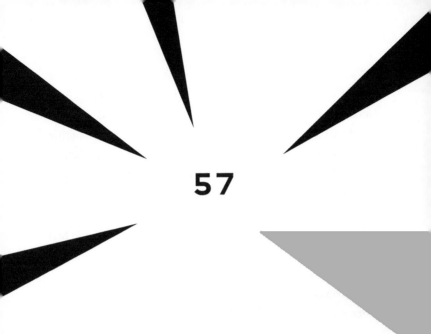

57

THE STORM HAD ARRIVED the morning of Luki's ninth birthday. Black thunderheads rolled in from the sea and piled up against the mountains, blotting out the morning sun. Wind shook the windows and howled through the trees. The air was thick with static. Dad's phone buzzed with an emergency weather advisory. When the rain came, it didn't form drops so much as sheets of water that threatened to drown Basque Country once and for all. His parents pretended to be cheerful, but Luki knew they were worried about the apple trees.

Right as Luki was about to blow out the candles, someone pounded on the front door. Dad looked at Mom, but she shook her head. None of Luki's friends were coming. Not in this weather. Frowning, Dad went to the door, and Luki sensed but did not understand the electric anxiety that was gathering around his father. But it was just a wet, bedraggled pilgrim who had gotten caught in the storm coming over the pass.

Her name was Aisling. Her clothes were soaked through, her bright red hair was plastered all over her face, and she spoke a foreign tongue, English, that Luki didn't understand.

Luki hadn't wanted to share his cake with her, but his mother had given him *the look* and he'd cut the stranger a slice to go with her coffee. His parents had helped her hang some of her gear to dry in front of the wood stove and Aisling had laughed and sang strange songs and by the time the storm finally broke and she was gathering up her things and lacing her boots, Luki had fallen in love with her.

As he was bidding her farewell, and Aisling was offering profuse thanks, Luki's father said something to her in English, and then repeated it in Basque. *Gure istorioa kontatu.* Tell our story.

It was something you said to pilgrims. A seed, planted.

And here in the pitch darkness of the basement, fear curdling in their guts, waiting for whatever summary execution awaited them, Luki, Devon, and Geoff were planting such a seed.

They sat cross-legged on the cold concrete floor, knees touching, hands bound behind their backs, voices low and urgent—the subterranean black rendering sound that much more intimate, that much thicker with emotion and subtext.

They were their voices.

Luki told his story haltingly, almost begrudgingly. He was a private person from a private people, a nation who knew the value of secrets, who respected their power. Devon didn't rush him, though there was every reason to hurry. She was quiet, gentle, held space for him to open into. The darkness helped. He could pretend that he was talking to himself, that there weren't thousands of people listening to his every stutter, that this wasn't their only chance to get the story out, that harpZkord hadn't hacked three-dozen leading investigative journalists and casually deposited Luki's stolen files in their inboxes. No. Luki was just floating through an alternate dimension where he happened to be reliving the harrowing drive along the dark roads of suburban Maryland in the passenger seat of Paul's car, the progress bar edging toward completion on his laptop, and the sense of wonder that had gotten him into science in the first place, before he realized the extent to which his ideals had been suborned. A dream. That was it. Nothing more. Don't stop. Keep talking. Though he had to admit that dreams didn't usually render how sore your ass could get sitting on bare concrete with this much accuracy.

When his turn came, Geoff was better. Much better. So much better that Luki was relieved he himself had gone first. Nobel Laureates were used to being interviewed, and Luki knew that Geoff had spent as much time advocating for science policy reform as he had in a lab. So he was used to talking to an audience. But there was something more than that too. Most people rambled when they spoke, reaching for and handling ideas as they uttered them. Where others spoke in sentences or maybe paragraphs, Geoff spoke in novels. His words were unerringly precise, his voice established a rhythm, and he introduced and reincorporated concepts like a juggler did balls. Even so, Luki could tell that Geoff needed the darkness as much as he did, that more than anything, the man was seeking refuge from himself.

Devon played on another level entirely. Luki hadn't noticed it at first. He thought she was just asking questions. And then he realized that every question was a threshold onto the next leg of a larger journey, that with the subtlest of interjections, the application of crucial moments of silence, she was constructing an invisible narrative architecture that elevated Luki and Geoff's stories, framed why they mattered, and illuminated the cascading implications. Devon was a master of her craft at the height of her power improvising with every tool at her disposal. Luki already knew what would happen next, was living it himself, yet he hung on every word.

Somewhere out there, people were listening. Maybe they were doing the dishes, or folding the laundry, or driving home from work, or walking the dog. What did they make of this tale that was too implausible to be fiction? What were they thinking when instead of sponsorship breaks, Devon regularly interrupted the broadcast to announce their precise location and plead for help? Whoever they were, whatever they thought, once they tuned in, Luki knew that they wouldn't be able to tear their attention away—disaster demanded you bear witness.

So when the lights snapped on, it didn't just blind the three of them, but shattered the vast, exquisite palace Devon was conjuring in their imaginations.

Squinting against the glare, Luki peered up at the door at the top of the stairs.

Sansome.

Thunder echoed faintly through the branching alleys of Luki's memory and he wondered where Aisling's path had taken her, what life had asked of her, who she had decided to become.

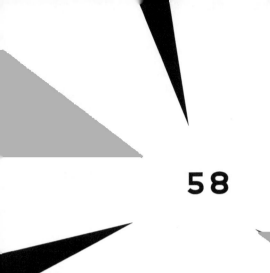

58

"I HAVE TO ADMIT"—said Sansome with a pained expression—"that you three have made quite a mess." He descended the steps slowly, peering at them like they were exotic additions to his zoological collection. "Frankly, I'm impressed. Or I would be if I wasn't so damn sad."

Devon knew she should be scared—this man had put a price on their heads and now they were entirely at his mercy—but she was so cognizant of the live audience, so absorbed in the work of braiding a story from disparate threads, that her doubts and fears, her very sense of self, faded into the background. She was still all too aware of what was at stake, it just didn't blind her to the fact that in a world brimming with things she couldn't control, she ought to focus on the things she could.

Sansome reached the bottom of the steps and stopped, clasping his hands behind his back. Without having made a conscious choice, Devon rose to her feet and faced him—her own hands bound behind her back, mirroring his, the raw terror pulsing off Luki and Geoff transmuting into something harder and brighter inside her.

Words flared across her glasses.

Seventy-seven thousand folks on the Rabbit Hole feed, which is trending across social. Live audience is doubling every one hundred and fifty three seconds. You famous.

"Especially you, Ms. Chaiket," said Sansome. "Mr. Zubiri and I go back a long time. Mr Rossi and I even longer. You, though." He shook his head. "Fuck... I am really, truly going to miss *Rabbit Hole*."

"Why?" asked Devon.

"Why am I going to miss your podcast? Why are you here? Why am I here?" Manic energy infused his words. "Why did Reap3r implode? Why did you all fuck everything up? Why have all the subatomic particles since the Big Bang bounced off each other in such a way that led to our being ourselves, together, in this moment?"

"Yes, exactly," said Devon.

Sansome laughed a big laugh that wanted to be more than it was, reaching for feral insouciance but grasping only the bluster of a bully attempting to reinforce a sense of righteousness that hadn't been built to code.

"I'm here to ask you many of the same questions," said Sansome. "Your curiosity is what sparked my interest in your work. It's a powerful thing, curiosity—our species' defining trait. We wouldn't be us without it. Geoff here wanted to pretend it could be quashed, that if we tried hard enough, we could pretend to be something other than human."

"How is anti-proliferation inhuman?" said Geoff.

"Do you think the inventor of firearms could have kept guns to himself by telling everyone else they couldn't use them?" asked Sansome. "Yes, your discoveries are dangerous, but you don't solve that by locking them away. You solve it by putting those dangerous tools into the right hands, channeling their power."

Geoff snorted. "And yours are the right hands? Or Paul's?"

"So the Pentagon funnels billions into your startups," said Devon. "They get deadly new toys and you rack up record profits."

Sansome shrugged. "Not everyone is content to let enemy labs develop god knows what while we sit on our hands. By trolling his own patents, Geoff is holding back the entire U.S. biotech industry. All Paul asked was that he and Luki contribute to keeping this country safe. And if not Paul, if not Molly, then who? That's not a rhetorical question. I would have been happy to back anyone you picked. But by baring your hearts, you, all three of you, are forcing my hand. It's a damn shame, if you ask me."

130k.

"What makes you think any country is equipped to make these calls?" asked Luki. "The American government is using Q to target American citizens. I bet Paul has been surveilling us the whole time and outsourced the wet-work to you."

Devon flashed back to a CIA staffer she'd interviewed on background for the harp story who'd explained that the most common misconception of government was that it was a cohesive whole, that you could ascribe sensible agency to an organization that large. In reality, human institutions weren't unitary rational actors but complex and often incomprehensible systems of warring, collaborating, contradictory factions of gifted, asinine, courageous, fearful, generous, greedy, ambitious, dependable, maddening, inspiring, flawed people. Secret programs were even less legible—even to insiders—because they so often wound up chasing their own tails in an effort to maintain said secrecy.

"Paul doesn't know shit about this mess you're making," said Sansome. "I've had Geoff's house bugged for years—sorry buddy, but your confession to Devon proved why it was necessary. And if Paul wasn't your customer, would you prefer someone else have Q's spyware? Beijing? Moscow? Delhi? Brussels?"

Ask him about Alice Tufekci and Frank Ngo.

"Motherfucker," said Geoff.
"We didn't build it to be spyware." Desperation tinged Luki's voice. "That's the worst possible use-case for Q."

Devon caught Sansome's eye. She didn't know where this new fork in the rainbow road might lead, but she trusted harp. "What about Alice Tufekci and Frank Ngo?" she asked.

Sansome blanched.
Geoff's head snapped around.

Now ask him about Lev Towles and Issa Lahiri.

Devon did.
Sansome's eyes narrowed to slits.
Luki hissed.

I'm untangling Reap3r's ledger. Looks like the three of you weren't Sansome's first bounties. I'm cherry-picking names that cross reference with your friends.

"How do you know?" the calm in Sansome's voice was far more terrifying than his anger had been.

"You killed them, didn't you?" asked Geoff with dawning horror. "You told me the night of the eruption. You asked why I thought my closest collaborators had passed away within a few years of Bakunawa. I thought you were just being an enigmatic asshole, trying to intimidate me."

"But Issa died in a car crash after she left Q to join Google," said Luki. "And Lev had a stroke."

"Lev was closing in on Q's approach independently," said Sansome. "Given another year or two, his lab at MIT would have connected the dots. And Issa knew too much about your chip architecture. It's not like she could wipe her memory when she started her new job."

"So you *murdered* them?" Panic ratcheted Luki's voice higher and higher.

"I *protected* you," snapped Sansome. "Both of you."

175k listeners.

Sansome had stood just as proud and defiant on the stage at TED. Devon remembered watching and rewatching his talk in preparation for the grant interview, sensing his vulnerability in front of an audience, the practice girding his apparent ease. What had he said under the glare of the lights right before applause washed over him? *We find the best people in the world, figure out what makes them tick, write them checks, and give them free rein* to do what only they can do. *That's the Human Capital formula. Only people can change the world.* Zoom out. Cut to faces lit by inspired smiles. Fade to black. Devon saw that what had seemed so complicated was in fact very simple.

"So, invest in the best," she said. "Pay whatever it takes to attract top talent. And if you can't tempt the competition, eliminate them. Human Capital is the anteambulo with a knife in his belt. Who were you planning to kill to accelerate my success?"

There was real sorrow in Sansome's wan smile. "See, I knew you were good," he said. "Esteban had his doubts, but I knew." He sighed. "Unfortunately, we can't have you three running your mouths, which you've proven you can't keep shut. I'd be failing the rest of the Human Capital family if I let your revelations undermine them." He turned his head to call back over his shoulder. "Esteban?"

Like sunlight through a magnifying glass, the energy burgeoning inside Devon converged into a single, brilliant point.

"I thought you said you were a fan," she said.

"An avid one," said Sansome. "Truly."

"And yet you're missing the most popular episode of *Rabbit Hole* ever?"

Sick burn. 250k.

"Excuse me?" Sansome cocked his head to the side.

"I'm told the livestream just hit a quarter million listeners," said Devon.

Something in Sansome's expression slipped for a moment before he was able to get his self-assured mask back in place.

"Then again," said Devon. "Why listen when you're the star, right?"

"Bullshit," said Sansome, but he was looking at Devon, *really* looking at her for the very first time. "You're not going to get out of this by spinning— Hold on." Suddenly he was striding toward her. "Those are *the* glasses. I've read about them. I—"

Just as Sansome snatched them off Devon's face, Geoff tried unsuccessfully to trip him. Sansome kicked Geoff savagely in the stomach and then examined the glasses. "Not even Esteban has been able to find me a pair."

"They're pretty neat," said Devon, summoning her widest shit-eating grin to cover the ineffable storm of emotions raging inside her. "Built-in mic and everything."

Sansome gave her an unreadable look, then slowly donned the glasses. Devon had no idea what harp might be painting across his vision, but all the color drained from his face.

"Esteban!" he bellowed. "Esteban!"

"Mr. Haverford," said a quiet voice. "If you'll please come with me."

59

A PETITE WOMAN STOOD at the base of the stairs. They all looked at her in consternation. Who was she? How had she gotten there? How long had she been standing there? Her hair was black and wild, her clothes stained a rusty brown. There was something almost mythological about her—an aura of unusually dense meaning—as if she'd stepped out of the pages of a dark fairy tale.

"Esteban!" shouted Sansome.

"Esteban is indisposed," said the woman. "And I'm afraid I must insist that you come with me."

Sansome just stared.

A pair of knives appeared in her hands. "Now."

"You are going to regret this," hissed Sansome as he stalked past her.

"I'm sure I will," said the woman as she made room for him to lead the way up the stairs. "Regret comes for all of us in the end."

She turned to follow, then glanced back at Devon and did a double take. Her gaze snapped to Geoff, and then Luki, holding there for a moment. Luki's heart froze and melted a dozen times in quick succession like a multiyear time-lapse of a northern lake. There was unspeakable anguish behind those eyes, and something else—recognition?

A frown creased the woman's forehead as she met Devon's gaze one final time. Luki had the sense that once again, in a way he couldn't begin to understand, everything hung in the balance.

"Wait twenty minutes," said the woman, reaching an inscrutable decision. She tossed something that glinted in the fluorescent light as it arced through the air and clattered across the floor to come to rest in front of Devon.

And then the woman was gone—along with Sansome.

Devon looked down.

A short, curved blade lay at her feet—more claw than knife.

Luki, Devon, and Geoff were alone in the basement once more.

Or maybe not entirely alone.

An odd scratching noise was coming from a large crate pressed up against the wall.

"Hold on," said Luki, struggling to his knees.

He could have sworn he'd seen that crate somewhere before… and suddenly he was grabbing Devon's elbow and pressing his finger to his lips as they stared through dense foliage at a battered pickup truck three thousand miles away.

Apparently that mysterious woman wasn't their only fellow traveler.

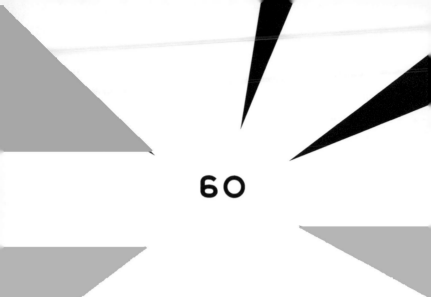

60

SANSOME STEPPED gingerly over the prone bodies of the security contractors. He couldn't see any wounds. Regardless, shouting for backup wouldn't accomplish anything. If his hired guns were out of play, the rest of his staff wouldn't stand a chance.

Pwned, asshole.

The text slid across the glasses next to the running count of listeners on the *Rabbit Hole* livestream that hovered in the bottom-right-hand corner of his vision like a guillotine—the *alleged* livestream. Devon was sharp. Maybe she was just trying to bluff her way out of a tight spot using these secret-brand specs as a high-tech prop. Because if she wasn't, heads were going to roll. Maybe even his. First Luki and Geoff inspiring each other's confessions. Then the Reap3r meltdown at the Ferry Building. Now this. What the fuck was going on? These were *his* people.

People he loved and admired. People he'd sacrificed everything to protect and empower. People who were breaking his heart. No. Don't even think about that. One problem at a time.

"Who put you up to this?" he demanded.

Just because you're scared doesn't give you the right to be rude.

For fuck's sake. Was someone on the other end of these things or was snide commentary an artifact of their infamous algomagic?

"Office," said the woman in her carefully neutral voice.

His heart couldn't decide whether to race or stop dead. His thoughts frayed before reaching firm conclusions. His resolve, the bottomless conviction that had always been his wellspring, evaporated like dew under summer sun.

"Look, whatever they're paying you, I'll triple it," he said, resenting the rising pitch he couldn't keep from his voice.

"Office," she repeated coldly.

It made no sense.

Unless.

And then they were there in his office where Sansome's beloved collection of Darwin's original papers filled the climate-controlled bookshelf—the intellectual flotsam of a genius whose ideas remade the world—and reflected sunlight glared off the glass just like the hot lights that had blinded him onstage at TED. Now, as then, his stomach twisted and his breath came fast and shallow. Crisis stripped you down to your bare essence, forced you to confront whatever dynamic was really at work within you, the source of your power and your suffering, a truth too darkly radiant to approach directly unless under duress. This was the same brink to which public speaking goaded Sansome, a feeling he abhorred and sought out, and so he reached within himself to tap the practices instilled by Esteban's rigorous training.

Inhale.

Exhale.

Inhale.

Exhale.

Esteban.

Human Capital's silent partner. Had Esteban sent this bitch with the knife? Sansome knew the possibility was real, knew how much it hurt even to consider it, and knew that he himself had hedged against this very contingency with a dead-man's switch. Were Sansome to be killed or incapacitated, evidence of his and Esteban's machinations would be automatically distributed to every major news service unless Esteban correctly answered the system prompt within two minutes. If Sansome was going down, he wouldn't go down alone.

Had their years of sticking their necks out to secure a better future amounted to so little? Esteban was so expert at adapting his personality to fit circumstances that perhaps circumstances had come to define him. When you could become anyone, who were you really? Sansome had waxed lyrical about how all of Human Capital's investees advanced their respective frontiers, but Esteban was the only one who truly inhabited the liminal, who thrived on the ragged edges of things. And surely it was natural for a resident of the fringe to gaze with jealousy on the man at the very center, to want to exert a gravitational pull, to draw worlds into his orbit. Sansome knew the feeling. He sometimes envied Esteban's ability to fade into the background at will, to slip away from things that Sansome had no choice but to face. But if Esteban had indeed betrayed him, what was the point? This was *their* project. Their partnership *was* the project. Sansome was cast adrift on a quicksilver sea. Had his only real friendship succumbed to realpolitik?

He quickly scanned the room as if the answer might be right in front of him: besides the bookshelf, there was his desk with his computer, keyboard, and iPhone, the kaleidoscopic Maximo Laura tapestry, the Isfahan rug he'd found in a—except he was standing on plastic sheeting, not hand-knotted silk.

That's when the unadulterated realization finally shattered the last of Sansome's coping mechanisms: he was here to be slaughtered.

Seriously though, RIP. I know what it's like to live in fear. May this be a mercy.

Sansome spun, shoes squeaking on plastic, and faced his captor. She stood in the doorway, eyes closed, head inclined, hands hanging just below her navel, left clasping right just above the fist out of which curved a cruel tooth of mottled-blue steel—as if she had plucked the waxing crescent moon out of the firmament.

Come on, he told himself, clenching his jaw. She was half his size, and he'd won a bar fight or two in his day. He sure could use one of Esteban's little pep talks right now, but he'd have to do without.

Bitch.

Bitch.

Never mind the knife, he could take her.

And then she opened her eyes, raised her head, and met his gaze, and he immediately saw that he couldn't—that he didn't have a chance in hell. Sansome had always prided himself on his ability to read people, and she was a veritable library of obituaries.

So he charged her because that's what you did when you were outmatched but still breathing, and she didn't so much move as flicker, and then he was on his knees and the plastic was no longer whitely translucent but bright, bright red and then he was on his back and noticing that he was tired, so very tired.

Except that it wasn't yet time for sleep. Not quite.

He must do the thing he could not do.

Esteban may very well have sent this fallen angel to snatch his soul, but Sansome would not die a prisoner of the prisoner's dilemma. He would not drag his friend overboard with him, even if his friend had pushed him.

What you did was who you were.

Friendship could not fall victim to anything, because friendship was a choice.

For the first and the last time, Sansome chose.

Reaching into reserves he didn't know he had, Sansome summoned the last of his fading strength.

"Hey Siri," he called out to the phone on his desk, blood bubbling from his lips. "Text Esteban: Audience. Send."

There. That was it: the password he'd set for the system prompt—inspired by Esteban's comment that an audience was the thing that Sansome loved to hate and hated to love—and that he was dying in front of. Esteban could now disarm the dead man's switch. He might still go down, but it wouldn't be because of Sansome. A parting gift for his coconspirator, because what was friendship if not whispering secrets in the dark.

Then the walls began to melt and the ceiling faded into liquid sky and something caught inside him in a place he could

never have named but somehow always knew was there and—
not unlike his kite lifting him up and out of the water—yanked
Sansome beyond the beyond.

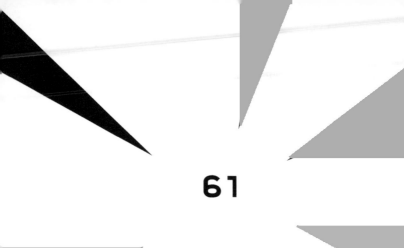

61

UNHOOKING THE LATCH, they pried open the crate.

Geoff had no idea what might be waiting inside and had had enough surprises to last him a lifetime. But Devon and Luki were determined to find out, and they had to do something during their prescribed twenty minutes or they'd go insane.

The wooden top finally came off, clattering to the concrete floor.

"Bernadette!" said Devon. "It has to be her."

Geoff peered in. The novel in his jacket pocket had helped cushion Sansome's kick, but now the edge of the crate pressed it against the bruise.

It took him a moment to parse what he was seeing.

"So *this* is what those men were after," said Luki, and then, darkly, "Typical Sansome."

Devon nodded. "The Center would never dare accuse their largest donor."

The poachers had laid the giant tortoise on her back so she couldn't move during transport, just like pirates, explorers, and mariners had done when dropping by the Galápagos to stock up on tortoises to eat on long voyages. Bernadette had been born when that was common practice. She slowly extended her head—flaps of leathery skin unfolding—and side-eyed them suspiciously.

Yet another prisoner for Sansome's private zoo.

"We need to get her out of here," said Geoff, feeling an unlikely rush of empathy for the animal. She'd been lumbering around Isabella Island when Darwin made his famous visit, when Ada Lovelace wrote the first computer program, when Einstein published his theory of special relativity, when Alexander Fleming accidentally discovered penicillin, when Geoff let himself be convinced that weaponizing biology was the best way to advance it, and when he managed to develop a vaccine to disarm the monster he'd secretly created.

Terry Pratchett's Discworld rested on the back of four elephants that stood atop a giant turtle swimming through the depths of space. Geoff squinted down at Bernadette, imagining that instead of lying inverted, she was in fact carrying Planet Earth on her back. Geoff, Molly, Devon, Luki, Sansome, Esteban, Paul, Bernadette, each of the 220 million hungry ghosts felled by Bakunawa, *every living being* was a world unto themselves, densely interconnected, interdependent at every scale, deserving of respect and simple kindness—even if it was nothing more than a trio of strangers offering a helping hand.

"We will," said Devon. "But we have to get ourselves out of here first, or we won't survive to rescue her."

"Has it been twenty minutes?" asked Luki.

"Close enough," said Devon.

Over the course of this extraordinary day, Devon and Luki had demonstrated a scrappy courage that Geoff admired and envied. He glanced around the basement. There were the zipties they'd cut off each other's wrists. There was where they'd sat knee-to-knee in the dark as Devon beamed their story to the world. In all the anxious fantasies he'd had about the world finding out what he'd done, who he really was, Geoff had never imagined a scene quite like this. Alice would have appreciated it.

Geoff led the way up the stairs and tried the door.

The woman had left it unlocked.

Out there, thousands of people knew his secret. Out there, his monolithic Reputation was coming apart. Out there, it was all finally starting. Geoff had always known he was a sinner, not a saint, but the world had just found out, and wouldn't be forgetting anytime soon. This was the first day of whatever the rest of his life turned out to be.

"Ready?" he looked back over his shoulder.

Luki stiffened and Devon nodded, the knife in her hand sending Geoff back to the *tenegre* sword lying on the floor of his house, the feeling of such profound emptiness that nothing more than gin fumes might be enough to buoy him up off the deck into the onrushing fog. The strangest part of this whole day was even as every vestige of his life sloughed away, how solid he now felt in his body, fresh cement poured into a mold.

So, without even needing to steel himself, he opened the door.

And there was Esteban, kneeling over the spread-eagled body of one of his goons, checking the man for a pulse. At the sound of the door opening, his gaze snapped up to Geoff who shuddered at the raw, wolfish hunger blazing forth from eyes stripped of their customary veils of finesse and misdirection.

Esteban looked like he was about to say something, but then, changing his mind, lunged for the pistol in his unconscious colleague's shoulder holster.

Geoff froze.

If he attacked, he might just be able to make it across the hallway before Esteban could bring the gun to bear.

If he retreated, he'd be momentarily out of harm's way, but the three of them would be back to square one.

There was no time to come up with a plan. But what did time mean to him anyway? Once the authorities started debriefing him, Geoff would lose whatever control he still had over his future. In Geoff's mind's eye, a moonlit tower of steam born of a boiling sea rose to blot out the stars, the churning column tinged red from flowing lava and shot through with lighting. Sansome had quoted Kant at him: *Whereas the beautiful is limited, the sublime is limitless, so that the mind in the presence of the sublime, attempting to imagine what it cannot, has pain in the failure but pleasure in contemplating the immensity of the attempt.*

There would be a reckoning. Geoff had crippled a generation and lied about it to save himself and his masters. Now the masks were off, and the gloves would soon follow. Whatever tomorrow held, he deserved worse, and would do whatever he could, not to make things right—that was impossible—but to make things better.

Devon and Luki had their whole lives ahead of them, lives they had devoted to standing up for what they believed in no matter the consequences, something Geoff had been putting off for far too long.

In his recurring nightmare, Geoff was always left standing in the ruins of civilization, staring out across the waves, hoping for a sail to appear over an unknown horizon so that he might deliver an unread letter to a nameless woman.

But he wasn't waiting for deliverance.

Deliverance was waiting for him.

His only regret was not getting to taste a Pastrami Ruskie one last time.

62

A FEW STEPS AHEAD of Devon, Geoff opened the door.

He stiffened.

"What is it?" Devon tightened her grip on the hilt of the curved dagger.

But instead of replying, Geoff rushed forward and out of view.

Devon sprinted after him, flinching sideways at the sound of one, two, three, four gunshots. Her shoulder slammed into the doorframe and she careened out of the stairwell and into the hallway, Luki charging after her.

Geoff lay facedown on top of one—no, *two* other people. Blood bloomed from two holes in the back of his jacket.

"Geoff!" Devon knelt at his side.

"Is that…?" Luke began, staring at the twitching body under Geoff.

"Yes," she said. Esteban. A bullet had gone up under his chin and torn apart one side of his face, but he was still recognizable. And under him, one of the assholes who'd kidnapped them from the *Cecco*.

"Look at this." Luki scooped up a blood-spattered paperback novel with a bullet hole through the middle.

Geoff moaned.

"He's alive!" said Devon.

She and Luki gently rolled Geoff off the macabre pile and onto his back. They startled when they saw the pistol Esteban clutched to his chest, but he was extremely, unambiguously dead. Geoff had tackled him, pinning the gun between their bodies at the very moment Esteban was firing it.

"Go," said Geoff weakly, waving them away. Crevices gaped in his chest and stomach. "Go."

"Come on," said Devon, and she and Luki helped Geoff to his feet.

"Leave me," said Geoff. "I'll just slow you down. Go."

"If you waste one more breath trying to convince us to abandon you, I'll salt your damn wounds," said Devon.

"Ride the endorphins while you can," said Luki.

"I've been here before," gasped Geoff as they got him moving, supporting him on both sides. "Sansome's office is this way, and then there's a side exit."

They limped up the hallway as quietly as they could, glanced into Sansome's empty office where evening light slanted down onto a Persian rug, and stumbled out onto a flagstone path that looped around to the front of the house—passing three more unconscious staff members along the way.

"Homegirl doesn't fuck around," said Devon. She still couldn't shake the haunted look in the eyes of that enigmatic avenging angel.

Coming up on the ranch's circular drive, birds darting through the gathering dusk, Devon realized with a shock that they had stood right here as dawn broke that very morning.

Time was a strange thing. You could keep on keeping on for years and then the world changed in a single day. Now the drive wasn't full of cars waiting to whisk them and their luggage home, but packed with an unlikely collection of vehicles: a vintage Land Rover with surfboards strapped to the roof, two black sedans with government plates, a Tesla squeezed between a pair of pastel pink Vespas, an electrician's truck, a Marin County Sheriff pickup, and a half-dozen bicycles. Even as Geoff, Devon, and Luki slowed, trying to make sense of the strange scene, more assorted cars pulled in off the road.

"Devon!" someone shouted, emerging from the oddball crowd of motorists and pointing. "That's her!"

"Vince?" asked Devon. "What are you doing here? What's going on?"

"These people"—murmured Luki so only she and Geoff could hear—"are *your* people."

"When I heard it on *Rabbit Hole*, I came right away," said Vince, hurrying forward. "We all did. There even a few FBI guys from the San Francisco office who said they've listened to every episode." He nodded toward four armed men in suits, flanked by the sheriff, striding over from the house's front door, where they'd apparently been about to try to gain entry. "But what's happening? Did you get out? Dumb, of course you did. How did you escape? Hold on"—he searched Luki's face, and then Geoff's—"that's *him* isn't it? And *him* too?" His gaze dropped to Geoff's wounds, "Fuck."

Devon raised her voice as she and Luki lowered Geoff to the ground. "We've got a casualty here. Two gunshot wounds to the torso." That got the crowd's attention and they began to gather. She pointed at a bystander in cycling garb. "You, call 911 and get an ambulance here stat." Then she lowered her voice and addressed Vince. "Gimme your phone."

"But—"

"Now."

He did. She plugged in a number and handed the phone to Luki.

"Wait a min—" objected Vince.

She met his eyes. "Do you trust me?"

"I mean, sure—" he said.

"Then get this man out of here before the cops realize who he is," said Devon, maintaining eye contact and summoning every ounce of urgency she could muster. She would protect her source, her friend.

Luki's gaze flicked back and forth like he was watching a ping pong match.

Devon grabbed his elbow, remembering how he'd grabbed hers right before he changed her life forever.

"Call Kai," she said, wishing there was time to say more, to offer a proper goodbye. "Do whatever they say. I'll buy you as much time as I can."

He opened his mouth. Closed it. Nodded.

And then Vince hustled him away into the crowd.

"Help!" Devon screamed at the FBI agents pushing toward her and Geoff. "For fuck's sake, help!"

Law enforcement couldn't resist a damsel in distress, and Devon had plenty of distress to offer.

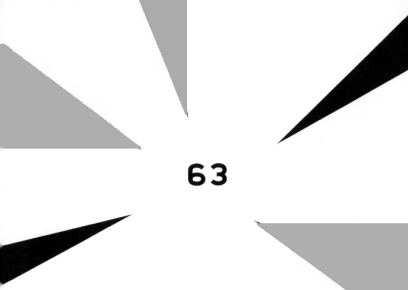

63

ISABELLA TOOK A BITE of pupusa.

The sourness of the *curtido* she'd been fermenting on the kitchen counter perfectly complemented the spiciness of the salsa, the sharp flavors combining to cut the natural sweetness of the heirloom corn and the richness of the *quesillo* and *loroco* stuffing.

Shame she couldn't taste a thing.

Her heart only had room for the ashes in the small glass jar on the table in front of her. She hadn't brought an urn—hadn't wanted to acknowledge to herself that she would need one—but The Baker had quietly fetched this from the main building.

Wondering why the tears wouldn't come, despising herself for their absence, Isabella took another bite.

He was the one who had given them the special cornflower. He was the one who had given them the tip: Reap3r. A kind man. A generous man. A cursed man whose every venture ended in spectacular disaster.

This was all his fault. This was all Isabella's fault. This was all Marisol's fault. This was all their families' fault. This was all El Salvador's fault. This was all the coyote's and the rabbit's fault. This was all everyone's, everything's fault. Everything was contingent. Everything was invented. Everything was fucked.

She took another bite.

Thirty-seven million dollars. Mind-boggling wealth. Numbers on a screen. When all today's kills were accounted for, all the bonuses and multiples applied, all the smart contracts settled, all the cryptocurrency funneled into their account, that's how much Marisol had cost.

How they had dreamed of this kind of payout, of having enough cash to retire, of building a home in this foreign, beloved, hateful metropolis.

Picking up the jar, she pressed her forehead against the glass, straining to loosen her soul from whatever bonds held it here, or call some fragment of Marisol's back, reaching past logic, past belief, fumbling in darkness that was not darkness but nothing at all. There was no communion to be had. It was nothing more than a jar of ash, as profane and as sacred as anything else in this universe.

Ever so gently, Isabella placed the jar back on the table.

She had been in elementary school when Bakunawa had swept through El Salvador, claiming life after life after life. They had said you needed to keep a distance from other people to slow the spread of contagion. She'd learned to note the angle of the sun and watch for shadows thrown around blind corners so as not to surprise—or be surprised by—other pedestrians. The habit had stuck. Only now did she realize that she had been watching the shadows for so long that she'd become one.

She took a long, shuddering breath.

Her last target, the man in Marin with the astronomical fee attached, had been holding the first three targets hostage— the two men and the woman they'd originally followed from Oakland to San Francisco, whose contract had been cancelled at the very last moment. Isabella had recognized them in the basement from their Reap3r profiles, and had recognized something *in* them, something desperate, something fierce, something familiar. Strange that she had left them one of her karambits. Or maybe not so strange: She was no longer two.

Isabella had secured unimaginable riches but lost the only thing that really mattered: someone to share them with. She looked around at their apartment. They had been so keen on making this work, on doing whatever was necessary to carve out a place for themselves, to belong. But all meaning had leaked from the cast iron pans, the torn *Rodrigo y Gabriela* poster, the pull-up bar, the small shrine to Our Lady of Peace, the resplendent orchid. They were just objects now. And beyond these walls, this phoenix-city that had burned to the ground nine times, always rising from the ashes grander and stranger and denser with beautiful, mad dreams than before.

Without Marisol, this was no longer home.

Nowhere was.

And all because of a godforsaken app.

Isabella raised her remaining karambit and mottled steel absorbed the light without so much as a glimmer. She would take her ill-begotten fortune and hunt down Reap3r's inventor, even if it took her to the ends of the earth and beyond the edge of time. She knew vengeance would be cold comfort, but she wanted numbness, not comfort, and nothing numbed like the cold.

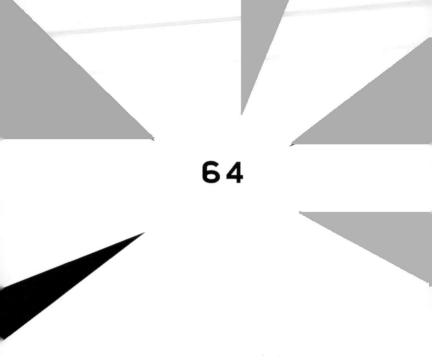

64

NEON BLAZED OVERHEAD, people thronged the narrow street, unfamiliar smells seeped through his cloth mask, and Luki tried and mostly failed to come to terms with the fact that an unlikely combination of Devon's lightning-fast action, Kai's fake papers, Vince's unquestioning helpfulness, general chaos, and a whole lot of luck had somehow managed to smuggle Luki off of Sansome's ranch, to the airport, and across the Pacific before Paul's hammer came down.

"Trust me, it's worth it," said harp, guiding him by the elbow to the end of a long queue that ran halfway up the block.

That was another thing he was struggling to come to terms with: harpZkord wasn't just a digital demigod inhabiting the space between lines of code, but a living, breathing human being who had volunteered to be his guide to whatever nebulous territory still lay, or could be created, outside the panopticon to which Luki had contributed. And she was female, explaining

Devon's pronoun slip-up during the escape from the Ferry Building. In fact, this was the closest Luki had been to the experience of going on a date in years. He swallowed the lump in his throat as he remembered his parents' exhortations over Zoom. When, if ever, would he be able to talk to them again?

harp had bought their freedom with devastation, using the access he had granted with Q to turn Reap3r on itself, cranking the vice until the system collapsed inward like a dying sun—sucking Sansome over the event horizon along with it. Q. *The troops can't wait for the next act,* Dexa had told him on the bluff right before she took him to the airport. He could only hope that the next act didn't wind up costing Dexa and everyone else at Q their careers, or their lives. And now that Luki's face was plastered across all the feeds—whistleblower du jour—he also hoped that they felt a small measure of pride at having helped, that he was giving voice to qualms that they felt just as acutely, that everyone felt who had helped realize the dream of quantum computing only to see it devolve into the most banal of nightmares. And that was the crux of what he'd done: the nightmare was no longer secret.

Would anything change, really? People expected regular software updates, but forgot that governance was also in constant flux, and began to fail when it fell out of sync with the culture. Without preventive maintenance, pressure built up like tectonic forces along a fault line until a new order snapped into place, often violently. Maybe these revelations were a leading tremor of an impending quake, or maybe they'd relieve just enough pressure that the status quo could stutter forward without fundamental reform for a while longer. Either way, the only thing you could do was your best, and civilization was the sum of everyone trying to do just that. Sansome might have aspired to be a master of the universe, but if there was one thing Luki had learned from a life dedicated to quanta, it was how thoroughly reality eclipsed human understanding.

They reached the front of the line and harp negotiated with the vendor. Dozens of small buns covered in sesame seeds sizzled in a shallow iron pan. It smelled fantastic.

"*Xie xie*," said harp, accepting the steaming bag.

Luki shouldered the backpack containing all his worldly belongings—including the bullet-pierced paperback he hadn't had the opportunity to return to Geoff—and they zig-zagged through the crowd back to the bikes, passing bustling micro-cafes outfitted with high-end Italian espresso machines that looked like tiny spaceships, design boutiques stocked with striking denim cuts, enough food stalls to feed a small army, a public basketball court in the middle of some kind of pick-up tournament, and an eighty-eight-story karaoke club.

"Welcome to Taipei," said harp, twirling a finger. "A city so interesting that nobody eats at home because the night markets are where it's *at*. The best part is with so much happening, nobody has time to notice you."

She unlocked their bikes, handed him a tiger-striped helmet complete with fuzzy ears, donned an elephantine one, and led him through a maze of densely packed alleys. The crowd thinned and then disappeared completely, and they pedaled through a sleepy residential neighborhood, apartment buildings rising high on all sides, tiny parks with playgrounds and exercise equipment tucked in every few blocks—empty and dark this late at night, but without the palpable sense of latent danger they would have exuded in any good-sized American city.

It had been so hard to learn the American way of doing things when he'd first moved to the States. Sometimes, it would feel just like a Netflix series, comfortable if a little surreal, and then he'd turn a corner and find himself in the middle of a tent city and wonder whether he'd stepped through a portal into some disturbing alternate dimension—or maybe into another genre: dystopian. But eventually he'd learned the ropes and America had become a part of him just as he became a part of it.

Could he really start all over again?

Could he really live the life he'd chosen?

Luki had spent his life learning to think, not run. The learning curve would be steep enough that even a stumble promised not just failure, but oblivion. The only silver lining was that by making no plans, he'd left no clues for his pursuers, but he was all too aware that failing to plan had been a half-conscious hedge against losing his nerve.

"We're here," said harp, swinging a leg over the bike frame and coasting to a stop.

The unfurnished apartment was on the eighth floor—*good luck!* according to harp. When she hit the light Luki saw it was packed with boxes of all sizes. He stepped inside, examining them more closely.

Ikea and Lego. An apartment's worth of furniture, an elementary school's worth of toys.

He looked at harp quizzically.

She shrugged and a shadow fluttered beneath her smile. "Believe me, you'll need something to distract yourself with," she said.

They sat cross-legged on the floor and ate. Luki nearly burned his tongue with the first bite. The buns were soft and fluffy on top, crispy on the bottom, and stuffed with pork. Oil and hot sauce ran down their fingers.

"So?" asked harp.

"Sure as hell beats airplane food," said Luki.

"Bomb," said harp.

"Bomb," agreed Luki.

And then suddenly he was weeping and he tried to get himself under control but the sobs wracked his body and he smeared oil across his cheeks as he tried to wipe away the tears and he was sneaking into the village library and losing himself in Richard Feynman's stories and celebrating *txotx* with his parents and watching the surfer rocket out of the boiling barrel and brushing his fingertips across the pitted surface of Paul's technicolor wall and swigging gin from Geoff's bottle and waiting for the file transfer to finish and snorkeling with Devon and fleeing the Ferry Building massacre and using every ounce of strength in his slim body to row that stupid fucking boat and charging their kidnappers and sitting in darkness with zip-ties cutting into his wrists and telling his story to the world—a story that might free the scientific project he'd dedicated his life to, but would end his free life as a scientist at the same time.

After what might have been seconds or minutes or hours, the storm passed, and slowly, very slowly, his breath, his heart, his mind rocked back into an ever so fragile equilibrium.

He looked up. harp hadn't moved, hadn't interrupted. She was just sitting there quietly. Listening. Being present. Holding space for him.

"I'm so—" he began, but she held up a hand to stop him.

He pressed his lips together and met her gaze. harp's luminous black eyes channeled bottomless determination—a life preserver thrown to a drowning mariner. "You're lucky there's someone to show you the ropes of this whole fugitive thing," she said gently, and not without humor. "There are *ever* so many ways to fuck up, and *ever* so many fates worse than death. So whenever the mind-numbing burden of maintaining good opsec starts to chafe, remember that unlike you, I didn't have me."

There was a message—polished smooth by time—that the elders in Luki's village would pass along to seekers like Aisling en route to Santiago de Compostela: the tourist demands, the pilgrim gives thanks.

From this day forward, if Luki was anything, he was a pilgrim.

"Xie xie," he said, the new words strange on his tongue.

"Yikes," said harp with a delighted, delightful guffaw. "We have *got* to work on that accent."

65

TONIGHT ALL THE rainbow roads led to Palimpsest.

People came from London, Tokyo, Manila, and Buenos Aires. People came from scientific research stations on Antarctica, far-flung suburbs of Istanbul, and cushy Beltway think tanks. People came from every nook and cranny to which Kai's glasses had spread. There would be press, lawyers, activists, engineers, federal agents, hackers, politicians, scientists, and poets. Each of them touched in some way by Luki's story, Geoff's story, Sansome's story.

Devon's story.

"You ready for this?" asked Vince. He'd become an ally, more than that: a friend.

"I don't know," said Devon, surprising herself with her candor.

"We never do," said Vince. "That's what keeps life interesting."

Kai had said something like that to her once.

Devon opened the door and stepped out of the car. Multicolored lasers danced in complicated patterns across the shade sails, as if Palimpsest was driven across its urban seas by shattered light.

As Devon crossed the street to the entrance, she saw that the murals had once again been painted over and she nearly tripped on the curb as she recognized a portrait of herself. Stepping back, she looked along the length of the exterior walls. There was Luki. There was Geoff. There was Sansome, Molly, Vince, Esteban, Paul, and even Bernadette. An intricately detailed quantum computer hummed in a secret lab buried deep underground. Thousands of pinhead-size faces aggregated to illustrate the numbers 220 million, encircled by the tail of a dragon that was preparing to swallow a crescent moon. *The Liminal* sat at anchor in a Galápagan inlet, lava flowing in the background. A vicious melee raged through the Ferry Building. On and on and on. It was so much. Too much. Devon was a teacup trying to catch a waterfall.

"Yo, bro," said Kai, stepping out onto the sidewalk. They wore a color-morphing, metalloid jumpsuit that created an effect on the naked eye that Devon could have sworn would have required the digital magic of the glasses. They grinned, and beckoned her in. "We're all set."

People seeking the meaning of life got it backward. You didn't ask life for an answer. Life asked you.

Palimpsest was transformed. They'd set up temporary bleachers around the outer edges of the space, all facing in toward the bar at the center of which stood a stage. Every seat was taken, and every place to stand was packed. As Devon and Kai entered, cameras began to flash and a tide of murmurs surged.

"The fire marshal is gonna give me hell," said Kai. "But screw it. Congrats on the launch, motherfucker." They winked.

"Remember, you're living my best life."

The launch. Right. That's why all these people were here. That's why Devon was here. She'd asked for Kai's advice on applying for the Human Capital grant. Devon had needed that funding because despite *Rabbit Hole*'s dedicated following, she'd never been able to make ends meet. Seeking sponsorship turned her listeners into products and made Devon dependent on the Sansomes of the world. It was time for a change. The live recording had gone out on the *Rabbit Hole* feed, sparking a flurry of investigations, Geoff's trials, Luki's manhunt, Human Capital's disgrace, and outcries from all sides. Having got the word out through improvisation, Devon had devoted herself to the research and production of a new episode that would go to *Rabbit Hole*'s famously absurd level of depth—teasing out the implications of every theme and following every thread to its conclusion. The difference was that you had to pay for it—she was publishing it as an audiobook instead of a podcast. Edges: they were terrifying—peering over a cliff—and powerful—bounding a problem or project, challenging people to choose whether they were in or out. There was never a right or wrong way with these things, only a right way for you. When Devon put out her SOS over the livestream, her fans had come through. Now she hoped they'd come through again so she could find a way to make a living making *Rabbit Hole*.

"Devon!" Only one person on Earth said her name that way, at once celebratory and imperative.

"*Phaw, Mae*," she said, beaming as her parents leaned in to give her a quick hug. How Devon had resented having to work in the restaurant as a teenager, glaring up at the photo of the king as she wiped down tables. But despite how hard they worked, her parents had never resented their own labor. For them, the restaurant wasn't a burden, but a path to freedom—a way to bring people together, to enrich lives, to share the food that was their creative medium. Now, Devon needed to channel their dauntless resourcefulness, their dedication to uniting passion and business.

The Human Capital grant had been the first stage of the kind of lucrative sponsorship deal she'd been chasing for so long, yet it undermined the very independence it was supposed to represent. The thing you think you want is rarely the thing you need. Letting go of the former to embrace the latter is how you grow. Sitting in her closet recording studio, Devon had imagined *Rabbit Hole* to be an oubliette. Now she saw that it was in fact a womb. To further her art, she must become an entrepreneur.

They reached the stage and Kai gave Devon a firm slap on the ass and said, "Go show 'em who you are."

The crowd roared as Devon mounted the stage. She looked out at the assembled faces, mirrored turquoise lenses reflecting back at her.

Palimpsests were manuscripts from which the text had been scraped or washed so that the page could be reused. Words layered over the shadow of words, sentences over sentences, stories over stories. Luki, now in hiding with harp, had crafted a master key and then distributed an infinite number of copies. Geoff, recovering from his injuries and on trial in a dozen different courts simultaneously, had taken the transformative and dangerous discoveries he'd been hoarding and open-sourced them so that anyone could advance the science, including Molly, but no one could monopolize it. Before he vanished, Sansome had assembled a cadre of pioneers and luminaries, accelerating their respective ascents and cutting down anyone who stood in their way. A week after they'd escaped the basement, an anonymous data dump had implicated Esteban with a mountain of evidence that corroborated Devon's story. Paul was launching counter-investigations to cover up his own role in all this and solidify his powerbase. There was no end-game. There was only the game itself. History, memory, life, identity. Everything was revision.

Devon reached up to touch the karambit hanging between her breasts in its necklaced sheath. We don't grow straight up. We branch and twist and turn back on ourselves, always reaching toward the light.

Taking a deep breath, she gave herself over to the story.

THE END

W R I T I N G   *R E A P 3 R*

Gene Wolf pointed out that you never learn how to write a novel. You just learn how to write the novel that you're writing. Writing *Reap3r* proved to me how right Gene is.

I began working on the book in the fall of 2019. My wife and I were in the middle of a round-the-world trip. We trekked the wilds of Patagonia, swam under endless summer sun in arctic fjords, walked the 500-mile Camino de Santiago, and marveled at ancient Incan ruins in the Andes. The year was a mosaic assembled from fragments of experience gathered in far-flung lands.

We read as we traveled, voyaging through internal worlds just as ripe for exploration. While we sailed the namesake archipelago, I devoured Kurt Vonnegut's *Galápagos* and fell in love with its strange combination of big ideas, lightning pace, and madcap glee. David Mitchell's *Cloud Atlas* lodged in my heart as well: fully realized characters whose loosely connected stories spanned continents and centuries. I realized that the structure of these novels echoed our journey: they were narrative mosaics.

That realization made me want to craft a mosaic of my own, and *Reap3r* was born. So I combed through my notes of disparate ideas for characters, scenes, worlds, feelings, moments, plots, themes, events, etc. and instead of asking how each of them might grow into novels, I asked myself how they might be synthesized into a single story. I had collected dots, and now I was going to connect them.

I blazed through the rough draft. My wife and I returned home to Oakland, and ten days later California locked down as COVID-19 swept across the world. In addition to being terrifying, the pandemic was eerie for me because I'd been writing Geoff for months before it arrived—it was almost as if I was seeing his backstory brought to monstrous life. But if anything, the isolation and uncertainty of quarantine accelerated my work on the manuscript. Writing, like reading, let me escape into imagination.

I finished the rough draft in June, and I knew it was the best thing I'd ever written. The story was alive. It moved. It danced. It coalesced. It was at once tight and sprawling, fast and deep. I sent the manuscript to the small handful of advance readers that constitute my braintrust, and waited for the accolades to roll in.

But instead of praise, I received questions, questions about why the characters did what they did and what the big picture really was—questions I was appalled to discover I couldn't answer.

The story was broken.

I had built a house on a cracked foundation.

The next few months were brutal. I cycled through dozens of possible fixes, some cosmetic, some profound. I considered shattering my mosaic and spinning each piece into its own standalone novel. I thought about scrapping everything and starting a brand new story from scratch. I tested the patience of my braintrust by soliciting feedback whenever a solution presented itself. But nothing worked. I felt like an overambitious juggler watching in horror as balls rained down on the stage around me.

An interviewer once asked David Mitchell about weaving six novellas into what became *Cloud Atlas*. "It was just the insouciance of youth," said David. "Sometimes your lack of experience can save you. Sometimes an underinformed decision is retrospectively the right decision, and had you had more wisdom, you wouldn't have done it." At that moment, I wished I had come across the interview before embarking on *Reap3r*. I wished I had had more wisdom, so I wouldn't have done it.

And that was when I remembered an unpublished short story that I had written in a single afternoon six months earlier, a story about a venture capitalist giving a TED talk while an on-demand assassin stalked his competition. An idea began to take shape, not like a lightbulb snapping on, but like pressure building along a fault line. Maybe I, the juggler, didn't need to settle for simpler tricks or quit the circus to pursue a career in accountancy. Maybe what I actually needed was to toss yet one more ball into the air, trusting it to complete the unresolved pattern of time and balance and gravity.

This turned out to be not the beginning of the end, but the end of the beginning. I set to work. I integrated the short story into the novel. I reinvented main characters. I rewrote much of the manuscript and added fifty percent more material. I refactored the narrative again and again and again and again. I incorporated input from friends, writers, agents, editors, and more advance readers. In the end, it took me more than twice as long to revise *Reap3r* as to write the rough draft.

That wasn't what I was expecting when, full of youthful insouciance, I set out to write this story, but it was what this story required of me. It didn't matter that I had already written nine novels. I needed to learn how to write *this* novel. I gave it my all in the hope that my all might be enough.

If you're still reading, I hope you agree it was worth it.

Best, Eliot

P.S. We all find our next favorite book because someone we trust recommends it. If you enjoyed *Reap3r*, please tell your friends, post reviews, gift it far and wide, and spread the word however you can. It might feel insignificant, but it makes an enormous difference. Books thrive on word of mouth. Culture is a collective project in which we all have a stake and a voice. Oh, and if you're curious about what I'm reading, I send a monthly newsletter recommending books I love that you might too. I also include writing updates and field notes from my creative process. Subscribe at www.eliotpeper.com

THANKS

Brad Feld and Amy Batchelor provided a generous grant that made *Reap3r* possible.

Kevin Barrett Kane designed the beautiful cover and interiors—inspired by concept art from Peter Nowell.

Tim Erickson and Ash Tyrrell edited *Reap3r*. Any remaining errors are mine alone.

Jackson Keeler, Josh Anon, Lucas Carlson, Sarah Fornshell, and Cameron McClure read early drafts and gave invaluable notes.

Michael Lewis shared practical tips for narrating the audiobook.

Seth Godin, Tim Chang, Barry Eisler, Robin Sloan, Hannu Rajaniemi, Elizabeth Bear, Matt Wallace, Don Burke, Jake Chapman, Josh Elman, Danny Crichton, Jason Bade, David Mandell, Malka Older, Ben Casnocha, Jessie Young, Mike Shatzkin, Ryan Orbuch, Manu Saadia, Kim Stanley Robinson, and John Cordier offered ideas, advice, and encouragement along the way.

Kurt Vonnegut's *Galápagos*, David Mitchell's *Cloud Atlas*, Ursula K. Le Guin's *Steering the Craft*, Derek Sivers's *Your Music and People*, William Gibson's *Agency*, John McPhee's *Draft No. 4*, Italo Calvino's *If on a winter's night a traveler*, Anne Trubek's *So You Want to Publish a Book?*, Carlo Rovelli's *Seven Brief Lessons on Physics*, Richard P. Feynman's *Surely You're Joking, Mr. Feynman!*, Edward Snowden's *Permanent Record*, Austin Kleon's *Keep Going*, Andy Matuschak and Michael Nielsen's *Quantum Country*, Ada Palmer's *The Will to Battle*, and Keith Johnstone's *Impro* influenced how I wrote this particular story.

Taylor Swift's "marjorie" and Monolink's "Burning Sun" were often playing on infinite loops as I worked on the manuscript.

Michael Sippey, Tegan Tigani, Salman Ansari, Dan Mason, David Brittain, Clare James, Bob Baskerville, Jim Pallotta, Cathie Mellon, Rob Roy Rankin, Mary J.L. Rowe, Guy Hale, Daniel Stafford, Louis J. Erste, Suzanne W. Strisik, Bernardo Hernandez Alejos, Mary Stofer, Lawrence Wilkinson, and Peter Neame invested in my writing so I could do more of it.

My brilliant wife Andrea Castillo was my creative partner at every step. Our dog Claire was a loyal assistant.

You brought *Reap3r* to life by reading it.

To all, a thousand thanks.

MORE FROM
ELIOT PEPER

Veil

Breach

Borderless

Bandwidth

Neon Fever Dream

Cumulus

Exit Strategy

Power Play

Version 1.0

ABOUT THE AUTHOR

ELIOT PEPER is the author of ten novels, including *Bandwidth*, *Cumulus*, and *Veil*. He also helps founders build technology businesses and tell stories that create change. Eliot publishes a blog, sends a newsletter, tweets more than he probably should, and lives in Oakland, CA.

Learn more at www.eliotpeper.com